"[*Into That Good Night* is] a sparse, beautifully written memoir about
fatherhood, bravery, memory and one man in particular."
—*Publisher's Weekly* (starred review)

"[*Into That Good Night* is] one of the most memorable and uplifting
books of the year."
—*San Antonio Express News*

"[*Into That Good Night* is] wonderful, absolutely first rate in every way.
It is beautifully written, with a strong voice."
—Dan Rather

(In *Sundays with Ron Rozelle*) "there's an element of Mark Twain, O.
Henry, and our own John Graves in these pieces—humor and wis-
dom with Rozelle's own special turns."
—Robert Compton, former book editor of *The Dallas Morning News*

"*Touching Winter* is the kind of well-crafted, elegantly written, char-
acter-driven literary novel that New York doesn't publish anymore.
Thank God for university presses."
—Robert Flynn, author of *North to Yesterday*

"Rozelle splices together two eras in a potentially tricky structure that
ultimately yields a spare, beautifully written memoir about fatherhood, bravery, memory and one man in particular. His recollec-
tion of his childhood in a small east Texas town also reconstructs
his father, Lester, a once vigorous, strong-willed man whose own
memory was decimated by Alzheimer's. Other sections from the
early 1990s compare Rozelle's still-new experiences of paternity with
his evolving relationship with his own father. When Rozelle, a high

school English teacher, was growing up in Oakwood in the 1950s and '60s, Lester was the school superintendent of the 'white' school, where he formerly taught, as well as of the town's 'black' school. While Rozelle offers many details of life in a small Southern town, this is not an exercise in nostalgia. Lester was an upright man who publicly supported the Supreme Court decision that mandated school integration. That same quiet strength helped Rozelle deal with the death of his mother, who committed suicide after she was unsuccessfully treated for cancer. The author's skillful and compassionate writing brings both the father of his childhood and the man who could not remember the names of his own children to life. Lester died of a stroke in 1992, but this serves, as his son intended, as a moving tribute."

—*Publisher's Weekly*

"Like a stone washed smooth by the sea, Rozelle's language glows in the light and feels good in the hand. He shares the story of his father's life as superintendent of schools in the east Texas town of Oakwood. His father was quiet, orderly, sensible, and fair: he began that town's long journey toward school integration. Chapters toothsome with memories of Christmas, the pull and tug of siblings, and bootleg beer alternate with those chronicling the elder Rozelle's slippage into memory lapse and dementia. There's not a shred of sentimentality here, however; Rozelle's crystalline little memoir brings not tears but the joy of good things remembered, like the scent of 'a nickel held tight in a sweaty palm on a hot day' or the childish lesson that half-past one was 'not thirteen-thirty.' Rozelle rejoices, and readers with him, in his sisters, in his tangled memories of his mother, and above all, in the legacy of his straight-arrow and genuinely good dad. Moving and joyous: like his dad, Rozelle is a teacher. His students are very lucky indeed."

—*Booklist*, GraceAnne A. DeCandido

LEAVING THE COUNTRY OF SIN

LEAVING
THE
COUNTRY
OF SIN

A NOVEL

Ron Rozelle

Texas Review Press • Huntsville, Texas

Published by: Texas Review Press
            Huntsville, TX

LIBRARY OF CONGRESS CATALOGING-IN-PUBLICATION DATA

Names: Rozelle, Ron, 1952– author.
Title: Leaving the country of sin : a novel / by Ron Rozelle.
Other titles: Sabine series in literature.
Description: Huntsville, Texas : Texas Review Press, [2021] | Series:
    The Sabine series in literature
Identifiers: LCCN 2020042332 (print) | LCCN 2020042333 (ebook) |
    ISBN 9781680032307 (paperback) | ISBN 9781680032314 (ebook)
Subjects: LCSH: Galveston (Tex.)—Fiction. | LCGFT: Thrillers (Fic-
    tion) Novels.
Classification: LCC PS3568.O994 L43 2021 (print) | LCC PS3568.O994
    (ebook) | DDC 813/.54—dc23
LC record available at https://lccn.loc.gov/2020042332
LC ebook record available at https://lccn.loc.gov/2020042333

Cover photo courtesy Ken Lund | Flickr

for
Pat Soledade
and, as always,
for Karen

"In passing out of the country of sin, one necessarily passes through it."

—JOHN HENRY NEWMAN

A cold, biting wind pushed down from the north, swooshing through the oddly shaped, thick evergreen trees we'd seen in abundance since we'd left the coast.

It had been a long trek, a little over thirty miles—the easiest parts beside rice paddies, the hardest the skirting of villages and up and down steep hills covered with dense forest—from the drop-off point between two tiny villages whose names on the map looked like random letters, mostly cees, that had been scrambled and let be. Navy boys had deposited the two of us uneventfully on the beach and then slipped back into the frigid sea under an overcast midnight sky. Then their job was done, except for piloting their small vessel not too many kilometers south into significantly friendlier waters of South Korea.

But for Gomez and me, we'd just clocked in. For the part of a mission we always called the Dark Side of the Moon.

The building we'd finally reached was as unlike a fortress as a house in the suburbs. Which wasn't surprising, since we didn't get sent into fortresses; those required the noisier attention of more traditional, rough-and-tumble firepower.

The General rarely let us in on how we were matched with particular tasks, but the close proximity to the sea and the border had to have been factors this time, though not as weighing as the fact that whoever the tip had come from had been positive that there would be relatively few bodyguards to deal with. Which was confirmed by the array of satellite photographs we'd studied, the most recent one just before climbing into the boat. Which meant the North Koreans were either amazingly naïve, foolishly overconfident, or we were about to walk into a trap. My money would go on a combination of the first two, since trapping the likes of Gomez and me would really benefit no one, and wouldn't make a headline anywhere in the world.

The house was washed in splotches of silver moonlight. It was low, modern, and big—sprawling over much of a hilltop—and was surrounded by a dozen or so acres of those odd trees, set to dancing now by the perpetual wind. The chain-link fence that surrounded the compound wasn't electrified and, once the lone sentinel had passed by in his jeep on the ring road, we'd scrambled over, listened close for barking dogs, didn't hear any, and settled into a comfy nest among some thick tree trunks to take turns eating, sleeping, and spending the remaining hours of daylight watching the goings on at the house. Which consisted of nothing more exciting than a trio of guards armed with rifles and side arms randomly going in and coming out again, and one civilian, small even for a Korean, who made a single appearance on the deck, spoke with the guards, and went back in. Just before nightfall, the guy in the jeep drove up to the house, got out and went in, and one of the others drove the jeep back out the road that zigzagged through the trees toward the fence.

If things went as planned, he'd be the lucky one.

When darkness fully descended, we nodded at each other, said nothing, and Gomez moved quickly along the edge of the trees, keeping, as always, awfully quiet. Gomez was a master of quiet.

I tried to locate him in patchy moonlight that filtered down though the racing clouds as he made his way animallike through the undergrowth, but he'd gone as invisible as a superhero in a comic book. Gomez was as small, lean, and chiseled as when he'd been the odds-on favorite to be the New Mexico state champion cross-country runner in his senior year of high school. If it hadn't been for the girl who'd dumped him a week before the state meet, and the subsequent bottle of tequila he'd chugged—which led to one guy getting his skull fractured and another, who happened to be an off-duty Santa Fe cop, getting his arm broken—he'd have ended up with a full ride at Arizona State, and a shot at making the Olympic team.

But, as it turned out, he'd ended up with the General. As I had at about the same time.

The two of us flew not only under—as the cliché goes—the radar but under politics and sanctions and bureaucracy as well. When it came to matters of last resort, the Powers That Be had at their disposal whole brigades of brawny commandos and any number of talented snipers, long-distance, high-caliber lads who could nail a sucker in either eye from an almost unbelievable distance. But the problem with using commandos or snipers was you left one hell of a calling card.

Gomez and I, on the other hand, left pretty close to nothing. We didn't have to locate shell casings or drop rifles into rivers or lakes because we never brought rifles. Just one pistol each, not of the huge Dirty Harry variety, as often as not never fired, and slender daggers, honed razor sharp, in scabbards on our boots. This time, the plan was to be in and out with nothing more in our wake than the three soldiers who, hopefully, would wake up with nothing more serious than a few bruises and a son of a bitch of a headache. And, of course, one guy who wouldn't wake up at all, one problem solved that no government or regime would ever mention, since what he was up to wasn't . . . mentionable.

The actual deed was always done quickly and was hardly the stuff of James Bond or *The Terminator*. Most of our assignments consisted of a hell of a lot of planning, followed by a hell of a lot of walking, then a hell of a lot of waiting, and finally a brief moment of brute force that any thug in any alley could provide.

All of my attention was on the brightly lit deck. The guard on the far side would be Gomez's problem. His two colleagues, chattering softly as they leaned against the handrail, would fall to me. One of them, obviously off duty, had left his rifle inside, so he'd be the second item on my agenda.

I moved from one tree to another to the opposite side of the house from where Gomez would be by now. We never wasted time or energy trying to find each other, since we always knew the other was in place.

Some wind chimes were singing out in the darkness, probably in the handsome garden filled with comfortable looking chairs we'd seen from our afternoon vantage point. Tall bamboo stalks tapped and rubbed against each other in the wind; lively oriental music drifted out of the house from a radio.

When Gomez's guy said something that caused my two to turn toward him, I sprinted across the wide, brightly lit lawn, pressing myself tight against the dark side of the deck. When the men above me resumed their conversation, I pushed the button on my wristwatch that activated a silent vibration on Gomez's. Which meant Now.

Which meant Go.

Gomez was over the deck's railing in a split second, leaving the guard not even enough time to lift, much less fire, his rifle before he had him twisted, turned, downed, and out cold.

Of my two, the one with the rifle—perhaps not the brightest light in the fixture, or the best trained—turned to see what the commotion was, presenting the perfect target for me to kick his firearm loose from his grip. Which was my desired result; the unmistakable sound of his wrist breaking was unfortunate.

His cohort, quicker than his buddy, charged in quick, mean, and headfirst, delivering one hell of a thumping wallop between my shoulder blades. Which probably gave him great satisfaction but wasn't nearly as effective as employing the pistol on his utility belt might have been. By now Gomez had gotten behind the one who I had relieved of his gun and had him in a headlock. Gomez required very, very little time to get behind things.

My soldier was still in the process of unholstering his sidearm when I had the end of the silencer on my own pressed hard against his forehead.

So far, so good. No shots had been fired, so I hoped the man in the jeep out at the fence would continue keeping his own counsel.

Gomez pummeled his fellow hard enough to keep him out of commission for a bit, while I kept my pistol affixed to his comrade. There was, of course, a remote chance that the little man inside would either come out blasting or slink around the side of the house and make a stealthier approach. But he was an aging academic and, more likely, if he'd heard us at all over the music, would either hunker down and hope for the best or find the nearest window or door and hightail it for somewhere else. In which case Gomez would overtake him before he crossed the yard. I generally left as much of the running as possible to Gomez.

When I'd settled the second guard down and administered the little injection that all three would be getting to assure enough naptime for us to be on our way before they awakened, we moved quickly through room after room, finally locating our subject behind a closed sliding panel in the kitchen. He was a small gentleman of late middle age who, in his robe and slippers, looked like an average enough grandfather ready for bed. Except for the fact that he was cowering on the floor, hugging his knees with his arms. And the fact that the General had told us he was his little country's best and only hope of perfecting some new and faster process involving nuclear physics especially applicable to long-range missiles.

He sputtered out something as Gomez lifted him gently to his feet. Then—just as the remainder of my breath was finding its way home after the sharp blow to my back—he turned him around, pulled his arms behind him, and locked them into a tight grip.

The sweet aroma of something fried in oil, pungent and peppery, filled the room. A mammoth wok in need of a good scrubbing sat on a gas ring. The music from the unseen radio clanged and clinked.

The man's eyes were wide now, as I stepped up to him. They were brimming with panic, of course, and a good bit of fear. And knowledge.

Almost every time, at the very end, there was a cold knowledge in a subject's eyes.

When he realized that this was how it would be.

• • •

Later, after we'd left a stack of notebooks in ashes, a laptop computer in fragments, and the three still snoozing guards tied up for the fourth to discover when he showed up for his breakfast, we'd put the place behind us and headed south, away from the sea. It was standard procedure to never leave the way we came.

We didn't talk for the first several miles, and kept to a steady course, stopping just once to drink some water and eat a couple of protein bars. Gomez said he'd hoped we'd see some giant pandas, and I told him I thought they only lived further north, in the high mountains.

He wiped some crumbs away from his mouth with the back of his hand, nodded, and said he'd wanted to see at least one.

An hour or so later I asked him, in a stage whisper we'd perfected long ago, if he still intended to reenlist.

He shrugged, didn't look back at me, and kept at his steady pace beside the dark road that was little more than a country lane.

We'd had the conversation before. Several times of late.

"This shit we do," he finally said, "ain't exactly a marketable skill in the real world."

I said it was in parts of it.

"Not any part I'd want anything to do with." He pointed at me. "You neither."

The first faint hint of headlights bled through some trees up ahead, where the road doglegged to the right. We jumped over a shallow ditch and rolled as far up under the brush beside it as we could. Then we froze into place.

In a few seconds an old sedan clattered past. The fact that it was neither a military nor a police vehicle was good, and that it didn't slow down was better.

We waited for long enough to make sure it wasn't coming back, then I double-checked our coordinates on the tiny GPS device that the General said was cheating, not as honorable as an old-fashioned compass.

When we were nearly home free, I tapped Gomez on the arm.

"Your problem, my friend, is that you don't have an Innisfree."

He pushed away some brush, leaned forward to see if there was anything up ahead that we didn't want to be there, then we moved back to the edge of the road.

He laughed. A short, smirky laugh quiet as a gust of wind.

"What the fuck is a Innisfree?"

I fell in beside him.

"This poet . . . ," I started.

Gomez shook his head.

"Oh shit, *here* we go. You and your goddamned—"

I brushed his usual response away with one hand, then we both were quiet for a long moment. Listening.

6

When the normal sounds of a forest was all we heard, I continued.

"In this poem, by an Irishman named Yeats, a guy has this special place where he wants to end up. A little island in a lake called Innisfree. He wants it so bad that even when he's standing in a cold, rainy, grimy city, with traffic speeding by, all he has to do is think about the place, maybe close his eyes, and he can hear the waves slapping up on that island."

A night bird cawed loudly. We looked around; then grinned at our edginess.

"Re-upping wouldn't be on your mind, wouldn't be a possibility," I said, "if you had an Innisfree. Some place to look forward to. Some place to aim for."

He held me in a long gaze that was a mixture of camaraderie and confusion. We'd come a long way, Gomez and I. In a very real sense we'd grown up together. Both of us had been eighteen when we'd been scooped up by the General, nearly two decades before.

"There ain't no hope for you," he finally said, "if you think there's places like that out there." He shook his head, his snort of disgust exploding into white vapor in the cold air.

Then we picked up the pace, took longer strides. We sensed safety now. And close by. We sensed, beyond the quintet of physical sensations, a small boat waiting in a small river, with a Navy kid gripping the throttle of an outboard motor calibrated to run very quiet indeed. And, a few miles beyond that, across the border, a tall man with a large cigar who was as close to a father as either of us could come up with, standing beside a jeep.

We made good time then, as we walked out of the Dark Side of the Moon.

The clouds of the night before had moved on, blown out with the north wind. I looked up at a wide sky full of stars.

One more mission, I figured. Maybe two. Then . . . something else. Another life.

Because, unlike Gomez, I *did* have an Innisfree.

And in the darkness of that cold forest I could very nearly hear warm waves lapping against its shore.

Part I
The Clerk Typist

One

The guy at the bar was misbehaving.

Talking too loud. Too crudely. Laying down entirely too much of the old *look at me, listen to me; ain't I something?* scent that such people employ to stink up otherwise perfectly fine places.

If you let yourself succumb to it, there'll always be a guy at the bar. So, usually I finish my drink, put down a tip and find the door.

But *this* guy. It hadn't taken more than a few minutes of *this* guy for me to know that a demure departure wasn't going to happen tonight.

In the first place, he was hitting too hard and too impolitely on the girls sitting down the bar from him. Second, he had that mean look about him, that squinty-eyed, scowling visage that lets you peg an asshole across a big room even in bad light. And—last but certainly not least—he was wearing a baseball cap inside the house, and backward.

And I just don't like that.

So I leaned over my martini and stirred the olive around a little. Max, the owner and usual bartender, already knew me well enough to start loading his silver shaker with cracked ice whenever he saw me come in, since it was always a martini I was after. And Max knew exactly how I wanted it built: a generous dollop of Bombay Sapphire with not much more than a rumor of vermouth splashed in, stirred briskly to the icy perfection of an alpine cloud and served in a well-chilled stemmed glass with a single pimento-stuffed Spanish queen olive impaled on a toothpick. None of the trendy new sacrileges for me, with apple juice or chocolate or other such garbage. Just the tried and true classic, and every so often either a neat Scotch or a cold beer. Beyond that specific trinity, I'm out of drinks.

Max's place was one of a handful of upscale watering holes in the Strand district. Close by the Tremont Hotel, it had all of the accoutrements of a good place to bring a date—oak paneled walls, framed photographs of the island a century or so ago, ornate light sconces and plenty of red leather and brass—or to come by yourself, sink into a comfortable booth, and let the world go by for a little while. It wasn't the kind of place where the guy at the bar would normally be, his natural habitat leaning more toward the dives up on the seawall. But, like I said, his ilk is likely to turn up anywhere. Like a bad penny.

He clinked the ice cubes around in his drink, probably bourbon. He looked like a bourbon man to me. Then he leaned up on his stool, planted both elbows on the bar, looked at one of the girls down the way, and stirred the drink with his big finger. He squinted some more, then rubbed his jaw, like a great thinker, a real sage, before casting a pearl of wisdom.

"What I don't get," he finally said, taking another drink, "is why a gal like you is out here sippin' a few with another gal, when you could be holed up somewheres nice and cozy with somebody who could do you some good."

He winked at her then, took a loud swallow of his drink, and nudged his companion on the next stool.

"How 'bout that, Bob. Do *you* get it?"

Now Bob, obviously this guy's perpetual sidekick, was another prize. More than a few teeth shy of a full set. A belly that had given up any attempt at staying within the confines of a muscle shirt whose sleeves had either been ripped away or had rotted out. A pudgy mug that might once have come close to being baby faced, but now was just plain ugly.

Bob grinned. "I don't get it."

"I bet that's right," the girl said. She was sufficiently attractive, and had probably sat at enough bars to have listened to all manner of bullshit, to have honed the only reliable defense to it: a surly comeback.

"I bet you don't *ever* get it."

Her friend laughed, then drank some of her beer. Bob looked bewildered.

A Nora Jones number floated out of the speakers mounted over Max's collection of bottled spirits and rows of glistening glasses behind the bar. The music bled into the chatter of the fifteen or so patrons in booths, at tables, or balancing on stools.

"Now me," the other guy said, the one with the sneer and the backward turned baseball cap, "I get it all the damn time." He stared down into his drink, sucked an ice cube into his mouth, and plopped it with a splash back down into amber liquid. "I was figuring on gettin' me a little of it tonight." He looked hard at both of them, then just at the first one. "Till I seen you were with your girlfriend."

He waited for some sort of reaction. Them turning to each other and giggling was definitely not the one he'd hoped for.

That mean glare turned even meaner. He sloshed the ice cubes around.

"One thing I can't stand, Bob . . ." he started, then resorted to just pointing in the direction of the girls. "I can't stand . . . *that*."

Doubtless, there were numerous other things that he and Bob couldn't stand. I doubt that black folk rose very high in their estimation—what was left of Bob's muscle shirt proclaimed in fat letters that the South *would* rise again, under a waving Confederate flag—and Yankees and foreigners probably came up short as well. I'm not black, nor a foreigner, nor a homosexual. But I probably did fall within their definition of a Yankee, being originally from Oklahoma, which is north of the Texas border.

These fellows were each thirty or so, give or take a few years. So, a full decade younger than me. Bob wouldn't be a problem; he was fat, probably stupid and slow, and almost certainly the type that looked for ways to stay out of brawls rather than opportunities to get into them.

But the other one, the one doing all the jawing, was something else. He had twenty or so pounds on me, and not all blubber, like Bob's. This guy might have actually lifted a weight or two, and might just be a scrapper. With that go-to-hell smirk and that line of banter, he'd almost have to be. This wasn't a problem, either. Just a detail that must be factored in.

One of the girls actually winked at him, then. And drifted her long, polished fingernails along the other girl's forearm.

That did it for the guy at the bar. The straw. The camel's back. The whole deal.

I waited to see what his reaction would be. Watched him gulp down the last of his drink. Watched him push the glass away and hold up a finger in Max's direction for a refill. Watched him steam a few seconds. Then he mumbled "*sheee*it," stretching it out into almost three syllables.

"Gotta piss," he announced, standing up. He turned toward the girls. "I piss standin' up, by the way. I bet you gals do, too."

I gave him enough time to walk the length of the room to the can, then another couple of minutes to finish his business. Then I made my way through the clinking of glasses and the chatter.

He was the only guy in the room, as I had hoped he would be, and was involved with readjusting his cap in front of the mirror. I made as if to get past him to the urinals; he caught my eye in the reflection, locked his expression into the frown that must have been his default setting, and flexed his big hands into fists.

It took all of about two seconds to have one of them clamped tight, the arm twisted high up behind his back and his belly wedged hard against the counter. I put the pressure on and flicked the cap off onto the floor. He gave the startled look they always give. Then I slammed his face into the mirror, not hard enough to break the glass, but definitely hard enough to get his attention. Hard enough to make his lights flicker, I imagine.

He started to say something. I couldn't quite make out what since he didn't get very far into it before I administered his second meeting with the mirror.

"Now," I said, almost whispering it into his ear, pulling tighter up on the twisted arm so that he was as paralyzed as a bass held by the gills. "What you've been saying to those ladies in there." I pushed him close enough to the glass to make him think he was getting another ride. "You're going to stop that."

His look, at the moment, was a mixture of surprise, hatred, and fear. Definitely a little fear. He struggled to break loose.

So more pressure was necessary.

"You're gonna break my fuckin' arm," he managed to garble out. His nose was bleeding, just a little.

"Maybe," I told him. "That's entirely up to you. But I *can* tell you this. If you bring a quick halt to your rude behavior regarding those ladies, then you and I will be done. And," just a touch more force now, "if you choose not to, then I'll cause you all sorts of embarrassment in front of all those people. Then, I *will* break your arm. And maybe your nose."

I let go, and backed away from him. His first impulse was to charge, then he thought better of it.

"They ain't no *ladies*," he said, rubbing his hand and arm.

"That's not something you have to concern yourself with." I pulled two paper towels from the wall dispenser and wiped my hands. "Your only concern is the decision you have to make. Either you shut down your little sideshow, or I mop up the floor with you."

I crumpled up the paper towels and tossed them in the garbage bin.

"Choose wisely," I said.

Then I left him there and returned to my booth.

In a few minutes he came out, downed the drink that Max had made for him, threw some bills on the bar, snorted at Bob to come on, and left. Never looking at the two girls or at me.

Not too much later, when things slacked up a little, Max brought a fresh martini over and sat down opposite me in the booth.

He leaned back against the cushion and watched the other bartender, the younger one, sit a foaming draft beer in front of a customer.

"I don't guess I want to know what you did in the john to lose me those two charmers."

I tried for a startled expression.

"I did what I usually do in a john, Max." I looked past him at the two stools where they had been. "Did those guys leave? I hadn't noticed."

He grinned, pulling the first martini glass, the empty one, toward him.

"You get the house you bid on?"

I raised my glass in a toast. "You are looking at a bona fide home-owner on this island. No more shabby, one-bedroom apartment. No more washateria. No more parking my jeep on the street and hoping it'll still be there in the morning. "

"Congratulations," Max said. "Where is it?"

"Down the island in Jamaica Beach. Right in the dunes, on the gulf side of the highway."

Max raised his eyebrows.

"On the *gulf* side, no less. That had to set you back an extra thirty grand or more."

I stirred my olive around. Took a long, icy sip.

"Now tell me again," Max said. "Just how *does* one retire before he's forty, and buy a beach house that is actually *on* the beach?"

I let the frigid Bombay make its slow, pleasant progress down my throat.

"One serves twenty years in the army of the United States," I told him. "Twenty years to the day."

· · ·

Outside, a moonlit, midsummer night had settled in nicely over Galveston. I gave not much more than a glance around the tiny parking lot for the two creeps, who were both of the variety of vermin who can be counted on to slither off into the darkness once thumped down.

I had the top down on the jeep, and the night felt fine as I drove up out of the Strand district toward the seawall. Once there, what looked like every star ever created shone brightly over the wide expanse of the dark Gulf of Mexico. I turned right onto Seawall Boulevard and headed toward the west end of the island, souvenir shops and eateries and motels and hotels on my right, the sprawling eternity of the dark sea on the left. The usual summer crowd of tourists wandered along the sidewalk that topped the seawall. On the other side of the wide street, more of them moved into and out of bars and fast food shops. Jazz blared out of one of the bars when I stopped at a red light, some local combo picking up a few bucks in tips.

Soon, the boulevard dropped downhill and away from the seawall and became the Bluewater Highway. The buildings began to play out, but the gulf didn't. Then it was just her and me for long stretches between other headlights. The little village of Jamaica Beach—a few stores, a gas station, a collection of beach houses on one side of the highway and canal houses on the other—had already shut down.

A couple of miles further on, I pulled up behind the small house on stilts that I had just signed the papers on the day before and I took a long look at what would now be home. The realtor had said it was a classic Cape Cod and, since I had never been to Cape Cod and knew little about architecture, I took her word for it. It was the steep-pitched roof, the wide front deck, and the fireplace flanked on either side with built-in bookcases floor to ceiling that had rung my chime. That and the perfect view of the beach over the low dunes, the salty, constant breeze coming in off the water, and an abundance of tall windows that would let in tons of light. Whole roomfuls of dazzling, cleansing light would be great on some days, and those high windows framing brooding, winter skies would be equally as pleasing on others.

In the light of a full moon, she—for I could not think of her as anything but a she—seemed a perfect thing in a perfect place. I hadn't seen too many of those, manmade things that looked like they had evolved naturally, having grown into their setting like the rocks and trees around them. The Lion of Lucerne, carved into its stony cliff in a tiny city park in Switzerland was one. An old Bavarian church at the intersection of two winding lanes in Rotenberg, Germany, was another. None of the army bases where I'd spent the last two decades even came close. And neither did most beach houses.

But Gull Cottage did.

I'd asked the realtor if it had been named for the one in *The Ghost and Mrs. Muir*, but she obviously hadn't had a clue what I was talking about. It didn't matter, anyway. It was a nice name, and I couldn't have come up with a better one. Besides, there was already a placard proclaiming it high up between two shutters.

She sat closer to the dunes than her two neighbors, lesser houses with less character, utilitarian structures with decks and windows and doors and roofs, perched on the requisite stilts like all beach houses, but with nothing of the soul and spirit that had pulled me in and stolen my heart on first glance at this one.

I killed the engine on the jeep, then noticed that one of my neighbors had arrived while I had been in town. An old Chevrolet was parked at the house on the right. The realtor had said that it was rented out most of the time, that the owner lived in Dallas and came down to Galveston rarely. She'd said that someone lived full time in the one on the other side of me, but that he'd been gone for a few days.

"He's a colored man," she'd told me, being of a generation and obviously a worldview that would use that antiquated designation, and feel the necessity to. Something akin to full disclosure, I had guessed.

"But he's awfully nice, seems like," she'd added, quickly.

I climbed down out of the jeep and leaned against its hood, kicked off my sandals, dug my toes into the moist sand, and watched the mocha-hued moonlight spill over Gull Cottage. Tall, rough-hewn shutters rose up beside each of her windows, real shutters on heavy hinges that could be closed against angry weather. The panes of the windows mirrored the starry sky. A stiff sea breeze worked its way through the wispy grass on the tops of the dunes that hugged the house on three sides.

For a guy who had never owned much of anything, and only one other house that had been left to me and quickly sold, this little place looked fine, indeed.

It looked like home.

The only other one I'd ever known—not counting the barracks and then the NCO quarters on countless bases—had been so long ago that I sometimes had trouble remembering how the rooms had been arranged.

The wind died a little; a fragment of music came from the house where the old Chevrolet was parked. Some sort of rap or rock or pop that was as foreign to me as Swahili floated out of one of the dark, high up windows.

Where I caught a glimpse, for the briefest of seconds, of someone watching me watch my new house.

Two

The next morning I watched the sun climb up over the straight-as-a-ruler horizon that divided the sea and the sky directly in front of my porch. By that time, I was already two cups of strong, black coffee to the good, had gotten in a three mile run along the beach, push-ups and sit-ups, a shower, a bowl of Raisin Bran, and was settled into an Adirondack chair that had set me back the better part of three hundred bucks. The *Houston Chronicle* I was leafing through had appeared, along with the *Galveston Daily News*, in my driveway while I had been shaving, the first newspapers delivered personally to me in my lifetime.

I had no idea what percentage of society crammed that much of their day into the two hours before sunrise. But the military forever left its boot print on me when it came to rising and shining. I am one hell of a riser and shiner.

Sad excuses for waves rolled up on the beach, just visible over the dunes from my elevated vantage point. The surf on Galveston was altogether tamer than the thunderous, crashing assaults I'd seen in other parts of the world. It could be feisty, I imagined, when pushed by tropical storms but, on most days, the old gulf sent in gentler efforts, with barely sufficient heft to keep a surfer aloft for more than a few seconds.

Seagulls, inevitable and plentiful, cawed and squawked and darted down and then up again at the water's edge. A squadron of graceful pelicans skimmed a few inches over the rolling blue-green surface, one of them plowing down into the bathwater tepid Gulf for a mullet.

It was several days before the Fourth of July, and the houses that dotted the dunes were already full of renters or owners encamped for the holiday week. In a few hours, when the sun was up high enough to broil everything and everybody, the beach would be covered with ice chests and lawn chairs, with blaring boom boxes and yapping dogs and an army of sweating people.

So I was determined to enjoy it for a little while. Just me, my coffee, the morning papers, and those boisterous gulls.

Later, when I made a run up to the convenience store in Jamaica Beach for lunch fixings, the Bluewater was practically bumper to bumper with vehicles.

This would get old, I realized, as the summer wore on. But it would make what would come later a gift outright. I envisioned wide stretches of deserted winter beach to walk and run on, blustery days and nights with a chilly wind blowing in off the gulf. One empty house after another along the highway, with only Gull Cottage's and a handful of others' lights on. Smoke floating out of my chimney into the cold night, from either the wide hearth in the company of books upstairs or from the smaller firebox built into the chimney underneath.

But for now, I thought, as I inched along homeward with bottled water, lunch meat, chips, and bread in tow, it would have to be this. An endless progression of jackasses playing their music too loud and honking their horns for no better reason than that they had them to honk.

By the time I'd finally climbed my fifteen steps, thrown off my T-shirt, slapped together a sandwich, and brought it out onto the front porch, the beach was a swarming ant bed of activity. I plopped down in my chair, felt the warm sunlight on my chest, and looked up at a huge kite—a dragon, from the looks of it—spinning through a series of gyrations on the end of its long tether.

"I guess about the only thing all this wind is good for," somebody said close by, "is flyin' a kite."

I leaned up far enough to see just a head over the porch railing. It was a small head, and a pretty one, with a nice smile and long brown hair tied back. She was somewhere between sixteen and eighteen, I guessed.

"Hello," I said.

She took a few steps toward the sea, and I saw more of her. Quite literally. Since she had on what had to be one of the skimpiest bikinis I had yet encountered.

"We're staying next door," she said, pointing a small hand toward the house where the old Chevrolet was parked. She had a lilting little voice. A little girl's voice. She unfurled a big beach towel she had been holding and spread it on the sand. "The beach is too crowded."

Then she plopped down belly first on the towel, the ten or so square inches of blue fabric she was wearing not quite able to cover up much of her.

She looked up at me.

"So I'll just lay out here for a little while, if that's alright."

I told her it was fine. In point of fact, she was probably straddling the property line between the two houses.

"My name's Holly." She tugged a little on the bottom of her suit, then on the top. "What's yours?"

I told her it was Rafferty, not adding the first name, since I'm always called just Rafferty.

She laid her head down and closed her eyes. Her fair skin was baked to a creamy tan, and fell in gentle slopes, amid the slight confines of the microscopic swimsuit, in a way that would be of great interest to a boy her age. Hell, it was more than a little interesting to a man *my* age. She lay there long enough for me to think she had fallen asleep; I went back to what I had been reading in the paper.

The wide, blue sky was perfectly clear, except for a few tiny patches of high, white puffy clouds that drifted slowly along. Gulls sang out to each other and darted down to investigate any possibility of food among the throng of beachgoers.

"It's pretty hot," Holly said, after a few moments. I lowered the paper. She was propped up on her side now, the bikini top having shifted sufficiently to show a tan line.

"I bet it's a hundred," she said.

I pulled my attention back from her, and made a point of shaking the paper before continuing reading.

"You rent this place?"

"I own it." I folded the paper and laid it in my lap. "As of a couple of days ago. Do you . . . do your folks . . . own that one?"

She squinted her eyes in the bright sunlight and watched the house I was pointing to for a long moment.

"My granddaddy owns it. He lives in Dallas and never comes. So my mom and me come here sometimes when it's not rented out. We sort of take care of it for him. We came down to mow the yard and put fresh towels and sheets in there for the people coming in for the Fourth."

"Do you live in Dallas?"

She turned her attention from the house to me, gazing hard enough at my shirtless chest to make me pick the newspaper up again and thumb through it.

"We don't live anywhere, exactly," she said, when her inspection was concluded. "We stay down here a lot, mostly in the off season."

A series of hacking coughs erupted in her grandfather's house. Her mother, I guessed. All the windows had been opened to let the place air out.

"That old man over there," Holly pointed a graceful foot in the general direction of the house on the opposite side of mine, "he lives here all the time. He's gone today, I guess." She slowly rearranged herself into a cross-legged Indian position, the bottom part of her bikini disappearing completely into the valley between of her tiny belly and the tops of her legs. "He used to be a school teacher, Joyce said. I guess that's why he's so mean."

"Who's Joyce?"

"She's my mom, but I call her Joyce."

I told her that the realtor had said that the man next door was nice enough. She considered it.

"Nice enough if you like bein' yelled at for playin' music too loud, I guess."

She pushed at a place on her leg. Then she wetted her thumb and rubbed it against it.

"What do you do?" she wanted to know. "You know, like your job."

"I'm retired."

She showed the same surprise at that that most people did.

"You're not old enough to be retired." She laughed. Which caused her nose to wrinkle up and the patch of freckles on her cheeks to stretch wider.

"I was in the army. You get to retire after twenty years in the army."

"Jimmy—he's my boyfriend—he might go into the army. Or the

Marines." She got to her feet, stretched, and wandered over to the bottom of my stairs. "How old were you when you went in?"

I told her I had been eighteen.

"Jimmy's almost eighteen," she said. She climbed four or five steps, sat down, her back to me, and hugged her knees with her arms. She thought a minute. "So that means you're thirty-eight."

She was only off one year; I'd just had a birthday.

"Your math skills are impressive."

"You couldn't prove that by the bitch that taught me algebra last year."

She was close enough for me to see the field of small freckles on her shoulders, like tiny almond bits baked into a golden pastry.

I asked her what grade she was in.

"I ought to a senior. But I failed a whole year, because Joyce and me move around a lot."

I considered telling her I needed to go make a phone call, or make a roast, or make a birdhouse. I could tell her, of course, that I still had a lot of unpacking to do, which would have been the truth.

"What did you do in the army?" she asked, letting go of her knees and leaning back against a step. "Jimmy wants to jump out of planes."

"I worked in offices. My official title—it's called an MOS—was a 71B10, a clerk-typist."

She continued to look out at the gulf.

"What's a clerk-typist?"

"A clerk is sort of like a bookkeeper, and a typist is . . . somebody who types on a keyboard. Actually, they changed the job title not long after I enlisted, to data processor. I like the old one better, though; it's got more character."

"So, what did you *do*?" Data processing must have seemed more than a little lackluster when compared to jumping out of planes.

"I was a company clerk for a long time, in lots of companies on lots of bases. Then I got promoted a few times and was a section chief, sort of like an office manager, over some other soldiers."

She turned her head around, and studied me for a moment.

"You don't look much like a clerk-typist."

I didn't know how to respond to that. I'd heard it before, plenty of times.

"Did you have a gun?"

"Everybody had a gun . . . a rifle. Mine stayed locked up in the company armory except for when I had to fire it on a range once a year."

"Were you in a war?"

"I was. Two, actually."

"Clerking and typing?"

She stretched her legs out if front of her. Her toenails were painted fire engine red.

I smiled.

"That's right."

She went back down to her towel, laid back down on her stomach, picked at the knot that held her top in place, and let the two narrow strings fall away. The pink sides of her breasts glistened in the sun, like tomatoes waiting to be picked.

She lifted up a tube of suntan lotion and waved it in my direction.

"You want to put some on my back?"

I told her no, I didn't think I wanted to do that.

She grinned one of the most fetching, playful grins that I had ever seen. A grin that would serve her long and well if she turned out to be the type to employ such a device. And the current evidence—laid out on the beach towel like a young lioness waiting for a meal—indicated that she just might.

"What's the matter?" she asked, clicking her tongue against her teeth. "It's just a little oil."

Her golden back sparkled. The tiny triangle of her bikini bottom stretched tight against a compact rump. She lifted one short leg up, rocking a slender, tanned foot slightly.

"Entire wars have been fought over oil," I told her, as I got up and went inside.

• • •

A little while later, when I had unpacked a couple of boxes of books and placed them in the shelves on either side of the fireplace, I heard the familiar series of coughs. Closer this time.

"I thought you were going out on the beach," somebody said.

"It's too crowded out there."

I stepped up to the porch rail just in time to see Holly sit up on her towel, the bikini top still untied.

"That's Joyce," she told me, not concerned in the least that one breast was quickly becoming unfettered.

"Get inside and put a shirt on," Joyce said.

Holly smiled, rearranged her top, got slowly up, waved at me, and pranced off.

"She's kind of a free spirit, I guess you'd say," Joyce said, shaking a cigarette out of the pack she was holding and stabbing it between her lips.

"She's a pretty girl," I told her.

"Oh, she's pretty, all right. Pretty enough to get herself into some real trouble one of these days." She cupped a disposable butane lighter in one hand against the wind and held it up to ignite her smoke.

She had the same slight build as her daughter. Something about her was attractive enough—cute, even—though she certainly hadn't made any attempt at it; she wore faded blue jeans that were beyond the help of patches in a few places, flip flops, and a halter-top. She had on no make-up or nail polish, and her light brown hair was close-cropped and danced around a little in the wind.

Two decades spent in places where plenty of people used plenty of drugs had left me with a pretty reliable Geiger counter, and it didn't take more than a glance to know that this little lady had done her share. Any spark that might have once been in her face or her eyes was gone. And she was left with the tired, sad look of a woman who the world had knocked around pretty good. The look that adds five or more years to a woman's appearance. When I subtracted those, I guessed her to be in her mid-thirties, so she'd have been about Holly's age when she'd had her.

"I'm Rafferty, by the way."

She stood in the bright yard and nodded at the information.

"My dad owns the house. We're just cleaning it up before some renters get here. We're leaving in the morning."

A blast of rock music exploded out of the windows above her.

"Holly tells me you come out here pretty often."

She considered that. Maybe she considered me. She took a long pull on her cigarette.

"Sometimes," she said, letting the smoke find its slow way back out through her nose and her mouth. "Not all that often."

Then she turned and walked up the steps into her father's house.

• • •

Late that night, I read by the light of just one lamp in the living room that was slowly taking shape around me, finishing off a second martini. Lindberg's life was moving along nicely in the pages of the big biography that I'd bought the week before. My books filled up the shelves beside the fireplace like they belonged there; empty cardboard boxes lay discarded around the room, like spent shell casings. The windows were open, to let in the sea breeze.

Across the way, one light was on in the neighboring house. The window was open, and Holly was moving around in there, talking on a cell phone. She stopped, glanced in the direction of Gull Cottage, and unbuttoned the top button of the long shirt she was wearing. Then the next one. She turned away then, and went on with her conversation, perhaps with Jimmy, who wanted to jump out of airplanes. When she turned back around, the shirt was completely unbuttoned. She let it slide down over her arms and fall to the floor and there she was, in just a miniscule pair of panties, her brown hair down now.

I turned off the light, watched the show that was obviously being played out for my benefit for a few minutes, then got up and went to read in the bedroom.

• • •

The next morning came as hot and humid as those before it.

By the time I had finished my three miles and lumbered along through the shallow swirling tide, sweating and catching my breath, the sun was making its first golden sliver of an attempt to break into the dark sky over the edge of the Gulf.

And there, in the odd half-light, stood what I had been dreading, wondering about, maybe even hoping for. Hell, when you were as screwed up as I was, who could know?

"Hello, General," I said.

He watched me for a long moment. He was dressed in corduroy slacks and a knit polo shirt, as informal and unofficial a getup as I had ever seen him in. He stood well back from the surf, lest his expensive shoes get wet.

When I got to him, he offered his hand and I shook it.

Knowing, as I did so, that it would be a long day. Knowing, too, that finding me on a relatively small island hadn't been a problem for him. He could have found me anywhere.

"Let's take a ride," he said.

He said it with the confidence of someone used to having things go the way he wanted. With the confidence of one—one of only three or four living men—who knew that I had never, not even for a single day of my twenty-year hitch, been a clerk-typist.

Three

Middle America stretched out to the far-off curve of the world outside the window of the small private jet. The engines hummed beyond the tight shell of the cabin, no louder than a vacuum cleaner being operated in a room down a hallway. I took a sip of my coffee and waited for us to get to wherever we were going; the most elemental reckoning put it somewhere north and east. Another foregone certainty was that we were going to see a third person, since, otherwise, the General would have just filled me in at Galveston.

He had fixed the coffee himself in the tiny galley, a task proving to be no great feat even for a man not accustomed to doing things for himself, since it involved placing a pre-measured, porous packet into the only obvious tray that it could go into and pushing a button. Our breakfast had been sausage biscuits from a McDonald's drive-through on the way to Ellington Field, the Air Force base close to NASA. Even with the time it had taken for me to get a shower and a shave, we'd beaten most of the inbound morning traffic on Interstate 45 and had pulled up beside the plane around eight.

The General had brought no aides with him, and had driven the rental car himself from Houston to Galveston and back again. I had no doubt that he would have piloted the plane himself if flying had been among the plethora of things that he could do. But neither of us could fly an aircraft, though we had both jumped out of our fair share of them.

I watched him as he looked out the window beside his own comfortable seat. It had been only six months since I had seen him, so he couldn't have possibly aged to any great degree. But he *looked* older, maybe owing to the clothes that seemed so wrong on him. Stiffly starched camouflage fatigues, razor-sharp at the creases, with pairs of black stars stitched on the collars was what I was used to. Or, less commonly, dress blues, with a cluster of decorations the size of a large saucer, the Airborne Ranger crest just above it.

He was closer to sixty than fifty, with a leathery face of the Ernest Borgnine, Lee Marvin sort, white, Methodist, widowed father of three sons, none of whom had served in the military. A grandfather several times over. He was a career officer who had been passed over for a West Point slot and had received his first promotion fresh out of an ROTC program in a state college. In his first tour in Viet Nam, he'd won a Purple Heart and a Silver Star. In his second, he'd received a field promotion and ended up one of the youngest Majors in the army. After that war was over—not *won*, he'd be quick to tell you—he'd pretty much disappeared into the hazier areas of special operations. He drank single-malt Scotch, smoked Cuban cigars when he could get them and large, expensive domestics when he couldn't, detested games of any sort with the lone exception of the Army–Navy football game, and prided himself on not having seen a movie since John Wayne died. He owned one television set, a thirteen incher, which he never tuned to anything other than the Fox News Network, believing all the other options to be too hopelessly slanted in the direction of a bleeding heart, liberal philosophy that he saw as a peril and a sin. This, and a little more, was what I knew about him.

And it was significantly more than most people knew.

We talked about a couple of things in the news, about how hot it had been in Texas, and about not much else. When the pilot began his slow descent, we'd been silent for maybe twenty minutes.

"Sir," I said, watching what a pretty well-educated guess told me was either Pennsylvania or West Virginia lifting up toward us. "I thought I'd made it clear that I was done with this."

He took off his glasses and wiped them with a handkerchief, one of dozens of polishes they'd get before the day was over.

"Just sit and listen when we get there," he said. "That's all I'm asking. Then, if you have some questions, ask them." He put the glasses back on and the handkerchief away. "If you don't, then go on home and watch the waves roll in."

The moment his foot hit the tarmac at Andrews Air Force base, the General reached into his pocket and took out a gargantuan cigar, then his silver lighter with the insignia of his infantry division inscribed on the front. I followed him toward two late-model cars of different makes and colors. He told me to stay a few miles behind him, which was an SOP that we'd followed before. Which meant he finally had to divulge our destination.

His expression didn't change when he told me where we were headed. Neither did mine, since it had been on my very short list of possibilities.

• • •

The man we'd come to see kept us waiting in his office while he attended to something that one of his minions assured us was important. The General looked at his big Rolex a couple of times, obviously put out; I just studied the gigantic room and listened to my stomach rumble. It was past noon, and the sausage biscuits were distant memories.

The entire wall beside us was dominated by three large windows that gave one hell of a view of a substantial number of the treetops of northern Virginia. The glass in the windows was bulletproof, undoubtedly, and the thick concrete pillars between them reinforced to such a degree that an airliner or a missile, while certainly able to achieve its purpose, would nevertheless shutter a bit in the final seconds. The furnishings in the office were eclectic, the bookcases filled with a spattering of leather-bound official manuals and some biographies and histories. A cluster of photographs showed our host with assorted presidents and other world leaders. There were several family portraits, on various beaches and mountains, with various grandchildren and large dogs in the forefront.

I wondered how many other men had watched the sky through the three windows, or stared at the bulky, horrific lamp beside the couch, with the agency logo imbedded in its ceramic belly. Each new occupant of the opulent office surely brought in his own keepsakes and favorite pieces, but that lamp looked like something that had been there a while. It looked downright territorial.

A table in the corner was set for four people, with a white tablecloth and immaculately placed china and silverware and crystal goblets. Note pads and silver pens lay beside each place setting. A small bowl of white roses was in the exact center.

I looked at the table, then at the General.

"Don't get your hopes up," he said, looking at his watch again. "We're not the sort of company that gets asked to stay and eat."

When he finally made his entrance, the man—short, late sixties, silver hair cropped almost as short as the General's—breezed through a door behind his massive desk, looked at some memos or notes on its surface, then finally looked up at the two of us, standing now. He was in his shirtsleeves, his necktie loose at his collar.

He leaned over the desk and shook the General's hand and then mine as I was introduced. Then he looked at his wristwatch.

"Well now . . ." he said, lowering himself into the big chair and making a face that said let's get on with it. He slipped a pair of reading glasses out of his pocket, picked up a file and made a noisy business of leafing through its contents, stopping occasionally to actually read something.

He pointed at our chairs without looking up and we sat back down.

"You mustered out as a sergeant," he said, eyeing me over the half rims that perched on the tip of his nose like a cat waiting to pounce. He put the paper back in the file, then closed its cover.

"You didn't exactly soar up through the ranks, did you, Sergeant?"

"I'm not a sergeant," I reminded him. "I'm a civilian."

The General leaned forward.

"His service record was my idea," he said. Any other officer, even of the flag-grade variety, would have added "Sir." But I wasn't surprised that the General didn't. He horded both compliments and shows of respect. And he spent them sparingly.

"A man of Rafferty's . . . expertise . . . didn't need to have any undue attention drawn to him, inside the service or out. In there," he pointed to the file, "you'll see that he was a company clerk for most of his career. Then that he moved into administrative duties with only slightly greater responsibilities."

The man picked at the edge of file's cover. Pushed it a few inches away from him on the desk.

"Well, then," he said. "Let's have the real scoop. These units that he was supposed to be working *for*? Did they actually exist?"

He relaxed a little, reaching across the wide surface of the desk and lifting a cup from its saucer. Whatever he'd hoped to find there was either cold or absent; he clattered the cup back into place.

"Either out-and-out fabrications, outfits on paper only," the General told him, "or, a couple of times, he was attached to three or four actual infantry or armored companies at a time, as a liaison from division headquarters. Because he had several places where he might be, the company commanders never wondered where he was."

The man turned his attention from the General to me.

"What did you *do* during all this time?"

I had begun to wonder if I was going to be included in the conversation at all.

"I waited for the General to send for me. I trained. I read a lot; picked up a few college courses." I had, in fact, completed a Bachelor of Arts degree, with a double major in history and literature, and a Masters in philosophy. But I didn't figure he'd be interested, and I wasn't interested in telling him.

He leaned back into the plush leather of his chair. The General broke in.

"Per special arrangement with the defense department, Rafferty drew pay—and some benefits somewhat . . . out of kilter with his official record. When he retired, it was actually with the comparable rank of a light colonel. There are no commendations in that file. There's not any mention of any medals whatsoever, other than the obligatory ones that every grunt gets for doing his time. "

He looked at me.

"There *should* be. But there's not."

The man waited a long moment, as if thinking something over one more time before making a commitment. Then he unlocked a desk drawer and lifted out a slender folder. He opened it, and laid it out flat before him.

"There's a problem," he said, "in France. The fact that it *is* in France being the lion's share of the problem."

He leaned back. Rocked a little. Which I'd been expecting him to do. What's the use of having a throne that carved several thousand bucks out of your budget if you don't put it through its paces every once in a while?

"France is . . . *France*," he said. He waved a hand slowly in the air, as if to push away any notion of the country whatsoever. "They're traditionally and historically our friends and comrades but, when push comes to shove, they're just as likely to put their airspace off limits to our fighters when we need it as not. They don't like the situation that I'm about to explain to you any better than we do. But what they'd like even less is letting us in on the . . . solution."

Now that he had made up his mind, he rolled on like he'd found a new gear.

"And, since the French government doesn't seem any more inclined to do anything about it themselves than they were to stand up to the Nazis in 1940, we're in a Catch-22 of sorts."

He shook his head. Maybe he caught his breath.

"I can't use my people. And even if I could, the network is so screwed up over there right now that it could all come flying back into our lap in spades. For the same reason, the military is out. We simply can't take any action on this that might be construed as being planned or carried out by this government, covert or overt."

He pointed at the General, but kept his eyes on me.

"Your old friend here got called in to see if he could come up with an idea. And what he came up with was *you*."

Which, of course, came as no surprise. They hadn't flown me up there to see the sights. Besides, I'd already seen them, plenty of times.

"Our dilemma at the moment is one . . ." he looked down at something in the file, "Jacques Deminelle."

I asked if I was supposed to recognize the name.

"There's no reason you should, unless you're up on international high finance, or the lifestyles of the rich and famous. He's a regular mover and shaker among the frogs."

He lifted a single paper up. Scanned it.

"Forty-six years old. Inherited a considerable fortune that might or might not have been made in collusion with the Germans during the war, then added to it through some rather dubious means of his own that landed just far enough over the right side of the line to keep him out of prison. He's an extremely vocal opponent of the war in Iraq, but then he'd be in an infinitesimal minority in France if he wasn't. He enjoys the highlife, and pops up pretty often in the Paris society pages, with some young model or actress on his arm."

He leaned back in his big chair, rubbed his neck. Took off his glasses.

"On one of the many occasions that he had *more* than one young lady to attend to him—and a very young *man* or two, we've come to understand—an underage girl ended up face down in the pool on his estate in Saint Tropez. The local authorities managed to gloss it all over, and our boy was never even brought up on charges. It seems that money talks as loudly over there as it does anywhere else."

I looked at the General, then back at the man. Shrugged my shoulders.

"He sounds like a real prince of a guy. But surely we have enough domestic scum bags to worry about without having to go abroad."

He leaned forward.

"Deminelle has some connections that we . . . don't care for," he said.

The General, who was no doubt as hungry as I was and probably needed a cigar and a drink, decided it was time to scuttle the gobbledygook and cut to the chase. He turned in his chair and looked at me.

"Rafferty," he said, not paying any attention to the third person in the room, "this man is the gold standard of bastards." He leaned toward me. "He personally helped finance . . ." He paused then, as if hovering between considering the best way to relay the information and being taken aback momentarily by recalling it. Finally, he breathed out a few more words.

I sat staring at him. Seeing, instead of him, the top of the two towers of the World Trade Center erupting into billowing explosions of smoke and flames, like thick matches just scratched into life.

A clock ticked somewhere in the big room. The three of us sat in complete silence for a time. It was the General who broke it.

"His own money, and a hell of a lot more that he helped raise, going straight to Al Quaida. Straight to Bin Laden. We *know* this!"

He jabbed his index finger hard enough on the table between us to make a crystal vase rattle.

"What's more," our host said, "the *French* know it."

He got up and walked slowly around the big desk, stopping to gaze out the middle of his windows.

"Something sticks in the French president's craw about killing a fellow countryman. Maybe it's all that liberty, equality, and fraternity horseshit. And he's just as adamant about letting somebody *else* do it."

"Why isn't the guy arrested and put on trial?" I asked. "It seems like it'd be a touchdown for the home team."

He was still looking at the view.

"I thought I'd already covered that, Mr. Rafferty." No Sergeant now; maybe we were making progress. "He's a French citizen. Of some renown. The French don't want the stigma, and we, at the moment, don't want to piss off the French."

He turned away from the window and looked at me.

"It's one of those vicious political circles that make readers of espionage novels wonder if they really happen . . ." He actually managed a slight smile, "That really do."

He buttoned his shirt collar, then pulled his necktie tight.

"The bottom line is this: there are people high up in both governments who want Mr. Diminelle to simply . . . not be."

I asked him *how* high up.

"I'm not at liberty to say. And you don't need to know."

He took a step closer.

"All you need to know is how to plan this thing perfectly, executing one of the precise surgical removals that the General assures me is your forte. Then get yourself home and wait for a significant deposit of taxpayers' money to appear in a secure bank account. Then you forget this, and we forget you. The world's a little better place, and you're a little better off."

He looked at his watch. Then he looked at the table in the corner. Three ravenous VIPs were probably waiting outside the polished mahogany doors, not the much smaller one that opened into a back hallway that we had been shown into and were obviously about to be shown out of.

"I've got another meeting," he said. The General stood up. I didn't. The man summed up.

"You'll be entirely on your own. You don't belong to us, or to the army, and you damned sure don't belong to the French or the UN or anybody else. There can be absolutely no trail of any kind—paper or electronic or anything else. Just set it up, do it quickly and efficiently, and . . . disappear."

He went back around his desk, picked up his suit jacket, and put it on.

"Needless to say, if you are apprehended, or killed . . . then you will quite simply be caught. Or dead."

He took off his glasses, folded them and put them in his shirt pocket.

"The General can help to some degree. With research. But damned little, and no tactical support at all."

He waited for me to get up.

"I haven't said I'll do it," I told him.

His neck colored slightly then. His eyes narrowed. He was new at the job, and his predecessor had famously botched things up badly. So both Congress and the media were eyeing him closely. He'd obviously wanted his own people to do this, but he'd had his hands tied. Lowering himself to even consider this idea had surely cost him something. And now the prospect of being deprived of even that really popped his cork. He pointed at the General.

"You could have *told* him that before you left Houston." He tapped the surface of the desk with one nervous finger. "Why'd you even *come?*"

I stared at him for a long moment, then let a trace of a nod tilt in the General's direction. That would have to be enough of a reason.

The man watched me for a long moment. Then he visibly relaxed.

"At any rate," he said, "thank you for making the trip. This is a thing that needs doing, and it needs doing soon."

His handshake was firm. Confident. The kind of handshake the General had long ago convinced me was admirable.

"I hope you'll give it some thought, Mr. Rafferty. I certainly do."

At the door, the General shook his hand and thanked him, adding "sir" this time.

• • •

After an excellent late lunch–early dinner of blue crabs and Chesapeake oysters at one of the General's favorite restaurants, he handed me an envelope that I could tell was fat with cash.

"There's a seven o'clock Continental flight with plenty of open seats from Ronald Reagan to Houston. Go home, knock back a few of those goddamn awful martinis, and let me know something. ASAP."

Outside, I whistled down a cab, and as it was pulling up he put his hand lightly on my arm.

"I could say something *real* shitty right now," he said. He took out another one of the monster cigars, bit the tip of it off, and spat it out. "About how much of a patriot you are."

I opened the door to the cab. Then I waited for the rest of it.

"But we both know I'm not going to do that." He fired up his lighter and held its flame to the cigar. "Just like we both know that I'm not going to say anything about how Gomez would have jumped out of his ass to do this one."

I turned and starred at him.

I could have come up with something shitty myself to say at the moment.

"Well, it's a lead-pipe cinch that Gomez won't be doing it." I kept my hand at my side, figuring we wouldn't be shaking. "Isn't it, General?"

He probably wanted to tell me to go to hell just then. But he didn't. He tried for a knowing smile.

"And I'm not going to ask you what your decision will be."

He puffed away at the stogie for long enough to get it going. Then he executed a half-hearted twitch of his index finger, and stepped back to the curb.

"Because we both already know the answer to that one."

Four

The packet of cash was more than adequate to cover a first-class ticket. So I splurged. I sank down into a wide, comfortable seat, had myself a couple of Heineken's, a not too shabby filet of sole, and worked my way through the copy of the *Washington Post* I'd bought at the airport before we touched down in Houston. Where I eyed the long line at the car rental counters, then eyed the remainder of the stash, then headed outside to where the cabs were waiting.

Gull Cottage looked inviting when the cabbie, a blessedly quiet guy who seemed happy enough to make one long run down to the island and back instead of a bunch of short ones in the city, deposited me at my driveway just short of midnight. I tipped him handsomely, and, when he had pulled away, counted out the remaining bills in the light of the full moon. Just about enough to provide a fresh bottle of Bombay at the Sand-n-Sea Liquor Hut the next day. Sort of a travel perk, was how I decided to consider it.

That was exactly what I was thinking when the world was yanked out from under me and I ended up on my ass among a great clattering of a distinctly confusing and unknown origin. Something—instinct, training, adrenalin; probably a heady mixture of all three—brought me up again quickly and twisting around to deal with the situation. Which turned out to be not much of one at all.

While there had been sufficient moonlight for me to count my money, there hadn't been enough to allow me to see the black metal barbeque pit in the dark shadow of the house. I had hosed it down and given it a good scrubbing the day before and left it out to dry. Now it lay in several pieces—grill, base, and cover, with one wheel off to one side—looking like the photos of the Titanic debris field on the bottom of the Atlantic.

A light came on behind me. I looked up and could just make out, in the house on the side of Gull Cottage where the commotion had just transpired, the figure of a man—a tall, slender one in what looked to be a pair of too-large boxer shorts—silhouetted against the bright light behind him. He was standing at the edge of his front deck, gripping the handrail in front of him.

"Jesus *Christ*," he said, not one bit happily. "What the hell's going on down there?"

The light that let me see only an ebony outline illuminated me and my unfortunate barbeque pit just fine. He looked at both of us.

"This is my house," I told him, lest he think I was a prowler.

"Is that right?" he said, his voice not as pitchy this time around. It was a mellow voice actually—with a gravelly undertone—that still retained an edge of aggravation.

"Then where the hell have you been all day. I've been here since this morning, and that jeep hasn't moved one inch. There hasn't been a soul in or out of that house as far as I could tell." He nodded at that, confirming, I guess, that he didn't miss much. "You telling me you been in there all day? What the hell, you some kind of a *monk*?"

"I was gone," I said, the words sounding as stupid to me as they must have to him. I rubbed the shoulder that had taken the brunt of my fall.

I told him I'd been brought home in a taxi.

He looked at the empty place beside the road where I was pointing. Looked at me. Shook his head. Pointed to my jeep.

"That's not your vehicle?" he asked.

I told him it was. He took a moment to think about it.

"Well," he said, "I guess if somebody wants to get a snoot full and have to get hauled home in a taxi, and then fall down in his own yard . . . that's his own business." Then he was silent for a moment, his speech dissolving into a barely audible *tsk, tsk, tsk* that reminded me of someone that I couldn't quite locate in my memory bank at the moment.

"But goddamn it, boy," he said. "Some of us want to get a little *sleep!*"

With that, he spun around, darted back inside as quick as a hiccup, slammed the door, and turned off his light.

So now I had made the acquaintance of the retired teacher who Holly had said was mean and the realtor had said was nice.

For a colored man.

• • •

The next morning I decided to put any consideration of anything other than my run, my toilet, and my breakfast off till they had each been accomplished. When they had, I dug into one of the larger boxes in the bedroom and found the huge artist's tablet that I remembered seeing there and took it and a mechanical pencil out to the front deck with a last cup of coffee. Then I plopped myself down in the Adirondack that had become my command center, feeling not a little like Captain Kirk on the bridge of the *Enterprise*.

Over the top of the big pad an ominous bank of dark clouds lifted slowly up over the gulf, boding ill for holiday revelers who were already making their pilgrimage down to the surf. The weatherman on television had given a thirty percent chance for rain, which was quickly looking closer to a hundred percent from my perspective. Independence Day was still two days away and, given the Gulf's fickle nature when it came to summer showers, conditions could go either way.

The pad of parchment-colored paper that I held looked like a particularly expansive bit of potential that might, or might not, be ultimately realized. When I had taken those college courses, every composition I had to write—up to and including a couple of lengthy senior level research papers on John Steinbeck's role as a propagandist in the run-up to World War II and Woodrow Wilson's futile League of Nations crusade, and a graduate thesis juxtaposing European and American existentialism—started with a blank sheet of paper or a blank monitor screen, either of which scared the holy hell out of me. Then, bit by bit, and word by word, ideas and phrases and finally complete sentences found their way into the emptiness and every hour was more of a minor victory and less of an impossible goal.

The cream-colored expanse that gazed back at me was roughly four times larger than either a sheet of typing paper or the screen of a laptop computer, but it was no less intimidating. Maybe more so. The end result of those empty slates had always been nothing more than an insignificant morsel of academic clap-trap that would have no more effect on the world than to further my progress toward one degree or another. The culmination of this one would, if I decided to go through with it, be of significantly greater import. If not to the state of the world, then at the very least to my stepping, voluntarily, back into a world that I had vowed to leave forever.

The first rumbling echoes of thunder rolled through the low clouds that hung heavy and dark over the water. Muffled lightening exploded deep inside them, like flash bulbs going off slowly somewhere in a hazy night. Beachgoers began packing up their gear and heading back to the safe havens of vehicles parked at the edge of the dunes or rented beach houses. In not too many minutes, the first solid pings of rain pattered on the roof over my deck. The sea breeze picked up, just a little, and the sweet, musty fragrance of rain and salt swirled over everything.

I rolled a few millimeters of lead out of the tip of the mechanical pencil, eyed it against the dark sky like a doctor inspecting the needle of his syringe before jabbing away at someone, and carefully printed a single word in one corner of the big page.

FRANCE.

I looked at it, thinking, as I did so, that there were many, many other words that I would rather have written in regards to the planning I was commencing.

The last time I had been there—carrying a passport, credit cards, a driver's license, and a library card all in a name other than my own—had been during one of that nation's frequent snits aimed at the United States. So I'd had to have a visa, issued by the French consulate in Milwaukee, the city that the General had selected as the hometown of whoever I had been for that visit. So I wrote the second word on the tablet. Smaller.

Visa?

I was assuming, of course, that, if I ended up doing the thing at all, I would be doing it in France. Which might or might not turn out to be the best plan. If the object of our affections had any travel plans that I could discover, it might be better to leave France out of the equation completely. In the bottom, left-hand corner, I printed a heading, leaving several inches beneath it for the list that would gradually emerge.

TO-DO

Then I penciled in the first item.

Itinerary for subject—Immd. future.

The society pages of a Paris newspaper might be helpful there. But it was a long shot; it would be damned near an unbelievable stroke of luck if *Le Monde* reported that Jacques Deminelle was enjoying the first part of his two-week holiday on the tiny Greek isle of Skyros, with a photo of him along with two young bikini-clad models and a grinning teenaged boy in a Speedo.

The best approach would be to have someone finagle the information out of this guy's personal secretary or—better yet, since it took another human being out of the mix—tap into his computer and find his planning calendar. But these were out this time, since the resources of any agency that could accomplish either of them were off limits. So I'd have to do the digging myself.

Somewhere in the center of the page, I jotted down:

Airlines—private / public.

Remembering what the fellow in the big office had said about Deminelle being substantially well-heeled, I crossed out public and circled private. If I could discover what charter service he used, or if he owned his own plane, then I'd be a step ahead toward learning where he might be going anytime soon.

The thing that had been tapping persistently at the back of my brain tapped again, so I wrote down what it wanted me to write.

SECURITY?

Given the lifestyle he led, and the company he kept—not to mention the activities he funded—he had to have at the very least a bodyguard or two. More than likely, more than that. Of the massive, thick-necked variety, with shaved heads, locked-in scowls, fists the size of small hams, and nine-millimeter Glocks close at hand. Electronic surveillance at his home, and at any villas and playgrounds he had scattered around here and there would be formidable. And maybe prohibitive. Cameras everywhere. Sensors. Guard dogs.

God, I hate guard dogs.

There would still be some level of security at places other than his residences, but it might be more easily breached. Not *easy*, of course; nothing about this would turn out to be anywhere near easy. But easier. Maybe.

I looked up from the paper. Maybe for the first time since writing the first word. The rain was falling harder, beating out a lively tempo on the roof of my porch. Some more of the thunder worked its way slowly through the clouds out over the Gulf. The beach was completely deserted now; everyone was inside their house or their car waiting to see if the bottom would fall out of the clouds and send down a pounding deluge, or if it would just be a little summer shower and, after a few minutes, quit.

It quit.

By the time it did, and sunlight crept over everything like a blanket being pulled back, I had covered the entire page with questions and comments. All of it neatly printed. Most of it in single words. Many of which were crossed through, with better, more specific words beside them. Some things were circled. Some had stars. The to-do list had quickly outgrown its little corner and had snaked up along one side to nearly the top of the other side of the page.

The legion of beachgoers plodded back through the dunes toward the surf, their umbrellas popping up like flowers blooming quickly in a meadow. Seagulls floated along in the freshly washed air. I scanned the page full of my careful lettering. There were damned few answers there, if any. And a bumper crop of questions.

But it was a start.

Enough of one for me to lift up the cordless phone beside my chair and punch in the numbers for the General's secure line.

Enough of one for me to speak the two syllables that we both had expected.

"Okay," I said, and pushed the off button on the phone.

• • •

I woke up to the sound of someone coming quickly up the steps leading to my deck. I closed the cover on the sketch pad I was still holding.

"Hello to this house!," the someone sang out.

Then my visitor stepped up onto my porch in a pair of oversized khaki shorts that came to his knees, a long button-down shirt the texture of grass cloth and the color of the paper I had been writing on for the last couple of hours, and a pair of reading glasses suspended over his narrow chest on a woven lanyard. He was as tall and lanky as he had appeared when silhouetted in the bright light the night before, and his movements were as rapid. Almost like a small dog rushing at anything new.

"My name's Tucker," he said, jabbing his hand toward me even while I was still getting up out of the chair.

I shook it.

"Rafferty."

He lowered himself, uninvited, into the porch swing close by my chair.

"That's your last name, I imagine." He said, pulling a wide bandana out of one of the pockets of his shorts and wiping it across his forehead. "Unless you're an Ivy League playboy or a Boston banker."

I was about to tell him I was neither when he kept on with his end of the conversation. So far, it had all been his end.

"I go by my last name myself." He gave one last swipe to the back of his neck with the bandana, folded it, and put it away. "I was the last of nine children in my family, and they had all but run out of names by my turn, so I ended up with an *awfully* ugly name—after my Mama's brother who'd drowned—that I never used, even as a child."

I realized, then, that I was still standing. So I sat down. He leaned against the curved back of the swing and slowed down his recitation, finding a more comfortable pace.

"When I was a little boy and my granddaddy was still alive he told me one day that I'd ended up with a damned silly name for a boy to go around with and that he had been against it. So he said I ought to just go by my last name. He—my granddaddy—had been called Tucker for so long that I don't think he even remembered what his first name was."

He rocked a little in the swing. His skin was the color of milk chocolate, his wiry, white hair cut in a short cropping. His face was a patchwork of creases and his tall, lean body of the sort that any clothes he might put on it would likely appear too large. He was in his late sixties I guessed, maybe seventy. The eyes he was studying me with were narrow.

"Are you sober?" he asked, speaking slowly now, as if he had shifted his way down through the gears to the lowest one.

"As a judge," I told him.

He laughed at that. He had a rich, deep laugh.

"Son," he said, "I've lived on this island all my life, and I've seen more drunk judges than sober ones."

"So you're a BOI?" I asked him.

On Galveston, BOI means "born on the island," and it constitutes a status akin almost to royalty in other parts of the world.

"I am indeed. Fourth generation. My great grandfather was a slave here, and my granddaddy—the one who went by Tucker— along with my grandmother, my daddy, and a couple of his siblings—all lived through the storm. Barely."

Saying *the storm*, on Galveston, was like saying *the city* in Oklahoma when I was a kid. There, it could only mean Oklahoma

City, and on Galveston, which has been in the direct path of many hundreds of storms, *the storm* invariably means the hurricane of September 1900. Between six and eight thousand people died in a single night when the entire island became part of the ocean floor for several hours, and it is still the greatest natural disaster in the history of the United States.

"I was sober last night, too," I told him. "Just for the record."

He nodded at the information.

"*I* wasn't," he said. "I'd been in the hands—literally—of too many doctors and nurses for the last couple of days, all of them prodding and sticking and being more intimate than I could enjoy under the circumstances. So I came home and had a couple of highballs and went sound to sleep. Till you decided to go dancing with your bar-beque pit, that is."

He took another long look at me. The kind that was full of questions he'd like to ask. But just a few minutes with him told me that he was the sort of man who would not overstep his bounds. I'm not inclined to make snap judgments about people or situations. But I caught myself thinking that I wouldn't be at all surprised if I ended up liking him.

"I usually mix up a tolerable batch of martinis around five," I told him. "If you want to drop by."

"That's neighborly," he said, standing up. Stretching. "And I'll take you up on it."

I got up and shook his outstretched hand a second time.

"At five, then."

He looked at the sketch pad in the chair.

"Are you an artist, Rafferty?"

I smiled. Shook my head.

"Can't draw a straight line. I was just tinkering with a few thoughts I needed to stretch out wide enough to see them."

He mulled that over.

"A thinker," he said. "And a planner." He nodded. "That's fine. We could do with a thinker and a planner around here." He turned his attention from the tablet to the house that belonged to Joyce's father. She and Holly were gone now, replaced with a family of milky white mainlanders who had spent several hours already at the beach and would no doubt spend the evening slathered with an ointment that wouldn't provide nearly enough relief to their lobster-red skin.

"Most folks," Tucker went on, "around here, don't think about a damned thing. Don't plan anything. They just wade into a situation till they either drown or somehow or another wade back out."

I told Tucker I had met the daughter and granddaughter of the owner of the house a couple of days before.

He frowned. "They're out here pretty often."

"Joyce said they look after the place for her dad," I said.

"Looking for a place to stay free," he said, "is more like it."

He glanced at me.

"Be careful there." He said, pointing at the house, then at me. "The little girl would screw a woodpile if she thought there was a snake it in. And her *mama*." He shook his head. Made the little *tsk, tsk, tsk*ing sound that he had made the night before, that I suddenly remembered one of my old First Sergeants used to make. "Well . . . all I can figure is that her mama has a lucrative little business going on here and there. Sort of like a pharmacy, if you get my drift. Without the degree to hang on the wall."

He went quickly down the steps, taking two at a time, raising one slender hand in farewell.

"If she *owned* a wall."

Five

The stately four-story Rosenberg Memorial Library sat halfway between the Strand and the seawall on 23rd Street, among sprawling shade trees that might be as old as the building. Which looked to be about as old as the ground it stood on.

Max, the bartender so adept at concocting perfect drinks, told me once it was the oldest public library in continuous use in Texas. He was a walking chamber of commerce, that guy, having migrated down the intercoastal waterway from somewhere on the east coast several years before and finding enough to keep him perpetually interested on the island, living on the boat that he sailed in at one of the marinas. He was a history buff, especially when it came to *the* storm, and he'd said this library was *the* place to go to dig around about it. And, I was hoping as I climbed her steep steps, it might be a good place to dig around for other things as well.

Max had told me he'd had to pass muster with the chief archivist before finally being allowed to handle some of the original newspapers and other documents from 1900. They'd made him wear white gloves, so he wouldn't leave any smudges. For what I was after, there wouldn't have to be either an interview or a pair of gloves. Just a variety of dependable databases and a good computer that couldn't be traced back to me. Unlike the laptop on my table in Gull Cottage.

Inside, I chose the last computer in a row of ten, sat down in a chair that couldn't have been designed to be more uncomfortable, and went to work.

A couple of hours later, I'd had made pretty good headway through the list of things I'd transposed from the huge artist's pad to a much smaller notebook. The third database I tried gave me a list of articles about Jacques Deminelle from various French publications. They were all in French, of course, so I had to do a lot of cross-referencing with the language translator on the computer program. Finally, one of the articles had a photograph with him boarding a private jet, which, luckily, included the big registration numbers on the vertical fin. It would be easy enough now for the General, on an invented pretext regarding some completely unrelated matter, to get some little cog in the big machine of cloak and daggerage to trace the plane, determine if it belonged to Deminelle or a charter service, and tap into a schedule of any imminent flights filed with the French equivalent of the FAA. Two of the articles mentioned Deminelle's keen interest in scuba diving and, it being July, he might just be jetting off to one tropical hole or another to plunge into in the next few weeks.

I scanned most of the articles, jotting down facts in my notebook, like three high-profile divorces, four high-profile affairs that resulted in other peoples' divorces, and what seemed to be an ongoing touch-and-go tap dance with officialdom in regard to questionable business practices. I printed out the entire texts of only a couple of pieces in English that I wanted to spend more time with later. None of the articles made any mention of the death of a young girl in Saint Tropez or—no surprise here—of any dealings with Al Quada or Osama bin Laden.

The dozen or so photographs of Deminelle that I came up with all showed a tanned, lean fellow invariably in an open-collared shirt and a wrinkled sport coat, a shock of brown hair that he had probably paid a Paris hairstylist a handsome fee to look unruly, and a confident—almost surly—grin that said he expected to live forever.

• • •

Later that afternoon, Tucker took a long, eyes-closed sip of his martini, then breathed out a remnant of icy vapor. He smacked his lips. He smiled. At the risk of bragging, I can attest that my martinis have induced similar reactions on numerous occasions.

He held the frosted glass by its narrow stem and twirled it around, watching the olive resting in the crystal-clear gin and dry vermouth. Rocking a bit on the porch swing, he hoisted the glass in my direction.

"You get an A plus, Rafferty." He managed to condense my name from three syllables to two. He leaned back against the cushion and got comfortable. "The first faculty party I went to back when the schools integrated," he said, watching the perfectly blue sky over the still crowded beach, "oh, about a century ago it seems like, a couple of the white teachers appeared downright amazed that I not only knew how to drink a martini, but how to *make* one." He laughed that rich laugh of his and took another sip. "One of the sons of bitches was so cocky about it, I told him I'd left my jug of Ripple down in the car, along with my watermelon and chitlins."

He'd come bearing gifts. A big bowl of spicy crab dip that was as faintly sweet as it was lemony tart, along with crackers and chips.

"You're a chef," I told him, downing another fully laden cracker.

He shook his head.

"I watch the Food Channel. And download the recipes." He tilted his glass, indicating that a refill would not be refused. "None of my wives—three, all told, before you ask—were very good cooks. So I became one. Simple as that."

I poured his glass full again from the shaker.

"And now," he said, settling back into the swing, "in my lonely dotage, it turns out it is a skill both enjoyable and convenient."

"What did you teach?" I asked, topping off my own drink.

"Math, when I taught. Then I was an assistant principal for a long time, and finally the principal of a junior high school."

"Here in Galveston?"

He nodded. Smiled.

"My entire life has been spent right here on this island. Other than a couple of years away at the express invitation of the draft board. And then college."

I calculated which war his would have been. He was too old for Viet Nam, even the earliest part, but maybe barely old enough for Korea. He must have seen the gears working.

'I was what we called, back in the fifties, a cold warrior. Which meant the only action was going on in politicians' minds. After boot camp, they sent me to Fort Hood, not five hours from here." He crossed one slender leg over the other, both of them emerging from his gigantic khaki shorts like gnarled branches growing out of a tow sack. "I spent my two years battling communism in the base laundry."

He lifted the toothpick from his drink, let the olive drip-dry, then bit into it.

"The one good thing that came from the whole experience was my going to college. On Uncle Sugar's nickel. I do believe the G.I. Bill was the wisest thing the Congress did since repealing prohibition."

"I was at Hood," I said. "For a little over a year."

He watched me drag another cracker through the dip.

"I wondered if you might have been a soldier."

Then we worked our way quickly through the usual banter. That I had been in both Desert Storm and Iraq, that I had retired after my stint. That I didn't look like a clerk-typist.

When the sun was a good bit lower on the horizon behind my house, the dip bowl was scooped dry, and the second shaker of martinis was nearly empty, he got around to asking the question that had obviously been on his mind.

"Why Galveston?"

I sat quietly for a moment, sloshing the remaining puddle of booze around in my glass.

"I mean," he said, leaning up in the swing, "if you managed to save enough army pay to buy this little beauty of a house—which I've always coveted, by the way—then there were prettier beaches, better climates, that you could have had."

I nodded along as he laid out the enigma. Which had never been an enigma for me at all.

"I came here when I was eleven," I told him. "As a matter of fact, I was *exactly* eleven. We got here on my birthday. My uncle and me. My parents had died in a car accident a few months before, and Donald—he was my uncle—had been unlucky enough to be my only living relative. So he won the jackpot. It was a birthday present, you see. I'd never seen the ocean, and I guess Donald thought it would help me . . . get over everything."

"Did it?"

"It was the best week of my life, I think. I fell in love with the place. We must have ridden the Bolivar ferry a dozen times—back and forth across the bay, standing down on the main deck in front of the cars, or up on the observation walkway. Throwing bread crumbs up at the seagulls and seeing all those ships anchored out there waiting to dock. Watching the lighthouse get bigger as we got closer or smaller as we moved away from it. And the water churning up when the pilot threw the engines into reverse right before we hit the pilings."

I leaned forward. Rolled my glass, empty now, between my palms.

"I was pretty much in heaven. We hit all the tourist shops, all along the seawall. Ate seafood platters at Hill's and Guido's; swam at Stewart Beach. I got brown as a berry that week. I damn near cried when we had to go back."

"To where?"

"Oklahoma City. Donald was a real estate agent. I always knew he had to work extra hard when we got back to pay for the trip. My folks had been way deep in debt, with most of the rest of the country, so I didn't arrive as any kind of a bonus package."

I held up the nearly empty fifth of Bombay and shot Tucker my best questioning look. He gave me back what was probably his best *What the hell?* reply. So I went in for more ice and mixed up a short, final batch.

"I remember telling him," I said when I was back in my chair, pouring our last round, "on our way home, that I would live on this island one day. And—it sounds crazy, I know—but I just always had that as the plan. I never deviated from it. And the rest, as they say . . ."

We watched the sun sink down to the flat horizon behind us, over the Bluewater Highway and the wide expanse of salt grass on the other side and finally over the intercoastal waterway, where a tug lumbered slowly along, looking, from our vantage point, like it was pushing its barge through Kansas wheat fields.

"Donald tried his best to share my excitement about the trip. And the island. But I always knew it had just been another place to him. That it had all been for me. He probably got so sick of riding that ferry that he could have killed me." I waited for a few seconds, watching the distant tug disappear behind the edge of Tucker's house. "But he kept taking me back. Hell, he was twenty-six years old that summer—my dad's kid brother—and he shouldn't have been saddled with a nine-year-old kid."

Tucker smiled.

"I bet if you asked him now what he enjoyed about that trip, he'd say it was watching you have that fine of a time."

I nodded.

"I'll tell you what he *did* enjoy," I said. "Sea Arama, the old aquarium out on the west side that had the trained porpoise show." I thought of him watching them sail through hoops and dance on their tails across that fake blue water. He'd laughed at the corny jokes the girl with the microphone had memorized, and laughed again when we got splashed. When we got home, he talked about that show over and over.

Tucker drained the last of his martini. He put the glass down carefully on the side table.

"Sea Arama's been gone a hell of a long time," he said, standing up to gather up his platter and bowl.

"So has Donald," I said.

• • •

Later. When I'd tossed and turned through a fitful half sleep for a few hours and finally gotten up and made a cup of strong coffee, I stood on my deck and listened to the waves wash up on the black beach just beyond the dunes.

I stood there long enough to realize that there wouldn't be any more sleeping. It was still a couple of hours before time for my run. I was restless. A little edgy. Generally out of sorts, for no reason that I could specifically locate.

I'd committed to the General. So there wasn't any more soul-searching to be done about that. Not that there had been any even before I had told him I was in. It would be an interesting debate, I figured, as to whether or not there was much of a soul there to search.

A half hour later I was dressed and in my jeep on the Bluewater heading into Galveston. A second cup of coffee in the cup holder. The starry night splayed out around me and the damp, salty fragrance of the gulf rushing into the open jeep.

In town, the seawall was deserted, except for a handful of straggling revelers making their stumbling way to somewhere. The shops and bars on the other side of the street were closed up tight; almost every one of the windows in the motels and the big hotels were dark.

Up on the east end, out by Stewart Beach, I turned off Seawall Boulevard and headed toward the harbor, past little side streets named Barracuda and Dolphin and Bonita and Albacore. Past palm trees standing tall and perfectly still in the hot night.

There were only two vehicles waiting at the landing, a pickup and an eighteen-wheeler. The ferry was already docked; a few cars and another truck rolled slowly off, picked up speed, and headed up toward the seawall. In a few minutes, a sleepy looking attendant in an orange vest motioned us on board.

By the time I left the jeep and climbed the steep stairs up to the narrow observation platform, we'd churned out into the harbor channel and were making a sluggish, wide turn toward the bay. Pelican Island lay dark and quiet on our left, the brightly lit Coast Guard station on the right.

The truck driver and whoever was in the pickup had stayed in their vehicles, so I had the platform to myself. When we made the last of the turn I could just make out the illuminated lighthouse over on Bolivar. The ferry was one of the island's three lifelines to the mainland. The causeway, tall and graceful and usually thick with traffic—either the headwaters of Interstate 45 or where it petered out, dependent on how you approached it—was, by far, the most used. Then there was the toll bridge at the other end that carried the Bluewater Highway over San Luis Pass toward Surfside and Freeport. Finally, there was the small fleet of ferries that made this run over to Bolivar Point, carrying on pretty days almost as many tourists wanting a free boat ride as drivers needing to actually get someplace.

As the big engines chugged away and we slid across the dark bay, a few lines of Tennyson emerged from somewhere. Such is the benefit—and oftentimes the burden—of being an English major who paid close attention: snippets of verse bubble up at the oddest times.

The lights begin to twinkle from the rocks, came the poet's perfect phrasing—as they actually did on the narrow strip of boulders and salt grass that is Galveston's last toehold in the bay—*the slow moon climbs; the deep moans round with many voices.*

Many voices.

The pilot sounded the horn, sending a sad, lonely echo out into the darkness. As I clutched the very handrail that I had almost certainly clutched nearly three decades before, I felt my eyes tear up just a little in the stiff headwind.

Many voices.

One cold tear crept down my face. And I knew it wasn't just because of the wind.

Six

Every time I thought about the city, I was running.

Not running while I was doing the thinking, but running *in* my thinking. Or in my dreaming, or whenever the city happened to emerge. Not running in the sense of running down to the store for a loaf of bread. And not running for pleasure, or exercise. This was vein-popping, heart-pounding, throwing one sneakered foot in front of the other, serious hauling ass.

Because screwing things up, and then running away, was what I did best when I lived in the city.

The accident that killed my parents would have killed me too, without question, if I'd been in it. By all accounts it was a doozie, as car wrecks go, causing veteran cops and emergency personnel who'd seen more than their share of carnage, mechanical and human, to go queasy.

I'd been spending the night at my friend Jeff's house when the big rig plowed head-on into our little AMC Pacer while my parents were on their way home from the movies. The driver of the truck hadn't lived long enough to explain why he'd been barreling down the wrong side of the highway at what officials guessed must have been close to a hundred miles an hour. Subsequent toxicology reports cleared it up; he'd popped enough amphetamines to keep an entire platoon buzzing for a while.

Of course, there was barely enough left of my parents—their AMC Pacer was a Jetson's-looking little contraption with more glass than metal—to gather up and bury. But we did bury what they came up with in a big cemetery on the outskirts of Choctaw, which was itself on the outskirts of the city. My dad had been a civilian welder at Tinker air base there, and my mom had been a cook in one of the mess halls. We'd lived in a trailer park in Choctaw, where my folks spent most of their time screaming at each other, and sometimes at me, until I pretty effectively took myself out of the equation by spending as many nights as I could arrange at either Jeff's or Gary's, my only friends.

It had been Jeff and Gary who stood nervously beside me at the graveside service, all three of us outfitted in denim jackets—it was February—and jeans, tee shirts, and sneakers. Gary's grandmother had thrown a little fit and said that even if there wasn't going to be a proper funeral in a church, we ought to at least be made to wear our Sunday clothes. Which meant nothing to me, since Sunday was just one half of a weekend.

A few people who had worked with them came to my parents' burial, along with Jeff and Gary and their families, including Gary's grandmother, who frowned through the short service. An Air Force chaplain from Tinker read a scripture and said a prayer, looked at his watch, and got in his car and left.

I had known that the man who shook my hand as people were leaving was my uncle. I'd met him once before, at somebody's funeral. Both he and my dad had lived in the area all their lives, but they'd obviously never found any reason to spend any time at all with each other.

"I'm Donald," he said. Many men in that place, and that time, had the whole early seventies thing going on, replete with mutton-chop sideburns, gold chains, and ridiculously wide lapels. But Donald was in a nice suit with a dark tie, his sandy hair neatly trimmed just long enough to part on one side. He had on sunglasses.

"The thing is," he said, shifting the weight of his slender frame from one foot to the other, "I believe I'm the only family you've got."

He took off the sunglasses and slid them in his shirt pocket.

"Your mom . . . , " he had to think a second. "Cindy . . . didn't have any brothers or sisters, did she?"

I shook my head.

"And her parents are dead."

It was more a statement than a question, so I realized he already knew the answer.

He looked over at Jeff and Gary's folks, standing off to one side.

"I've talked to your friends' parents, and they said you could stay with them for a few days. Just till I can make some arrangements."

"What kind of arrangements?" I wanted to know.

"Well," this very nearly complete stranger told me, "till I can bring you to live with me."

I looked closely to see if he was joking. Then I looked over at the two little families and their downcast expressions long enough to know that he wasn't.

I never could remember if I started crying before or after I told him I didn't want to live with him. But I remember he told me he lived in the city. That he was a real estate agent. That he owned a cat. Which I suppose he thought might sweeten the deal; which it didn't, since I'd had no previous association with cats or any interest in striking one up.

A week later, Donald and I moved my not too many possessions from Choctaw into Oklahoma City. Four months later, in June, we went to Galveston for a week.

A few years after that, I started running.

• • •

Many readers of S. E. Hinton's novels about teen gangs in Oklahoma City probably doubted that the level of violent juvenile delinquency described in *The Outsiders* could have actually occurred out there in the boondocks, amid the yokels and a stone's throw from the wheat fields.

But they would have been wrong.

I was in my first fistfight when I was eleven, dislodging one of my front teeth that Donald had to pay to get fixed. I told him I fell on the concrete slab during PE, and he'd bought it easily enough.

I took up thievery when I was twelve and, by the time I was a bona fide teenager, I'd progressed from slipping candy and gum into my jacket pockets in TG&Y and Sears to working in tandem with my new buddy Sammy to pilfer cigarettes or beer from 7-Elevens, one of us diverting the attention of the cashier while the other one lifted the goods. We had a couple of close calls, but were too quick on our feet to get caught. Sammy could run as fast as I could.

He was my most reliable confederate, and the closest thing I'd had to a friend since Gary and Jeff who, though they both still lived less than twenty miles away, might as well have been on Mars.

I was one cocky little bastard in those days. I had the smart-ass attitude down pat, had enjoyed several rolls in the hay—once *literally* in the hay behind the girl's farmhouse on the outskirts of the city, the other times in cramped back seats of cars—had smoked dope when I could get it, had popped a few pills when they were offered, but mostly subsisted on a pretty steady diet of beer that we stole in convenience stores.

I lied to Donald constantly about where I'd been, who I'd been with, and what I'd been doing. About the lousy grades I made in school, and the trouble I was always in with one teacher or assistant principal or another. I was confident enough of my invincibility and Donald's naivety to share Sammy's confidence that we were ready, when we were seventeen, for the next step in our life of crime. For our intricately planned rite of passage into a lifestyle that looked awfully enticing at the time.

As it turned out, of course, I wasn't all that invincible after all. And Donald wasn't in the least bit naive.

When the proverbial shit hit the proverbial fan, Sammy and I had cased a liquor store, a little Mom and Pop shop in the bad part of the city. In other words, in what we considered *our* territory.

Problem was, a couple of guys with more smarts, more years, and more balls than we had considered it *their* territory. So when we did the deed, leaving the old man who ran the place at night none the worse for wear and the cash register relieved of its two hundred and thirty two bucks—we left the change—it wasn't two hours before the older punks who had been charging the owners for a little protection actually provided some. They waylaid us outside a games arcade that we hung out in, pushed us outside and around the corner into an alley, recovered the money—along with almost fifteen dollars that I had *before* the robbery—knocked us around like a couple of rag dolls and, when Sammy finally located the switchblade in his jeans pocket and snapped it open, they pulled out a pistol and shot him in the leg.

In less than ten minutes a policeman was looming over Sammy, the two fixers had made a clean getaway, and I nearly busted a gut hoofing it as far away as I could manage, having to stop several streets over to gasp in great gulps of air.

If this was an S. E. Hinton novel, Sammy wouldn't have made it to the hospital. The flashing hazard lights would have danced across his pale face, the wail of the siren would have filled the close confines of the ambulance. The attendant would have bucked him up, saying something like "Hang on, kid. Just a little further." And Sammy would have remembered just enough lines from a Robert Frost poem to burble them out before slipping away.

But Sammy didn't know Robert Frost from Robert Redford. And the attendant just called him a dumb shit and shook his head. He was at the hospital only long enough for a doctor to determine that the slug had just skidded past, leaving little more than a scratch. Then Sammy was driven over to the juvenile detention center, where he soldiered on heroically through their interrogations for all of ten minutes before providing them with my name and address.

It was Donald who answered the door and let the two cops in. He listened to what they had to say, came into my room and told me to get dressed, and then told them to keep me as long as they needed me, that he wouldn't be making any effort to get me out on bail. That jail seemed like the best place for the likes of me.

Two days later, after alternating between long hours of sitting around in orange warm-ups two sizes too big and being taken out to pick up cigarette butts and candy wrappers all over the city, after eating damned bad food, and managing to refrain from beating the holy hell out of some of the scum bags in there with me, I was brought before a judge.

Who, without actually ever looking at me, sorted through the papers in front of him and found me guilty of armed robbery—Sammy had shown the old man in the liquor store the knife that would later get him shot—and quite unceremoniously sentenced me to several years in the slammer.

What I didn't know then, standing there probably openmouthed, was that the system didn't work nearly this quickly. But I did recall one thing from TV shows and movies.

"Don't I get a lawyer?" I asked him. "I thought everybody got a lawyer."

The judge pushed the papers into a neat stack. Straightened its sides. Then, he took off his glasses and *did* look at me.

"You're fortunate, in one sense," he said, looking awfully judicial as he leaned back in his big chair and clasped his hands together in front of him. He was probably in his early forties. But he looked, that morning, to be as old as wisdom itself.

"You've got quite an uncle," he said, pointing to something behind me. I turned and saw Donald then, sitting in the front row of seats. "Who has gone to great lengths the last few days to convince me that you might be worth a second chance."

He leaned forward then and pointed his finger at me.

"I doubt that you are, you understand. But I've done a little checking up on your uncle, and not only can't I find anybody to say anything disparaging about him, I can't locate anyone who knows him that doesn't think he's the best thing since sliced bread."

The judge went on singing Donald's praises, and I felt the noose slackening. He found it admirable that such a young man had stepped in and raised a child he didn't even know, how he worked so hard to keep me clothed and fed. He went on and on and, by the time he finally got around to what he was wandering toward, I had turned completely around and looked at my uncle as if I was seeing him for the first time.

He looked exhausted. I guess from all the legwork he'd done and the arguments he'd concocted. And he looked sad. And why wouldn't he?

Donald would tell me later—after the judge finally put his glasses back on and commuted my sentence to a few months behind bars and then a probationary period, dependent on my getting myself, once I turned eighteen, into one of the branches of the military service for a hitch of at least four years—that part of his motivation to get me off was the fact that he hadn't been around enough to see the warning signs. He'd become one of the most successful young realtors in the city by then, and was gone almost all the time. Anything in the way of a social life was conducted away from our house. So, I'd had free reign, and he regretted it.

As the bailiff took me out of the courtroom at the end of it, I stopped and shook Donald's hand. And he gave what I thought, at the time, was an odd farewell.

"We know what we are," he said, stealing the words outright from Shakespeare, unbeknownst to me, who hadn't spent enough time or attention in school to realize it, "but not what we may be."

Seven

Joyce and Holly returned a couple of weeks later. On a Monday.

I was on my oyster shell driveway beside the house, refurbishing a fifteen-foot sailboat I'd bought from a guy a few miles down the Bluewater toward San Luis pass. And it was turning into a bigger project than I had anticipated.

I could have used either a big jar of industrial strength Ben Gay or a damned good masseur after the first day I spent stripping her of several layers of paint and shellac and barnacles. Two days later, when I had her down to bare wood, I went carefully over all of her one more time, this time by hand, using a fine-grade paper rather than the courser stuff I'd used on the first round.

The purchase of the boat, then beginning her restoration, had taken up much of my time since my trip to Washington. But the business I'd committed myself to with the General had taken up just as much. I'd made three trips to the computers in the Rosenberg Library in town and had called the General twice on a secure line and learned that my subject—we'd always avoided referring to them, in planning or speaking or thinking, by their names—would be flying to Bermuda the second week in September for a holiday. A little more digging around got me the resort he was booked into and the most popular spots for scuba diving in the area.

So, I was slightly less than two months away from doing, one final time, what the General had made me very, very good at.

I was a sweaty mess in only a pair of soggy cutoffs when Joyce's old Chevrolet rattled to a stop beside her father's house. All the windows were open in the car—an Impala; I guessed an '83—so, on a morning like that one, in the mid-nineties and not a cloud in the sky, either these two were complete idiots or the A/C was busted.

Holly threw open her door, jumped out, and bounced over to where I was.

"You bought a boat," she said, popping a wad of chewing gum

loudly. She leaned against it, running her hand along the starboard side.

"She's not just a boat," I told her, tossing the used piece of sandpaper into her bow. "She's a Herreshoff Buzzards Bay. Built in the thirties; one of not too many still afloat."

"How do you know all that?" Joyce asked, wandering up with the perpetual cigarette dangling from her lips.

I wiped the sawdust off my hands with a towel, then some more of the sweat off my shoulders and arms.

"The guy who sold her to me told me."

She smiled, drew in the last pull of her smoke. Tossed it in the sand.

"Then you don't *know* anything, do you?" She patted the scrubbed wood. "There might be thousands of these things all over the place. "

Holly laughed. She had on a pair of short shorts that she must have poured herself into, a brief halter top, and she sported a shiny little bauble in her bellybutton that I didn't remember seeing there before. She was barefooted.

"Did you get screwed, Rafferty?" she asked, through more popping of the gum.

"I hate to disappoint you ladies," I said, picking up a half empty can of Diet Coke and gulping down the rest of it. "But I burned the midnight oil online, and found out that this little charmer is actually worth more than I paid for her." I patted the vessel as if she were a well-behaved dog. "The owner just wanted her off the place and out of his way. Seems like she got left at the house when he moved in, and he figured she wasn't worth the time and effort it would take to bring her back to life."

I smiled. Probably I beamed.

"This time I actually found a bargain."

Joyce smiled, too. She had an attractive smile when her mouth wasn't locked into its usual down-turned motif, or when there wasn't a cigarette attached to it.

"You know what they say," she said. "Even a blind hog finds an acorn every now and then."

She turned and headed toward the house.

Holly stretched up on her tiptoes so that her tanned stomach—from the top of the skimpy shorts to the bottom of the equally skimpy top—was arched out in my direction.

"You know *how* to sail a boat?" she asked.

Joyce turned around, probably considering it a legitimate question.

"Not exactly," I told them. There had been one particularly harrowing night in the Baltic Sea just off Finland a few years back when I'd had to sail one for twenty or so miles, the owner of the little ketch having inopportunely died during a bit of bad business. I'd figured I'd run into land sooner or later, which I did. Of course, I couldn't tell Joyce and Holly about it.

"I'm planning on taking a course, and getting certified."

Joyce stopped, turned around, and shot me a look that said I might, indeed, *need* to be certified.

Late that afternoon Tucker came over and watched me sanding away.

I felt a sneeze coming on—I'd been sneezing all afternoon—and stopped long enough for it to erupt. Then I wiped the residue away with a cloth.

"Must be all this dust," I said.

"Probably a summer cold," Tucker said. "Nothing's better for a summer cold than alcohol."

He waited for a response. But got just another sneeze.

"Gin is fine for a summer cold. And a little vermouth."

He squinted his eyes and gazed out over the Gulf at a brooding, purple thunderhead that filled up the horizon.

"Looks like a gully washer's moving in off of Her Majesty," he said.

I studied it, figured he was right, and went back to work with the worn section of sandpaper.

He glanced at his wristwatch a couple of times to remind me it really was time to stir up a batch of martinis, and told me they made electric buffers nowadays and sold them over at the Home Depot.

"It's a mission," I told him, wiping my brow. "Like Alan Ladd and Van Heflin chopping out that stump in *Shane*. They could have just hitched up a mule to yank it out. But they saw the value of the struggle. The beauty of the *battle*."

He considered it.

"Another way to look at it," he said, "is if Alan Ladd and Van Johnson *had* used a mule, they could have been sitting down to a jug and supper a few hours earlier than they did."

The approaching storm sent out its first roll of growling thunder. The air grew rich with the aroma of encroaching rain. The gulls overhead screeched more frantically ahead of it. I backed up, surveying my progress.

"She's a dandy. Isn't she, Tucker?" I let my gaze wander down her clean, curving gunwale. The smooth mahogany shone in the sunlight.

"She's yar," I added.

He grunted out a few bars of his deep, signature laugh.

"Hell, the only thing you know about *yar* is that you heard Grace Kelly say it in *High Society*. You're from Oklahoma, son. What the hell do you know about sailboats?"

I looked at him.

"Probably more than you do. And you grew up on an island."

He nodded.

"And one of the first things I learned was to have enough sense not to climb into one."

The first, fat drops of rain plopped around us. Tucker helped me push the boat on its trailer between the tall stilts and under the house.

"My suggestion, my friend," he said, dusting his hands on his shorts, "in case you're interested, is that you finish getting this little beauty all fixed up. Get it right on out of your system. Then lean her over sideways in that pretty dune out by the highway and plant some ivy in her. Because if you're planning on sailing her tiny ass out there," he spayed one big, bony hand in the direction of the gulf, "then my next bit of advice is to take out one hell of a life insurance policy."

I pretended to pay him no attention whatsoever.

"And list me as the sole beneficiary, please." The rain came down harder. He ambled off, making the *tsk, tsk, tsk* sound my old top sergeant used to make.

"Because I need a new car."

Then he went up into Gull Cottage and, our relationship having quickly settled comfortably into whatever it was, he started making the martinis himself.

• • •

It rained all night. And that is an understatement.

It was more like somebody up there threw open the windows and poured out all the water that could be located. It gushed down in torrents, splashing hard into pools among the dunes, sending winding little rivers around and through them out to the beach. The rain pounded away at the roof of Gull Cottage all night long and collected in puddles on the concrete slab beneath her.

A different pounding woke me up a little after three, this time at the front door. I emerged from my grogginess just enough to bring the numbers on the bedside clock into focus.

I climbed into a pair of cutoffs, looked out the window, and opened the door to Holly, who was somehow crying and shouting at the same time. She fell into my arms and commenced a frantic cadence of heaving sobs that she had to get under control before I could make any sense of what she was trying to tell me. I held her tight, and let her catch her breath.

"*Joyce!*" she finally managed to get out.

I clutched unto her shaking shoulders and pushed her away so she would have to look at me.

"What's wrong with Joyce?"

"Got her!" More gasping. "Trying to *k–k-kill* her!"

By the time she was finished I was halfway down the steps.

I barely glanced at the pickup parked out by the highway. The stinging rain shot needles into my bare back as I ran through the standing water and up the steps to the house beside mine. The front door was wide open; all the lights were on.

The man standing over Joyce was administering what must have been the finishing touches to a pretty bad beating; without slowing down I could see that her face was a bloody mess and that she was cradling her stomach. Without even seeing his face, I pegged him as the sort to kick a woman in the stomach.

The guy was big. But not big enough to keep him from going down like a house of cards when I threw him the side body block the General had taught me two decades before. Then he just lay there, and I stepped over to make even more of an impression.

It was the second gorilla, the one that had been in another room or outside looking for Holly when I made my entrance that turned the tide. The one who coldcocked me with a resounding blow to the back of my head. Then, when he saw that it didn't put me down, he did it again. Harder.

So there I was on the floor—which was filthy, I noticed; Joyce hadn't gotten around to vacuuming—when Goon number one, up now from his tumble, decided, once he'd collected his wits and some of his wind, that it was time for a little payback.

While his confederate held Holly, no doubt copping a feel into the bargain, the first thug planted one boot in the small of my back, grabbed my left arm with one huge hand, and twisted it into the awkward contortion necessary for him to do what I knew he was about to do. As he made the one, fierce jerk that was all that was required to dislocate my shoulder, all I could think of was that he wasn't very good at this. When it came to the dislocation of shoulders, you should always go for the right one, since most folks are right-handed and the ensuing inconvenience would be greater.

But what he lacked in expertise, he made up for in pure meanness. The job was completed at the first effort, but he made several more big yanks just to drive the point home.

Every one of them them felt like a long, slender knife slicing first into and then out of tender, moist muscles, sucking my breath away each time. Then, when he had landed a single, solid kick into my ribs, slapped Holly for good measure, and made his exit with his buddy, what I concluded was the absolute worst possibility arose. The itchy, sniffly tickling that meant I was about to belt out one hell of a massive sneeze.

Which I did.

Which turned out to be not the worst possibility after all. Since, though it pummeled me like a sledgehammer, it also delivered me into complete unconsciousness.

• • •

Donald was there when I woke up.

He was sitting in the bleachers of the old Sea-Arama, and everything was hazy around him. Like an old, jumpy black and white home movie that is a tad off center, a tad out of focus. He was laughing, and watching the trained porpoises jump through hoops held by disinterested teenagers.

Then Donald was gone. Replaced by a guy named Siminsky. A kid from Idaho back in boot camp at Fort Knox. Looking always like Sad Sack in fatigues that engulfed him. Thin as a rail, dumb as a post, hounded unmercifully by the drill sergeants, one of whom said he figured "the best part of you, boy, must have ran down your daddy's *leg!*"

Just as suddenly, Siminisky was gone and a man I saw only once, years earlier in Turkey, stared back at me. His eyes gone wide with the sudden realization of what was happening to him. Of what *I* was doing to him. Which was the last thing he would ever realize.

Then, there was Donald again. Clearer this time. Much older now, or, at least *looking* much older than he actually was. Toward the end of it. Thin, ashen-faced, much too frail to be sitting upright in a chair beside my bed reading a magazine.

Finally, it was Tucker who was sitting in the chair, his reading glasses perched on the tip of his nose. In the bright light of either morning or afternoon that came in the hospital window. He looked at me. Closed the magazine.

"I got a little mixed up," I think I said. "For a minute there."

He nodded, tossing the magazine on the foot of the bed.

"Well," he said, "you do realize they've got you doped up like a ten-dollar hooker?"

I blinked, to make sure it was really him. Then I conducted the short inventory I'd had to do before. When waking up in other places, other times. All the fingers worked, and all the toes.

"How bad?" I asked, wanting confirmation.

He stood up, looming over me. The countless dots on the tiles over his head began to swim around.

"Your left shoulder was pulled out of its socket. The doctor got it back into place with no problem. The muscles around it are torn. Swollen. You've got a cracked rib. Some scratches. Bruises." About what I figured.

"They'll let you go home tomorrow morning, most likely. Once the doctor's been by. Then I just hope I can push your woozy behind up the steps to your house."

I asked him how I got there.

"Via yours truly. Once I got a look at you, I figured you could make it okay in my car." He sat down on the edge of the bed. Turned the magazine over. It was *Gourmet*. "Figured if I called an ambulance, there'd be more questions about that girl and her daughter than you'd want. Since you saw fit to charge in there like Don Quixote."

It was coming back to me then. Slowly.

"Not that they're worth it, you understand," Tucker said.

"How did you . . .?"

"Lifted you up and got you to the car. The girl, that little horny girl—Holly—she was a little help. Not much."

"How did you . . .?"

"The admitting nurse in the ER and I go *way* back. We dated, back in the stone age. I never married this one, however, and it's a damned good thing. Or you and I would have been in a jam."

A single drop of liquid splashed almost imperceptibly from one part of the IV tube into another part.

"They know me here. I've been in and out for some tests, then for some plumbing work. Hell, I taught about half the people working here. The doctor down there, who I had to paddle one time because he stole a teacher's pocketbook, took one look and knew that an old codger like me—even a black one—couldn't have given you an ass whipping like this one. So when I hinted that it might be best to not ask too many questions, he didn't."

Things were shifting now. And getting foggy. I had to hurry.

"Where's . . .?"

"Holly and her mama?" He made a guffawing sound.

"Hell!" he waved his hand in front of him, as if shooing away gnats. "They blew out like two leaves in a north wind." Then he was slowly tidying things up on the bedside table. "Joyce was beat up pretty bad. Damn near as bad as you." He pushed the water cup back from the edge; aligned the box of tissues with the edge of the telephone. "But she wasn't about to go to any hospital. Too many questions at a hospital. Too many police."

He stepped over to the head of the bed.

"It was a couple of pushers, Rafferty. I'd bet my teacher's pension on that. A couple of badass pushers who Joyce probably got behind with who came around to make a believer out of her."

He moved closer. Put his hand on the chrome rail beside my head.

"They're bad news, son. I told you that before." He pointed at the sling on my arm. At the tape around my middle. "They're not anywhere worth *this*." I think he said something else.

But his voice had eased into a slow, rhythmic modulation, like the throbbing of an electrical impulse. Then his face was going all over the place, and I wondered if the sound was actually my own heartbeat, amplified somehow in the machine hooked up to the IV.

I closed my eyes and listened to it.

It sounded exactly like the heart that I sometimes imagined when I watched, from the deck of Gull Cottage, as the tide slipped back into the Gulf.

The great, good heart that I imagined out there somewhere. Beating steadily along thorough eternity, sending the waves in and then pulling them back again.

Part II
The Rule for Islands

Eight

July became August.

The faraway places in the Atlantic that are the perennial birthing grounds of hurricanes had sent several storms churning toward the Americas, none of which found their way into the Gulf of Mexico. But it was early yet, as hurricane seasons go. September still loomed ahead, and that is when most of the meanest ones had come calling on Galveston. That is when *The* storm had come, a little over a century before. When the next big one came, as it surely would, it would probably come in September.

So, the stretch of beach in front of Gull Cottage lay placidly under scorching sun and starry nights, under the brief squalls that made up quickly and then moved on, and under the endless legions of beachgoers who sought solace where the land meets the sea.

It had been almost two weeks since Tucker had brought me, groggy and wobbly, home from my short hospital stay. I'd taken the pills the doctor had prescribed, stayed off the booze while I was taking them, and was ready to get back to some sort of daily, useful activity. To working on the little boat that had not yet—for lack of a good enough name coming to mind—been christened. To not hurting in my middle and my shoulder every time I moved. And to the first sip of an icy cloud of a martini on my deck with Tucker.

I wondered about Joyce and Holly. Joyce had been in pretty bad shape when I last saw her, curled up in the fetal position on the floor of her father's beach house. Tucker said, several times, that we were well rid of them and that, if we were lucky, Joyce would be sufficiently frightened or embarrassed to stay away for good. What he said made perfectly good sense, I realized. Still, I caught myself listening closely every time I heard a loud, clanging engine out on the Bluewater, half hoping that it would be the old Impala huffing its way home.

I'd managed to drive myself, awkwardly and not a little

uncomfortably, into town to the library to use the computers once. Tucker would have gladly taken me—he was always on the lookout for things to do; sometimes I wondered if retirement was proving not to be all that he had hoped for—but he would have wanted to know what I was up to. More specifically, he would have wondered why I didn't just use my own laptop. So being driven there was not an option.

I was almost entirely past the research stage of the mission, anyway. Other than double-checking a few things and making sure the subject didn't change his flight plans or his booking into the resort in Bermuda.

What I needed then, just a bit more than a month out, was a hell of a lot more physical conditioning than I could handle with my shoulder in a sling and my rib cage bound tightly in a contraption covered over with laces and clamps, like some medieval instrument of torment. The doctor said I would be free of both of them in a few more days and could commence some exercising.

So, on that trip in to the library, I stopped at the nicest fitness center on the island and bought myself a membership. For no other reason than it had a lap pool.

Tucker had played the mother hen for the first few days, until I told him to get the hell out and let me do things for myself. Then he just wandered in occasionally.

"You're not nearly as sociable," he said on one of those visits, shaking his head, "when you're off the hooch." He gathered up some empty dishes that he'd brought over full of culinary delights.

"I've got to drive up to Huntsville tomorrow. You'd better tag along. Maybe it'll help you over this case of cabin fever you're suffering through." He cradled the dishes and plastic containers in his arms. "I'll try not to hit too many bumps."

I begged off. But he wasn't having it.

"I personally don't care if you stay around here all day and play with yourself. What I'm offering you is a nice road trip with a delightful, intelligent, and witty fellow who wouldn't mind the company."

Who could pass up an offer like that?

• • •

We left the next day, a Wednesday, in the early afternoon. Tucker's eleven-year-old Oldsmobile rode comfortably enough and was sufficiently spacious to offer some stretching room. He kept the radio tuned to a Houston jazz station and hummed along with some of the songs.

"Now, tell me again," I said, as we topped the causeway that connected the island to the mainland, "just why we're making this trip."

He said he'd never told me the first time. That we were going to see an old friend of his who taught at the college.

"We've got this thing we do every so often."

I asked him what kind of thing. Huntsville was a couple of hours up Interstate 45—with one of the largest cities in the nation smack dab in the middle— so, unless this was one *hell* of a good friend, the thing was bound to be more elaborate than grabbing a cup of coffee and saying hello.

"Oh," he said, easing off the gas and letting the Olds glide down the other side of the long bridge. "Oh, that would take the mystery right out of it."

Colonies of gulls glided along on either side, some zipping under the bridge and out over the bay that sprawled all around us, others swooping and darting for no other apparent purpose than to celebrate a nice afternoon. More doggedly determined pelicans kept to a perfectly straight flight pattern over the shimmering surface of the water. A couple of big tugs pushed heavy barges up the middle channel; a few tiny sails dotted the blue water, pushed by the slight breeze.

Tucker and I talked some, but not too much. One of the best things about the friendship that had taken root was that neither of us felt the need to ramble, to keep the air filled up with useless chatter. Much of our time—on either of our front decks or anywhere else that we happened to be—was passed in complete and blissful silence.

Sometimes days went by without our laying eyes on each other. Tucker was away some nights and, while I first feared that he was back in the hospital for whatever ailed him—he hadn't broached the subject, so neither had I—the spring in his step and satisfied look on his face the next morning convinced me that romance had been involved.

He had introduced me to an attractive lady one late afternoon before serving her the dinner he had prepared. Tiny lights had sparkled and danced in his dark windows later, so it was a candlelit occasion. Then, a couple of days later, he'd introduced me to a different lady, also attractive, before a different dinner in the flickering shadows of probably the same candles. So Tucker, I had to conclude, was a bit of a rover. A free agent.

In regards to me, I was, sadly, the *very* freest of agents. So free, in fact, that I had not served dinner to anyone in Gull Cottage, other than the occasional ham sandwich to Tucker. In the more than a month that I had lived there, I had waked up, other than the one night in the hospital, in my own bed every morning. Alone.

When we were getting close to Houston, Tucker asked me if I needed to make any stops. I didn't. On the north side, we took a quick bathroom break at a convenience store in the Woodlands, and then kept on through Conroe and finally caught our first glimpse, down a long, straight stretch of the freeway, of the miniscule outline of the gigantic statue of Sam Houston still several miles ahead. He grew more distinct as we got closer. The hero of San Jacinto, twice president of Texas when she was a republic and governor when she became a state, epic drinker of whiskey and teller of tales, he had lived the last years of his life in Huntsville, then died and was buried there. The university we were headed for bore his name.

I had never been in downtown Huntsville, having only skirted the town's western periphery on the interstate. Tucker glided the big Olds through a busy courthouse square surrounded by shops and cafes, although the old county courthouse that should have sat in its center had been replaced at some point by an austere, utilitarian building that I would bet good money had gone up in the sixties or seventies, when function nearly always trumped aesthetics. We went down one hill and up another—all of Huntsville seemed to reside in hills and valleys—to the university. Tucker pulled to a stop in a numbered parking place in a small, tree-shaded lot.

I told him, as he was climbing out, that we were in what looked to be a faculty lot.

"I'm an old man. And I'm black." he said, slamming the door. "I doubt there's a security guard on the place with the balls to make me move it."

• • •

"All built by convicts," Tucker told me in the spacious lobby we were walking through. He waved his arms around as if he had designed the place himself. "The state pen's two blocks away, so they just brought truckloads of cons up the hill every day and put them to work."

In the elevator, a complete stranger and I listened to Tucker exclaim that this was one of the finest criminal justice departments of any university in the world.

"Right here at Sam Houston," he said, tapping the wall as if the Otis elevator was a sacred symbol of the college. He looked at the stranger and nodded. He winked.

"Got my masters degree here," he said.

When we got out on the third floor, I said that I would have figured his masters would be in education.

"It is," he said, heading determinedly down a hallway. "I never took one class in this building. I just said it was a damned good department."

The door was open to the small office I followed him into. The short man behind the desk wore a wrinkled, powder blue Oxford shirt and a loosened necktie, and sported a short ponytail that somehow looked fine on a man not too many years younger than Tucker. His white beard was kept close-cropped; a small ring in his left earlobe reflected the late afternoon sunlight from the lone window.

When they had finished shaking hands, Tucker turned to me.

"Rafferty, meet Andy Lewellen. That's *Doctor* Lewellen, Distinguished Professor of Criminal Justice, to anybody who's looking to be impressed." We shook hands. Tucker slapped him on his back. "But it's Andy to the poor old colored boy who had to room with this milky white Yankee from New England back in the day when such cohabitation was frowned upon by the numerous rednecks hereabouts."

Andy rolled up a journal he had been reading and tapped Tucker on the arm with it.

"It wasn't so bad," he said, tossing the journal on his cluttered desk. "I learned to eat ham hocks and cornbread that year."

"And butterbeans," Tucker chimed in. "Don't you dare forget my butterbeans."

Andy looked at my shoulder sling and, probably, at the bulge of the contraption under my shirt. He asked if I'd been in an accident. I told him something like that.

While they caught up, I scanned the plaques and framed certificates on the wall. Bachelor of Science from Cornell. Masters in Criminal Justice from Sam Houston State. Doctorate from Stanford. Memberships and accolades from numerous institutes, standing committees, and societies. Along with a signed photograph of Jimmy Carter. A quick glancè at the bookshelf found two volumes by Andrew Lewellen, PhD.

The window looked out over a parking lot bordered by a thick stand of trees and a few housetops. Just beyond, there was a long, unbroken length of tall, red brick wall with guardhouses in the middle and on the corners, each with a guard armed with a slung rifle visible even at a distance of several hundred yards. Gothic style buildings lifted up over the tops of the walls. And a narrow steeple.

"That's the prison, I'm guessing."

Tucker and Andy stepped closer to the window.

"That is *the* prison," Tucker said. He pointed in its direction.

"That's the Walls."

He very nearly whispered it, making it sound somehow mythical. Like Dorothy first hearing the words Emerald City. I told them I had always heard of it, but had never seen it.

"Built in 1846," Andy said, sitting on the edge of his desk. "One of the first orders of business when Texas transitioned from a republic to a state."

I must have sounded a little amazed when I asked if it was still used.

"Used, hell," Tucker said. "It's a regular Grand Central Station."

"Every inmate being paroled out of the Texas Prison System," Andy explained, "—and it's one gigantic system—is processed out of that old cluster of buildings. So, every weekday, a bunch of buses full of inmates come in from all over the state, every one of them having to be strip-searched and logged in. This, in addition to the couple of thousand convicts assigned for the length of their sentences to The Walls."

"And in addition," Tucker said, looking at his watch and then tapping its face for Andy's benefit, "to the other little chore that's carried out frequently in there."

Andy glanced at his own watch. Nodded.

"More frequently than anywhere in the free world," he said, standing up from his desk, grabbing his worn leather briefcase, and shooing us out ahead of him.

Nine

We had dinner in a barbeque joint not far from campus. The owner, a jovial mountain of a man who must have been a constant partaker of his own fare, knew both Tucker and Andy.

The little place was crowded and loud. Smoke from the outside pit drifted in through the screened windows. The brisket and the pork ribs were first class, and the owner insisted that we try his homemade peach cobbler for desert; he served it piping hot in deep ceramic bowls with a generous scoop of Blue Bell vanilla ice cream on top.

Back in Tucker's car, we followed Andy back toward campus.

"So," I said, relaxing into the comfortable seat and letting the heavy grub settle into place, "what's next on the secret agenda?" I belched as quietly as I could. "As impressed as I am with your friend, I doubt that you make a round trip of four hours just to eat barbeque."

Tucker sucked at the toothpick he'd taken when he paid our bill. He listened to the music on the radio for a block or two.

"I guess it's time I filled you in on this thing we do," he said. Three coeds walked by on the sidewalk in front of what looked like a library. An impressive football stadium filled up the top of a hill on the other side of the street. The girls wore short shorts and shorter tops.

"Damn," Tucker said, taking the toothpick out and jabbing it in the direction of the girls. "That's nice. How come the gals didn't dress like that when I was in school here?" Then he was quiet again as we drove past the criminal justice center and down the hill toward The Walls.

"Back to this thing you two do," I reminded him.

Several media vans were parked along the street that rose up beside the red brick walls. Huge satellite dishes perched high above them on extended towers. One of the newsmen was already standing in front of a cameraman, sending a live feed back to the Houston station.

I could see the guard clearly now in one of the small houses called pickets perched on the wall. It was a shotgun he was holding, not a rifle. Which made good sense; you wouldn't want rifle fire zinging around in the center of a town.

Two crowds had gathered in front of the prison, maintaining enough distance from each other to convince me they were in opposing camps. A quick glance up at the old building, then at the people assembled and the news vans, then at the several state troopers and city cops milling around told me what I needed to know without my having to squint to read the wording on the several signs that bobbled around in the crowds.

"We've come to an execution," I said.

• • •

Tucker drove past the crowds and parked across the street beside Andy's car.

"Not exactly," he said. "In fact, we won't get anywhere near the little building inside there where the deed is done." He turned off the engine and looked over at me. "But we get as close as we can. As close as they let us."

I sat and looked back at him.

"Every time there's an execution?"

"Damn near. Andy hasn't missed *any* since he came back to the university to teach. Not a single one in over four years. I generally make one every few months or so. The cost of gas and all, you know?"

"Wait a minute." I held up my hand. "How often do these . . . happen?"

Tucker smiled. But it wasn't a cheerful, nor even an amused, smile.

"This is Texas, Rafferty," he said, taking the keys out of the ignition. "The state that dispatches condemned folks at a faster rate than any government, anywhere, in the civilized world. There's an average of over twenty a year."

I let that sink in. Then I figured it was time to ask him which side of the fence he and Andy stood on the issue when I saw Andy passing out white candles to several people at the edge of the parking lot.

So I knew.

When I started to open the door, Tucker reached over and laid his hand on my arm.

"I don't expect you to take part in this, you know. I just wanted you to meet Andy, and to get out of the house for a while. You're welcome to sit right here, or to take the car and go catch a movie, or drive around campus and look at the little tight-assed girls."

I gave it a few seconds of thought. Then I reached for the handle.

"I guess I'll stick around. It might be fun to see how two old farts get their kicks."

• • •

The vigil was a quiet thing, and completely uneventful. The members of our group stood on a sidewalk, holding burning candles and watching the old building. The other, larger group was almost as quiet. There was no singing. No chanting. No shouting. I got the impression that these two congregations had been at this often enough and long enough to be respectful of the other and to let the evening run its regular course without incident.

When the big clock at the top of the prison read six, Tucker told me that, unless there had been a last-minute stay from the governor or the Supreme Court, the lethal mixture of drugs were about to be injected into the condemned inmate. Neither Tucker nor Andy had given me a name or a sex, but I assumed it was a man in there on the gurney. I would learn later that only two women had ever been executed in Texas, at least in modern times.

At about half past six, people started coming out the big front door. No announcement was made. Neither group disbanded. We all just stood there and watched the people get in their cars and leave.

A little while later, everybody blew out their candles and shook hands. Two members of the other group came over and visited with some people in ours. We told Andy goodbye and went back to

Tucker's Olds. It was still light outside, and I thought they ought to do this like they did in the old movies. At midnight.

On the way home, we were quiet for a while in the big car. Several miles south of Huntsville, I made the first attempt at conversation.

"How did you get started doing this?"

He stretched. Thought.

"Andy and I had some hellacious arguments about it, when we roomed together. This was a good many years ago, when we were working on our masters, both of us just divorced, and the hot topic around here was whether or not the Supreme Court would reverse itself on the death penalty. There'd been a moratorium for years, and it wasn't any great mystery that Texas would be one of the first states to jump back on the bandwagon when they got the green light."

Outside in the darkening night, the pine-covered hills of East Texas yielded gradually to flat pastures and then to concrete and clutter. To strip centers and malls and parking lots all the way into Houston. There was a clear sky overhead that would have offered a profusion of stars over Gull Cottage, but not here, over all the head-lights and taillights, the billboards and streetlights.

"I had myself down as a hard ass," Tucker went on. "You know, an Old Testament eye-for-an-eye, tooth-for-a tooth fellow? Hell, I was a vigilante, if you want to know the truth."

"So it was Andy that convinced you."

He shook his head.

"We finished our degrees before the court saw fit to change a thing. Went our separate ways and lost touch till he came back down here to teach."

I could barely make out his broad smile in the lights from the oncoming traffic.

"My conversion came a good bit later. Indirectly due to a beautiful lady named Belle."

He leaned back, settling into the comfortable seat and into the story.

"Now, Belle was a devout Roman Catholic and was, coincidently, the second of my several wives. She believed every tenet in the

Roman Catechism, even though she couldn't have told you what any of them were beyond the two or three biggies. She was the blindest of the blind followers among what my sweet little Baptist mother called the papists."

"Belle dragged me along to mass every Sunday, even though I couldn't take communion with her. Truth is, she shouldn't have been taking it either, since she'd married me in a civil ceremony preformed by a former student of mine who was a justice of the peace. That, and the fact that I was divorced. Finally, after two or three months of watching her go up there to get the wafer and the wine, I got up and went with her. "

He laughed.

"She was shaking like a leaf. Afraid that the priest was going to make a scene, and turn me out like a teenager in a liquor store. "

He turned the radio off, maybe wanting to pay full attention to his story. Maybe ensuring that I heard it correctly.

"I liked that priest. His name was Father Ross. His homilies were short, but every one of them was aimed right at me, seemed like. I had just been named principal at the school then, and had a lot on my mind. A lot of doubts, you know?"

"We had more than a few long talks about one thing and another, Father Ross and me. Usually over drinks in the rectory. There was a lot about the church that I couldn't go along with. Like no women priests. And the divorce thing. Though I'd hardly be the one to ask about that."

Tucker raised one hand from the wheel, waving it just a little.

"The most spirited discussions we had were about killing people. About capitol punishment. Abortion. Euthanasia. And I never gained an inch of ground, couldn't come up with one argument good enough to dislodge him one iota. Because he was damned sure, concrete *sure* of himself and his belief when it came to any taking of life."

The northbound traffic we met was heavy on 45 with people coming home late from their jobs in the city. People who lived in handsome houses in the suburbs, with manicured lawns and pools and children who rode bikes and skateboards. Normal people, who never had to give any thought to death beyond its eventual inevitability.

"So," I asked Tucker from my dark side of the front seat, "what was this padre's magic formula that cleared everything up for you?"

He grinned.

"Nothing magic. Just simple. He believed what he preached, that God made life, and he's the only one that has any right to take it."

I sat quietly for a long time, past Loop 610. We were down among the tall downtown skyscrapers, sparkling like jewels, before I had worked my way through first surprise, then anger, then confusion, then to something that was none of the three.

"So," I said, "let's say this guy that we just lit the candles for was a crack addict who killed a store clerk for the money in the register so he could get his next fix. You're telling me that society doesn't have the right to rid itself of a douche bag like *that*?"

Tucker was shaking his head before I finished laying out the scenario.

"Let's say what he *did* do," he said when I was done. "He *did* murder a woman and her four-year-old son in a home robbery for no other reason than they were there when he was. And because he was just one mean, cold-blooded son of a bitch."

He paused for long enough to let that sink in.

"That's why the television people were there today, and the reporters. Because it was a heinous crime, and a child was one of the victims. Did you honestly think the media trots up to Huntsville every time there's an execution? Hell, they'd be up there every other week." He sighed, then *tsk, tsk, tsk*ed into the dark interior of the car. "It's old news."

It was quiet again, until we were over the Pierce Elevated and headed due south toward Galveston on the gulf freeway.

"All the more reason," I said. "Anybody capable of doing something like that, something that inhumane, should be put down like a mad dog."

He smiled again. The all-knowing smile he used when nothing more could be done with a situation. I suspected he'd employed it regularly as a teacher and then a principal.

"I used to use the same argument, my friend. I even used the same simile. And do you know what Father Ross would say? He'd say that there's not a reason good enough. Ever. That's what he believed." He tapped the wheel. "It's what *I* believe."

I was quiet enough for long enough for him to know that I was upset.

"No need to get pissed off about it."

I tried for a grin, and probably didn't even come close.

"I'm just not all that religious, Tucker. Not that much of a believer, in fact. I guess we've never talked about religion before."

"We're not talking about it now," he said. "That priest lit the fire in me, but it's not a church thing that takes me up to Huntsville every few weeks. It's a people thing."

I shifted my weight, trying to find a more comfortable position. My shoulder was hurting, and my side. I was overdue for one of my pills.

"We just can't kill people, Rafferty," Tucker finally said. "It's one of the unalterable rules, the way I see it. Surely we've come far enough, and been here *long* enough, to have at least learned *that*. It's not just that it's not right. It's not *our* right."

I watched the busy freeway that led straight as an arrow in the dark night toward the island. I listened to his last words again, like a fragment played over and over on a tape recorder.

But it wasn't Tucker's voice that I heard saying them.

Ten

February, 1987. Switzerland.

A light snow had fallen quietly and steadily all night, so a white blanket covered the pitched roof and the tops of the hand rails of the bridge. Several feet under the wooden floor, the swift currents of the Reuss gurgled and sloshed as it charged into Lake Lucerne.

I'd had breakfast—a huge flakey croissant, butter, jam, and strong coffee—in the dining room of a lakeside hotel that fell somewhere between the best and the worst the city had to offer, and not the establishment in which I had slept. Then I'd walked along the Haldenstrasse, peopled on a winter morning, in the absence of tourists, with only the stern and somber Swiss in topcoats and mufflers determined to make their hearty way to work in the cold without benefit of streetcar or bus.

I'd slowed down to look out at the lake a few times, had stopped to gaze at the abundance of timepieces in the windows of the Bucherer clock shop, then had bypassed the wide bridge busy with morning traffic, and opted for the narrow fourteenth-century Kapellbrucke, careful to look up once or twice at the famous paintings wedged into the triangles of the eaves of its roof.

The wristwatch I pulled the top of my glove aside to look at was a Timex, a brand probably not to be found at the Bucherer. Eight twenty. Gomez would be at the landing by now, leaning against a wall pretending to read a newspaper or a railway timetable, or sitting on a bench, pushing up and down on the balls of his feet, flexing his shoulders, his compact body ready to break loose. To fly.

Sitting and waiting came hard for Gomez back then. And for me, to a lesser extent. But sitting and waiting was what we did most of the time.

Once across the bridge, I didn't have to wait long before climbing into the cable car that made the short run to Kriens, the village on the outskirts of Lucerne where the gondolas loaded before lifting people up the mountain.

• • •

A month before, in another cold city beside another cold river, Gomez and I had watched the General, then a colonel, go through the elaborate ceremony of sniffing a gargantuan cigar—Cuban, we suspected—before clipping its end and firing it up with his sacred silver Zippo.

When he had it going, and churned grey smoke out into the frigid air, he'd turned his attention to us.

"Thing is," he said, "the big man is going over there in June."

I'd looked out at the slowly moving Potomac and the skeletal winter trees beyond it, and waited for him to continue or for Gomez to ask one of his innumerable questions.

"Going over where?" Gomez asked. He was the stickler, of the two of us, for details.

"Berlin," the colonel growled around the clinched stogie. "Didn't I say Berlin?"

It was a rhetorical question, of course. Gomez left it unanswered.

Our little machine—Gomez and I called it The Colonel and Company—though just a few years old, usually ran like a precise, well-oiled dynamo, according to a well-established division of labors and an unwavering operating procedure. Well established, and kept unwavering entirely by the colonel, of course.

First, he was handed a situation by the Powers That Be, which might be the White House, the CIA, or the departments of State, Defense or—years later, near the end of our run, when the colonel was a two-star general and Gomez and I were old hands at the company business—Homeland Security. We even proved useful, once, to the Department of the Interior. Gomez called that one the Smokey the Bear Affair.

Next the colonel took a day or two to mull over every aspect of the possible project—relying on multiple cigars and bottles of single-malt Scotch as Sherlock Holmes had bowls of pipe tobacco, long sessions on his violin, and cocaine.

Finally, if he had determined that the plan was doable, he brought Gomez and me into the mix, the three of us working it from every angle, considering every possibility, no matter how minute, that might surprise us.

When we had it worked out completely, the colonel called the Powers That Be, and the situation that had become a possible project that had grown into a plan became an official mission.

We were between the second and third stage that cold morning, where the colonel was done with his analysis of the conundrum and was letting us in on the nuts and bolts of how to go about cracking it.

"So he's gung-ho to go over there and make this speech."

He tried to make himself comfortable in a wicker chair that wasn't built for his stout frame. We figured he must have an office somewhere—in the Pentagon or at one of the military bases in the area—but we'd never seen it. He always met with us at the small army base where we trained in Delaware or, usually, at an open-air eatery with lots of space. Like this one, even on a day when the temperature was struggling to stay above freezing.

"It seems he intends to," he waved the cigar slowly around in the air, "in this speech, in front of the fucking Brandenburg Gate, tell Gorbachev, who won't be within a thousand miles of the place, that he needs to make the Berlin Wall disappear."

I knew that not even Gomez would ask what the significance of that would be. And I knew that the colonel, who spent no time whatsoever on things he considered obvious, wasn't likely to speculate on how the Russian brand of communism, strained already to its philosophical and economic breaking point, would probably eventually come tumbling down along with the wall.

"So we're going to Berlin?" Gomez asked. He always asked, usually right before when the colonel would tell us. I never asked, but just went where I was told to go.

The colonel looked around. Not because he was worried that he'd be overheard—we had the frozen patio of the restaurant to ourselves—but because he always looked around when Gomez asked a question. Some people roll their eyes when exasperated, the colonel looked around.

"You're going to Switzerland."

He took a sip of his coffee, which must have gone stone cold by then.

"Maybe you can buy yourself a cuckoo clock."

• • •

Over the next several days, the three of us worked out the logistics.

The subject was a prominent KGB officer—the son of one of Khrushchev's important henchmen in the old days—who saw himself as a hardliner elder statesman, keeper of the old, true faith, loyal to Mother Russia and a way of life that Mr. Gorbachev seemed to be wandering away from. He intended, the Powers That Be had it on excellent authority, to shake things up a bit in the Kremlin in the way of an old-fashioned coup. Which would mean Gorbachev would not be the recipient of President Reagan's impassioned speech, and the old school KGB fellow would simply snub his nose at any demands regarding the tearing down of walls or governments. If, that is, the president made the speech at all which, under those new circumstances, was unlikely.

All the colonel had needed to know was that the subject would be in Lucerne on a certain date with his wife and their grandchildren. That and the fact that neither Gorbachev nor Reagan would shed any tears if the subject did not return to Moscow from his travels.

All Gomez and I needed to know was the time and the place.

At least I thought it was all Gomez needed to know.

During the very last of our planning, when we were tired and hungry, he asked one question too many. And it happened to be the one that we both knew full well, knew without having been told, was the one never to be asked at all. The unforgivable query.

The colonel looked at him long and hard before he attempted to respond.

"Right?" he said, making it should like the most ludicrous concept that could have been introduced. "What *right* do we have?"

I mumbled something about us all being exhausted, but he colonel waved it away with his big hand. He still had his gaze locked firmly on Gomez, who stared back at him stoically.

After a long moment, the colonel asked him if he had grown up in the country, knowing full well he had grown up in downtown Santa Fe, New Mexico, knowing even the street address and the names and ages of Gomez's siblings.

"You know where I grew up," Gomez said. "Sir."

The colonel nodded.

"*I* grew up in the country," he said. He began rolling up the maps and other pages we'd been working over. "I used to walk into town from our place when I was a kid. It was a little piss-ass town. But, when you lived on a farm, it was worth walking a few miles to get to it."

He put the papers and the maps into his brief case. Closed it.

"There were a few mean dogs in that town. Not chained up or kept in pens. They just ran loose, wherever they wanted to."

Gomez and I watched him tidy up, not offering to help. Both of us standing, nearly at attention.

"There's no negotiating with a mean dog," the colonel said. "No befriending them or trusting them. There was an old saying back then, and it was true. If you run, they chase you. And if you stand still, they either try to bite you or fuck you."

He walked over to Gomez and moved in as close as a drill sergeant about to tear into a recruit.

"The only way to deal with a mean dog is to kill him."

They stared at each other. I stared at both of them. The clock on the wall said it was midnight.

"We deal with mean dogs, son," the colonel told Gomez. "That's our job. That's our *duty*. So don't let me ever hear another fucking word about anybody's *rights*."

What seemed like thirty minutes, but was in all likelihood more like thirty seconds, passed before the colonel smiled, pushed his hand against Gomez's shoulder, and asked who was up for a strong drink and a rare beefsteak.

• • •

The ride up to the top of Mount Pilatus on the gondola was smooth, beautiful, and, most important, uneventful. The subject—one year shy of eighty years old, a general and an officially designated and decorated Hero of the Soviet Union—stood with his wife of over forty years, a dumpy woman who was the daughter of a long dead admiral who had also been a Hero of the Soviet Union. Their two grandchildren, a boy of seven and a girl of five, were not yet to the age where children feel compelled to be bored by everything, so they oohed and aahed and pointed at the panorama of alpine splendor that surrounded us. The children would be starting school near here the next week, in an exclusive private institution far removed from what the subject knew would happen soon in Russia. Where their parents were, or if they had had any say in the matter, had not been part of our briefing.

Gomez and I had followed, separately and at safe distances, the little family for two days. They'd taken a boat tour of the lake, had visited a train museum, had strolled into the small park beneath the famous Lion of Lucerne monument twice, and had saved for their last day this expedition up to the top of Pilatus. Where legends nearly two millennia old said the tortured soul of Pontius Pilate howled in remorseful agony on windy nights.

Gomez had gone up on the first run, and would be waiting up top, where there was a hotel, a gift shop, and any number of small trails along cliffs and crests and outcroppings. We'd both gone up the day before—separately while the other watched the subject and his entourage—to make like tourists as we snooped around.

The big gondola rose up through low clouds into its final, and steepest, climb up the sheer cliff's face to the top. The little plaza in front of the station was so socked in that the traditional alphorners who welcomed new arrivals were almost invisible behind their twenty-foot horns, booming out the same deep groans into the mist that I had had to endure the day before.

The subject let the children watch them for just a moment before herding them along with their grandmother into the restaurant of the hotel. Where they were given a table by a window and brought hot chocolate and sugary pastries.

I shivered, meanwhile, by a guardrail on a narrow path at the back of the building, looking down the cliff into a white cloud that dissipated in occasional small patches to show the straight drop of several thousand feet.

Inside, Gomez sat at a table across the room and waited for the subject to excuse himself. One given that the colonel said we could always rely on was that, when the subject is an old man, he will make frequent trips to a restroom.

Gomez followed him in, quickly and unceremoniously placed one hand over his mouth and with the other locked his arms behind him. Then, peeking out to make sure the short hallway we'd both studied the day before was clear, he pushed him along through the back door and to me.

I was there in case it turned out to be a two-man operation. It didn't. Pushing an elderly man over a low wall into a cloudy oblivion required no great skill and not much effort. A child could have done it. He'd had no protectors, which the colonel had predicted, given his considerably less than venerable position in the new regime, and he'd been old, a bit wobbly. A grandfather. Gomez shook his head in disgust. I thought for a moment that he might be sick.

The General screamed, of course, on his way down. But the alphorners were still bellowing away, and anyone hearing the rapidly receding shriek through the murkiness might have attributed it to old Pilate, wailing out his misery.

• • •

There wasn't a ride down in a heated gondola for us, nor on the oddly angled stairstep-tiered cogwheel train that depended entirely on good brakes. For us, it was a steep descent down a part of Pilatus that hikers and climbers rarely used, especially in February.

We'd wandered around the milling crowd on the observation plaza for a few minutes, and Gomez had watched the old woman and the two children as they looked for their companion, slowly at first, then more frantically, the woman asking questions in quick outbursts in a language that no one understood, the little girl crying. Then we'd made our way through the fog down a winding trail.

Half way down, Gomez muttered something.

"Can't hear you," I said, pushing the millionth tree limb out of my way.

"Not our right," he said again, not looking back at me.

We were perfectly silent in our descent. Even when we dropped out of the clouds and came to a ridge which offered one hell of a view of the lake, the Alps, and Lucerne, her steep old roofs tiny and bunched close together far below.

"It's not our fucking *right*," Gomez said again, moving more quickly to get down the mountain.

Eleven

Sleep didn't come easily the night Tucker and I returned from Huntsville. In fact, it didn't come at all until the night was almost gone.

I sat alone on the porch swing on the front deck, watching the moon complete nearly all of its graceful arc. Watching silver moonlight shimmer on the slowly churning surface of the Gulf.

And listening to Tucker's words. And Gomez's.

Over. And over.

Finally, I went in and flipped through the channels until I found a movie that was just beginning and was sufficiently old and sufficiently good, and I nestled into the plush cushions of my recliner. It was *Ice Station Zebra*, one of my favorite submarine sagas. But before the submarine even made an appearance, while Rock Hudson and Lloyd Nolan were still knocking back shots of single malt in Scotland before the mission, I nodded off completely.

In the morning, I drove up the Bluewater into town, along almost the entire length of the seawall, the gulf sparkling beside me like a grand lady in her best finery. One turn, on Seventh Street, took me across the narrow width of the island to John Sealy Hospital, for my follow-up visit with the doctor who had patched me up a couple of weeks before.

He looked younger than he had on that fateful night. In fact, he looked barely old enough to *be* a doctor. Something that I might be excused for having missed under the circumstances, when I had been in considerable discomfort and when he had been shooting me up with a fast-acting narcotic.

Something that I supposed I would have to get used to as I got older was people who were my juniors seeming too young to do important things. All those years with the General I hadn't wondered or worried about getting older, since the odds were pretty good that I wouldn't be doing it. But now, at the end of all of that, with just the one last thing coming up, it was on my mind.

The doctor examined me in a small treatment room full of stainless steel and linoleum and the pungent presence of pine-scented cleaner. A single poster on the white wall—a cut-away view of the digestive system—was the lone attempt at decoration. A wicker basket on the floor offered several magazines, each of which was at least two years old.

The doctor read my chart, took my blood pressure, felt of my pulse, pulled my left arm toward him, rotated it, looked at my side, and declared that I was healing nicely.

"Where's your driver this morning?" he asked.

I told him he was probably digging through his recipe file in preparation for one of his romantic rendezvous.

He laughed. Then he touched the cold medallion of his stethoscope to a few places on my back and chest. Listened.

"Always was one for the ladies," he said, poking around on my still tender rib cage. "We used to make bets on how many of the single teachers he'd put the move on."

He jabbed a little too hard in the exact place where the bigger of the two lowlifes had driven his point home with a size eleven or twelve boot. I winced.

"Good guy, Mr. Tucker," the doctor said. "He busted my ass a couple of times in junior high." He took the stethoscope out of his ears and let it dangle on the front of his white smock. "He had this paddle with 'Black Power' carved into it." He leaned back against the counter. Held his hand up, as if taking an oath. "Swear to God."

He smiled, shook his head, told me I could put my shirt back on.

He was scribbling some things down on my chart when he spoke again, looking at the paper. Not at me.

"You watch him, Rafferty." He handed me the sheet to give to the receptionist out front. "Don't let him overdo."

I maneuvered my polo shirt into place, yanking the folds out straight.

"Is he okay?"

He hesitated.

"Just don't let him overdo," the doctor said.

• • •

On the way home, I made my first visit to the fitness center I had joined. It was on Seawall Boulevard, down in a strip center full of dentist offices, a sandwich shop, a pharmacy. Nestled down there among palm trees and manicured hedges and a curving flagstone walkway that meandered through them.

The girl at the desk who swiped my membership card had the prettiest smile I'd seen that day. Of course, I hadn't seen many, other than the doctor's, two nurses, and the receptionist at the clinic, who, when I thought about it, hadn't made much, if any, effort in the smiling department anyway.

But this smile was the hands-down winner, and would have been even on a day with an abundance of smiles. It involved perfect teeth that were perfectly white, pretty lips set nicely in a smooth, olive-dark face. The eyes were champions, also. Dark. A little mischievous. Like Audrey Hepburn's eyes. A cute button nose that would have fit as nicely on a sixteen-year-old as it did on this girl in her late twenties or early thirties. Brunette hair pulled back. Slender body nicely outfitted in the same uniform of blue shirt and khaki shorts that the girl standing beside her was wearing, but not nearly so well. Her legs were toned and tanned and long and magically dark against the white socks that peeked over her tennis shoes.

Her nameplate said *Kelsie*.

I thanked her when I took the card back from her.

She said, "You're welcome." Which bumped her even higher in my estimation, since what I usually got was "No problem."

Then she used my first name.

"It's just Rafferty," I said.

That smile materialized again. To perfection, again.

"Well, Just Rafferty. You have a nice swim."

Which I did.

And, when I was done, and a little sore from the several strong laps I pushed myself through in spite of the pounding in my shoulder and side, and showered and changed, I stopped by the front desk and asked Kelsie for a schedule of aerobic classes.

Which I had no need for. But I got a good look at her ring finger when she handed me the brochure.

• • •

When I got home a blue pickup, maybe five or six years old, was parked at the house next door. It had one of those cartoon decals of a little boy taking a piss on the back window of the cab. Along with a bumper sticker that said *Don't Like My Driving? Dial 1-800-Eat Shit.* The kind of crap that jerks put on their vehicles to announce themselves as bona fide assholes, when their personal appearance and conduct is always more than enough to get the job done.

Rock music blared out of the open windows upstairs.

Tucker's car was gone; he'd probably gone down to the market in Jamaica Beach or into Galveston to Midsummer Books, one of his, and my, favorite haunts. If he'd been home, he'd have already been over there raising hell about the racket. I'd seen him march through the dunes out to the beach once to recite the local noise ordinance to confused looking tourists.

Holly came out on to the front deck of her grandfather's house, tying the tails of a button-down shirt into a bow just over her stomach. The teenaged boy who came out behind her was zipping the fly on the only thing he was wearing, a pair of scraggly cutoffs.

So, there was little doubt as to what *they'd* been up to.

Holly looked over the railing of the deck; saw me. Waved.

The boy, done with his zipping, came up close behind her and ran his hands over her bare stomach. Then down the front of her thighs, along her skin-tight short shorts.

She made a half-turn, so they could initiate a sloppy, slushing, prolonged kiss that I could hear from down in the yard.

The cemented spikes of the boy's short hair bobbed up and down as he rammed his tongue deep into Holly's mouth a couple of times.

When the suction of the procedure was disengaged, she leaned against him, resting her pretty head against his shoulder, just over a wide tattoo that snaked around his bicep. One hand rested at the top of his low-cut pants; with the other she drifted her fingertips along his bare, tanned chest.

"This is Jimmy," she called down to me.

The boy made one quick jerk of his head, which I had to suppose meant "It's good to meet you," and locked his mouth into a pout.

"Hello, Jimmy," I said.

He just stared at me, as if I had spoken in a language unknown to him. So I tried another phrase. Louder this time.

"Think you could turn that music down a little?"

When I had changed into shorts and a T-shirt and settled into my Adirondack with the Houston paper, Holly bounced up my steps and plopped down cross-legged on my porch swing.

"Where's your friend?" I asked her. He'd glared even harder in my direction with narrow, beady eyes before stomping inside and turning the music off altogether.

"He's asleep."

She smiled, not as magically as Kelsie, the Fitness Center girl, but in the same ballpark.

"We're tired." Then her smile grew even broader.

I glanced at the headlines. She watched me.

"You growing a beard?"

I hadn't shaved for a couple of days, and didn't intend to until my business on Bermuda was concluded. No haircut till then, either.

"Just going scruffy for a while," I told her, rubbing my stubby jaw.

She looked at my face and hair for a long moment. Took off her sunglasses and sucked on one of the earpieces.

"It looks good," she finally allowed.

We sat quietly for a moment. Me reading the paper. Her reading me.

"Where's your mom?" I finally got around to asking.

She gave a noncommittal shrug. Then she looked out at the Gulf, squinted her eyes at the bright sunlight and made the little patches of freckles beside her nose go wider.

"Does she know you're here?"

She kept looking at the horizon.

"Does she know you're with Jimmy?"

More staring.

"As if she *cared*," she said.

Twelve

Later, when I was inside studying a very large, very expensive topographical map of Bermuda and her surrounding waters that I had sent away for, I heard the door slam next door and watched, through my open windows, Holly and Jimmy run down the steps, through the dunes, and out to the beach.

It was late afternoon on a weekday late in the season, so there were only a few small groups of folks out. From the deck I watched the two lovebirds holding hands as they strolled out into the surf, stopping when they were chest deep to enter into one of those slipshod, marathon kisses. So, I thought, a little frolicking in the swirling, tepid seawater was on the agenda, as a warm-up to even more lusty shenanigans that night.

Somewhere between envy and prudishness, I turned away from the notion of carefree youth and back to the notes I was making on the map that spread out over my coffee table like a small blanket.

Tucker came back from wherever he had been and hollered up that he was doing beef stew for supper if I got hungry. The kids came back up from the beach after a while, wet and glistening and locked tight onto each other, Holly smiling and Jimmy still frowning.

Around six, when there was still plenty of light left for a long walk along the shoreline, I folded up the big map, locked it and my notebook away in the file drawer where I kept such things, and took my running shoes and a pair of socks out to the front deck to put them on.

The hood to Jimmy's pickup was open, and he was leaning over into the engine making some kind of repair or adjustment. Something clanged—metal against metal—and made a quick, hissing noise. Jimmy said "shit" a couple of times, the second time raising up so quickly he banged his head on the hood. Which caused him to say "shit" again. A screwdriver rattled down through the engine and fell on the sand. He waved his hand around, so he must have burned it on something. Or shocked it.

After he'd hopped around for a minute, he reached back into the engine and yanked out a short hose. Then he stood there and inspected it.

He was still wearing only the pair of faded, ragged cut off jeans that hung low enough to keep the chiseled cleft between his cheeks on constant display. His filthy tennis shoes were untied. No socks. His hair was still plastered into that short, spiked configuration. A bird of some kind—maybe an eagle—was tattooed on one side of his hairless chest, and the muscles of his abdomen really did, like the oft-used metaphor, resemble a washboard.

At the risk of sounding egotistical, my own abdomen was not all that shabby—for a guy tapping hard at forty—but I had to work like hell to keep it that way.

This kid didn't, I was pretty sure.

He smoked like a chimney—one after another—probably ate every morsel of junk food he could get his hands on, probably drank copious amounts of beer—not the lite variety—and I'd be damned surprised if he got much exercise at all, other than whatever acrobatics were necessary to satisfy Holly, in addition to whatever other little girls he lured in with that bad boy, sulky persona that would make a grown woman laugh out loud.

Holly came out onto the porch next door, wearing the same miniscule bikini that she'd been in when I first met her. And wearing a big pair of sunglasses that looked—not at all ironically—like the ones Sue Lyon wore in *Lolita*. She leaned against the rail and watched Jimmy.

In a minute she told him she could make him a sandwich if he wanted one. Peanut butter.

He kept to his inspection of the hose, and maintained the silent facade that I had determined he had polished to perfection. Sneering lip. Furled forehead over narrow eyes. Habitually flexing his firm biceps, one then the other.

Attitude seeped out of this little jackass like acid out of a Styrofoam cup.

Holly watched him while he reattached the hose, then started the engine and listened to it as he gunned it. She waved in my direction, and went back in.

I was just finishing tying the knot on the second shoe when an unmistakable clattering announced the arrival of Joyce's old car. By the time I was back out on the deck, she was out of it, across the yard and screaming at Jimmy. Screaming, in fact, like the proverbial banshee. And so directly into his shocked face that he must have been getting quite a shower of spittle.

"Low life son of a bitch jerk off sack of *shit*!" got screamed. Like rifle fire.

So did "worthless little *prick*!" She used that one twice.

All of it brought Holly back out, making her own attempt at caterwauling. But her mother was better at it than she was so she resorted to crying.

On the other side of Gull Cottage, Tucker came out on his deck, wearing an apron that said *Kiss the Cook* and holding an enormous butcher knife.

He shook his head, waved the knife in a slow circle as if casting a spell, said "What the hell?," and retreated into his house, almost certainly making his *tsk, tsk, tsk*ing sound. But the ruckus was too loud for me to hear it.

Now Joyce was pointing up at Holly, but her acerbic glare was still locked on to Jimmy.

"Do you think she's a *whore*?" she demanded. "You treat her like a *whore!*"

Jimmy yelled back that it took a whore to know one and that bought him a resounding slap in the face.

It also brought me down the stairs.

They both shut up then, and just stared at each other. Jimmy wanted badly to hit her back. I could see it in his eyes and his clinched teeth. In his heaving chest. The little tattooed bird seemed to be trying to take flight.

But Jimmy looked over at me. And probably bit his lip.

Holly went back into the house and came back out with a backpack that obviously contained Jimmy's belongings. Probably the lacquer he'd need to produce those pointed barbs of hair. Maybe another pair of cutoffs; shirts didn't seem to weigh heavily in his wardrobe. And hopefully—for Holly's benefit—a pack or two of condoms. She dropped the bag down to the ground.

"He needs money for *gas*!" she said, coming as close to a demanding pitch as her mellow little voice was capable of mustering. Then, more softly, as if comprehending the futility of it, "Just give him some money for some gas."

Joyce dug down into her jeans pocket and came out with a ten-dollar bill. She threw it against his chest.

Jimmy reached down, picked it up, and threw it back at her.

"*Fuck* you!" he said, reaching down to pick up the backpack.

Joyce was about to step toward him again when I walked over and picked up the ten spot and the backpack and carried them over to him.

"You've got a lot to learn about how to talk to ladies," I told him, shoving the backpack into his chest. He grasped it tight with both hands, pulling it in close like a basketballer about to launch a pass to a teammate. "Maybe you ought to read *How to Win Friends and Influence People*."

He slammed the bag into the back of the pickup, then turned quickly to face me, his arms, empty now of their load, stretched out in my direction, his hands balled into fists.

"Maybe I ought to kick your *ass*!" he spat out, taking the step forward that he might momentarily regret.

I had one of those hands locked tight and all of him twisted around and slammed into the side of his truck before he even knew what was happening.

"Now, Jimmy," I told him, when my face was in close enough to the side of his head to get a good whiff of whatever putrid concoction he used to lock that pathetic hairdo into place, "I've never really been *into* teaching manners to teenaged punks."

I pulled up on the besieged arm, and got the groan I wanted.

"But my life is changing lately, and I might as well take it up."

With my free hand, I rolled up the ten that he had thrown back at Joyce. I curled it up tight and shoved it down into the butt crack that protruded a good two inches over the tops of his cutoffs. Then I let him go and backed away.

"Now click enough brain cells together to get the hell out of here."

He made a move to come toward me. I held up one hand.

"Or . . . ,"– it always came down to the need for an *or* with these clowns, at whatever age—"I'm going to have to stomp a puddle in your little ass right here in front of Holly. And that would be embarrassing to her, to me, and, provided you're smarter than you look, to you."

He rocked up and down a couple of times, like an engine attempting to work up enough momentum to break loose from its mounts.

"We ain't done," he said. Then he pointed at me.

I laughed. And told him that I suspected we were.

He threw open the door, pulled himself up into the cab, and slammed the door shut. Then he executed the departure we all expected, with the gunning of the engine, the spinning of tires in the sand, and the screeching departure down the Blue Water Highway.

Holly watched it all. Then she watched me. She put her Lolita sunglasses back on, popped her gum, and leaned far enough over the deck railing to treat her mom and me to a panorama of her tanned, glistening chest, barely contained by the tiny bikini top.

"I think you're a couple of assholes," she said, with no more emotion than she might use to call us Democrats or Anglo-Saxons. She waited for a response, didn't get one, and wheeled around and went inside.

Joyce dug a cigarette out of the pack in her jeans pocket and lit it.

"Well," I said, "one asshole to another, how about a beer?"

We had them on my deck, where I stayed quiet long enough for her to start the conversation. It took a cigarette and three big swallows of brew before she did.

Then, when she finally did, she spilled it out quickly. Pointing her small hand in front of her as if the whole little drama were being played out in the dunes between us and the Gulf.

"She just up and hauls ass with that little creep. We're in

Channelview, where I work some at this bar, and when I get off—last night after midnight—she's just *gone*."

She hoisted her can of beer to show me how gone Holly had been.

I was envisioning the bar where Joyce worked. Probably a carbon copy of dozens up and down the Houston ship channel. Dingy. Dark. Mean. Catering to workers on the docks and in the cluttered chemical plants that loomed up as eerily as Mordor.

"No note. No phone call. Not a damned thing."

I told her they hadn't gotten here till this morning.

"Well, hell," she said, taking the second beer I handed her. "There's plenty of places to stop and screw between here and Channelview."

She relaxed a minute. Visibly, physically relaxed, like any mother after the initial, frantic worry and rage and then the ultimate showdown.

The bruises on her face and forearm were dark blue. And I suspected the ones on her belly were even darker. Her busted lower lip was on the mend.

"I guess since I'm *here*," she said, rolling what was left of her cigarette between the tips of two fingers, "and you haven't either told me go to hell or called the cops . . ." She took a deep drag on the smoke. "I might as well spend the night."

She located a place out on the darkening horizon to focus her attention on. Then she didn't stray from it.

"I'm damned sorry you got busted up," she said.

I took a long pull on the ice-cold beer.

"You got busted up, too."

"It had nothing to do with you, though," she said.

"You want to tell me about it?"

She tossed the cigarette butt out over the railing into the sand below.

"Fair enough," I said. "But you should know this." I crumpled the beer can into a wad and dropped it beside my chair.

"I'll find those guys."

I pulled another can from the plastic sleeve.

"And we'll settle up."

She looked at me then.

"We'll settle up for what they did to both of us."

She was quiet for a long moment.

"You're serious?" she asked, lighting another cigarette. "You're going after them?"

"Not just yet."

"You're a goddamn idiot, you know that, Rafferty?"

"I've heard it rumored."

"I'm not kidding. These aren't a couple of local yokels." She shook her head at what she considered to be the absurdity of the situation. "You could end up real dead, *real* soon."

The perpetual chorus of seagulls squawked away at the gloaming. The sun sank lower toward the horizon behind Gull Cottage. We drank two more beers each. Then Joyce went to deal with her daughter and I went to eat some of Tucker's stew.

Thirteen

Joyce and Holly spent the night next door. Then the next night. And the next. After five or six nights, Joyce must have felt an explanation was called for.

"My dad doesn't have the house rented out for a while," she said. "So, I figured, what the hell?"

I said something about it getting to be late in the season, then something about there being fewer people on the beach. I asked her about her job at the bar in Channelview and she said it was a part-time arrangement with the owner. There when she wanted it. There when she needed it.

We were walking along the beach, sidestepping putrid red seaweed that lay in reeking clumps everywhere, the Gulf's gift on the last few tides.

I'd decided to take a stroll and called up to her porch to see if she'd wanted to tag along. She'd hesitated, fiddled with the cigarette that I had begun to accept as an extension of her hand, and finally came downstairs.

A fine breeze pushed against our sides off the water, bringing along with it the rich blend of salt and sea, the rich mixture that must be the oldest on the planet. Slight waves lapped at our bare feet; a persistent little sandpiper squawked and pranced along as our companion; towering white clouds filled up the sky.

It was a few minutes after nine, and already hot. But stifling temperatures should start subsiding soon; September was just a couple of weeks away. I took some comfort in the knowledge that the world was spinning through enough of its necessary circumnavigation of the sun to bring everything closer to winter, the season I most looked forward to spending in Gull Cottage.

And closer to fulfilling my commitment to the General. To making the trip of several thousand miles, doing the deed, and coming home again. Then being done with such business forever. For, since my trip up to Huntsville with Tucker, I had felt myself wandering closer to the Doubt camp. A place that I had never visited before.

I pointed back in the general direction of the houses, where Holly was sleeping. Some days she didn't make her groggy, nearly naked appearance on her grandfather's deck until after noon.

"What about her school?" I asked. "Won't it be starting soon?"

Joyce had managed to light a fresh cigarette in the stiff wind. I had little doubt that she could have fired one up in a hurricane.

"If they even let her back *in*," she nearly yelled, over the waves, the wind, the cawing gulls, and the chattering commotion thrown up by the sociable sandpiper. "She's supposed to start her senior year at the high school in Channelview next week. She's on some kind of probation. And now they're saying that they might not give her credit for the time she was in alternative school last year." She took a long pull on the cigarette. "So that means she *definitely* won't be graduating next spring. Instead of *probably* won't."

I asked if Jimmy went to her school.

She made a face that incorporated anger, disgust, and exhaustion.

"He dropped out. Or they kicked him out. Depends on who you believe. And thank God. The further away I can keep her from that shitbird, the better off we'll both be."

I asked her what the story was there. How they got together.

She snorted, and blew out a long line of smoke that curled sharply into the wind and quickly floated off a good thirty feet over the sand and seaweed, finally dissipating in the dunes.

"How do you *think* they got together? They pulled off each other's pants and went at it like rabbits."

She looked at me then. Her face wasn't quite as pale, not quite as harried, after a few days in the sun. Her eyes sparkled just a bit. Her attractive mouth was still bent down into a frown, but showed the slightest potential of being able to work its way into a smile. Her short hair flew every which way in the stiff gust.

"It's not like those old movies that you always go on about, Rafferty. Kids don't go down to the soda shop and share a cherry coke after school anymore, if they ever really did. Nowadays, they find the backseat of a car or an empty bedroom in somebody's house, and they go at it."

A vision materialized; words tumbled out. It happens.

"The beast with two backs," I said.

She flashed me a look that said she didn't get it.

"In *Othello* Shakespeare called it the beast with two backs."

"Well, ain't you just the source of every little tidbit of information."

Her voice, a little raspy because of all the smoking, still held on to some of its original pitchy twang—southern, or piney woods East Texas—and still had just a trace of a lilting quality like her daughter's.

"You ought to go on *Jeopardy* and make you some money."

I laughed, and told her that if the *Jeopardy* people ever came down to Jamaica Beach to audition contestants, I might just try out.

"That'll be the day," she said, tossing the butt of her smoke into the sand. The sandpiper waddled over, inspected it, and went off in search of more interesting people or things. "The only reason anybody ever comes here is to plop their fat ass down on this beach because they can't afford to go to Cancun or Hawaii. And, some-times, to slip off from the husband or the wife to make the—what was it?—the beast with two backs with somebody else."

It was the perfect opportunity for her to ask me why *I'd* come there. But she didn't, and I'd have been damned surprised if she had. She seemed pretty adept at minding her own business, and staying out of other peoples'. Commendable traits, to my way of thinking.

We didn't talk for a few minutes, until we had wandered far enough away to quietly and mutually agree to turn around and head back.

"What will happen with Holly?" I finally asked her. "About school, I mean. Will she drop out, too?"

Joyce put her hands in the pockets of her blue jean shorts. Shrugged.

"Damned if I know."

She kept her hands buried in the pockets, lurching her shoulders forward into the wind.

"Believe it or not, she's got a pretty good brain in her head. It's places further down that get her into trouble. That and her temper."

She dug out her pack of Marlboros and her butane lighter.

"She locks horns with her teachers and her principals. Always has."

A cigarette found its way out into her hand. The package slipped back down into her pocket.

"She's as stubborn as a goddamned mule."

We walked on for a moment.

"I wonder where she gets *that*?" I said.

She pushed at me with the fist that held the cigarette and lighter. A playful, spirited push that made me sidestep, splashing, out into the shallow surf.

When I'd regained my footing, I broached one of the reasons I'd asked her along for the walk.

"When are we going to get around to talking about that night?"

She stopped walking in mid stride. Looked over at me.

"Far as I'm concerned, we're not *going* to get around it."

We were almost back to the houses now. We could see Tucker on his front deck, reading the paper. His American flag, on a short pole mounted to his banister, popped smartly in the wind off the Gulf.

"Why do you feel like you *need* to go after those guys?" She shook her head. "Why can't you just let it be?"

I kept walking, formulating my answer. When I delivered it, it came out not unlike a mathematic equation.

"They hurt you. They hurt *me*. They scared Holly. That one asshole had his hands all over her. And he was liking it."

I stopped at the dunes, and let her catch up.

"Rafferty," she said, "it shouldn't come as breaking news that more hands than that creep's have been all over Holly. And I've been hurt before."

"Who the hell are they, Joyce?"

No response.

"Why don't you *want* me find them?"

Still no response.

"Are they dealers?"

She shot me the glare that usually comes when stupid questions are involved.

"Sure," she said. "That's part of what they do. They deal drugs. To be specific, they work for a man who imports and then sells illegal drugs."

All very slowly laid out, as if trying to explain something that should be obvious even to a simpleton.

She put her hands on my shoulders then, and turned me around to face her. To make me look at her.

"But that's not it, Rafferty. I swear to God. I don't buy or sell that shit."

I noticed she didn't mention not *using* it. When I must have looked doubtful, which I most certainly was, she said it louder.

"I swear to *God!*"

I just stood there.

"So," she said, her features hard as flint, "fuck you, I guess."

Then she did a swift about-face and made a beeline for her house, almost sideswiping Tucker, who was making his way down to the beach.

"You know anything about women?" I asked him, when he got close enough for him to hear me.

He folded that morning's *Houston Chronicle* into a smaller configuration then it was already in, and tapped it several times into the palm of his other hand.

"Son," he said, "now we have finally stumbled into an area where I have considerable experience. Good and, alas, bad."

• • •

On one of the computers at the library in town, I double-checked, for perhaps the twentieth time, the various details and timelines that all had to fall into place for my upcoming jaunt to be successful. And it pretty much *had* to be successful, if I stood any chance of getting back undetected, unmolested, and undead.

Jacques Deminelle was booked into The Outrigger, unquestionably the swankiest—which meant the costliest, the most exclusive, and the most *reclusive*—private resort on Bermuda. He had a suite for himself, and enough other accommodations for a party of ten, this information courtesy of the night manager of the resort, thinking he was confirming the reservation. There would be a security staff of two or three, I figured, and a personal staff of maybe two more. I had to factor in that the crew of the aircraft would be staying for the two weeks—the fortnight, as it would be called on Bermuda—since no flight plan had been logged for a return to Paris and then back again. But flight plans for small aircraft were iffy things at best. Some outfits filed them; some didn't. But I wagered that the plane and the crew would stay on Bermuda; high rollers like Deminelle like to change their minds at a moment's notice.

A party of ten might seem enormous to a guy who grew up in Oklahoma City who, other than that one visit to Galveston with Donald, spent his vacations taking a dip in Lake Thunderbird once or twice a summer. But, for a guy like Deminelle, it meant he was traveling light. When you subtracted the goons, the flunkey, and the pilot and co-pilot, it only left four guests.

And, unless this particular tiger had changed his stripes, those four people would be young, beautiful, and willing.

One question kept tapping at the back of my mind as I worked through the databases.

Why Bermuda?

Everything I could find about the tiny curling group of islands inconveniently located in damned near the middle of the Atlantic Ocean told me that it was laid-back, quiet, and absolutely steeped in English tradition. Down to high tea and dressing for dinner.

Deminelle was definitely of the sort that would find things more to his liking in the Caribbean. Complete with reggae, Carnival, topless girls and tanned, lean island boys, and any number of vices he might wish to partake of.

Also, the middle of September was bound to be getting late in the season for diving. I realized that the Gulf Stream kept Bermuda semitropical, but, after all, it *was* on the doorstep of the north Atlantic.

I had to assume that skin diving was on Deminelle's agenda. He was an avid enthusiast, making numerous dives each year. And, though diving was certainly one of the reasons so many tourists flocked to Bermuda, I still had to wonder why he wasn't heading further south. Into warmer waters.

Another three hours at the computer in the library only made the conundrum murkier. In the last twenty years, according to a handful of French society reporters, Deminelle had made more than forty trips to the island. That I could find. Probably he'd made more. And every column put him as a guest at The Outrigger.

So, either it was one hell of a resort, or there was another reason, one that I would have to search hard for. Because there were diving locations just as good, or better, all over the world. And I just didn't see this sleazy character getting his kicks sipping a cup of Earl Grey and watching a cricket match.

I shut down the computer, rubbed my tired eyes, stretched, and wrote two words in large letters in my notebook. Then I underlined them. Then I circled them.

Why Bermuda?

I drove from the library to the fitness center, already feeling the cramping ache settling into my back and shoulders after nearly four hours of sitting at a computer.

Kelsie was nowhere in sight. The other girl—the one who found it harder to smile and didn't do nearly as much justice to the khaki shorts, blue shirt uniform—signed me in.

The lap pool was full. It was after five, and I tended to forget that real people who go to real jobs tend to go to places like gyms after five. The fellow sharing the lane with me was making a slow progress at moving his three hundred or so pounds along, and I had to wedge past him on occasion. But I had to give him credit. He was making the effort.

I did four quick laps. Then, when my injuries started protesting and the ache brought on from the afternoon stooped over a keyboard started subsiding a little, I slowed down my pace.

A half hour later, I leaned against the side of the pool, caught my breath, and listened to the echoes of splashing reverberate in the cavernous room. I plunged my head down into the cool water a couple of times, shook it off, and more than likely snorted like a plow horse.

And there, when I looked up, was Kelsie.

She was leaning down toward me, and the view of those perfect, olive dark legs was more than a little impressive.

"Hello, Just Rafferty," she said.

Then she launched that world-class, killer smile.

"You're favoring your shoulder and your side."

Had I been a lesser man—or a better one; who knew?—or, at least, a quicker and a wittier one, I would have come back with "No, what I'm favoring is *your* shoulder and *your* side, not to mention a few other parts."

What I did say was safer. Blander.

"I had a little accident a few weeks ago."

She nodded at that. The illumination from the skylights caught her dark hair just right, setting it aglow with tinges of gold.

She stood up.

"Maybe we need to design an exercise regimen for you, Just Rafferty."

Somebody called her name.

"Maybe we need to discuss that over dinner pretty soon," she said as she was turning to go.

Then she turned back.

"Maybe you'd better stop by the desk after your shower so we can set that up." Then she was gone.

Fourteen

I felt a little cheated, actually.

I felt a little bit robbed of the opportunity to use a bit of the old banter. A smidgen of the blarney that sometimes gets the foot in the door.

I'd had a few ladies tease their way into being asked out. One or two had been about as subtle as a bulldozer about it. But never, ever, had an attractive woman—*damned* attractive, as a matter of fact. A hottie of the highest magnitude—walked up and blatantly issued the invitation.

Yes, sir. I felt a little cheated at being beaten to the punch. And not a little out of the loop; a remnant of another era with other conventions.

But I got over it quickly enough.

So, one pleasant late afternoon I picked Kelsie up at the fitness center. Probably because she'd just had time enough to shower and change after her shift, but maybe because she didn't want me to know where she lived. Which would have been perfectly understandable, in sad and scary times filled with stalkers and oddballs and closet goons.

I waited at the counter for her, suffering the cold stare of her unsmiling associate. She came out wearing a bright yellow summer dress, its spaghetti straps perfect against her tanned, Mediterranean skin. She told the other girl goodbye, said she'd see her tomorrow.

On the short drive down into the Strand district, we managed to get the uncomfortable, mandatory chitchat out of the way. She liked the jeep. I liked her outfit. We both liked the island. And, in no time at all, we were at an eatery and bar located in an old tin warehouse that sprawled along the waterfront. Our outside table overlooked the harbor, where a big cabin cruiser churned loudly along and two shrimp boats were returning from their day's work.

Galveston's pride and joy, the century-and-a-half-year-old tall ship *Alissa*, floated in her moorings right beside us, her majestic forest of masts and lines lifting up into the hot late August dusk.

"The stuffed flounder is great here," I told Kelsie, over the top of the menu.

"I know, I've had it."

"And the crab cakes."

"Had them."

"The lobster ravioli is good, too."

"They don't do lobster ravioli here," she said, still behind the menu.

"Just testing."

The waiter came over, scribbled on his pad, saw Kelsie, and smiled.

"Back again."

She flashed him her magic smile. Then flashed what was left of it at me.

"I'm a sucker for good food. What can I say?"

She ordered the broiled seafood dinner, a house salad with honey mustard dressing, and a cup of gumbo.

The waiter scratched away at the pad, trying hard to keep up with her.

"I'll have the fried oysters," I told him when he was done. I closed the menu and handed it to him. "With a baked potato and coleslaw."

She put her hand on his arm as he started to turn away.

"Let's have some of those bacon-wrapped shrimp thingies to start."

She asked me if I liked wine. I lied.

"A bottle of Sauvignon Blanc, I think. Not the best bottle in the rack. But a good one. As cold as you can chill it."

When he was gone, she leaned over toward me, that dark hair dancing just a little in the slight breeze off the harbor.

"I'm not a dainty eater, Just Rafferty." She picked up her goblet of iced water and drank half of it. "I grew up with six brothers, and was glad to get anything they left on the table."

I laughed. She asked if I had brothers or sisters.

"Just me," I said.

Then we dispensed with the "are you from Galveston?" business—neither of us were—and were just getting into the "how did you end up here?" when the waiter brought the wine and the appetizer.

She'd grown up in some little town in central Texas, had gone to college at TCU, and was working on her masters in marine biology at Texas A&M's Galveston campus.

"Impressive," I told her, hoisting my wine glass in tribute. "What are you planning to do with it?"

"Anything that's outside," she said, steadily working her way through the shrimp.

"I want to do research, or work in the environmental department of some big company that can pay me tons. Or even for the EPA, who can't pay me tons. Charting migration patterns for whales. Doing fish counts. Cleaning up oil spills."

She managed to say all of it while eating.

"Well," I said, "by my count, you've cleaned up most of the appetizers."

She threw a shrimp tail at me.

I gave her the short version of my trip down to the island with Donald when I had been nine. The waiter was sitting an enormous platter of broiled fish, scallops, a couple of crab cakes, and shrimp kabobs in front of her when she asked if Donald ever came down from Oklahoma to visit.

When my plate was in its place, I dipped a golden corn-bread-crusted oyster in tartar sauce. "He died when I was nineteen." I swallowed the nutty-sweet bite and speared another one. Then, for no better reason than I felt the need to tie it all up neatly, I gave her the whole shebang. "My folks died in an accident when I was a kid, and Donald was my only relative."

She drank some of her wine. Sloshed what was left around in the glass. Watched the late afternoon light fall perfectly on the harbor. Said she was sorry about my family.

"So," she said, lifting a heaping forkful of crab cake, "unless there's an ex-wife or two, or a current one that you haven't sprung on me, it really *is* Just Rafferty."

• • •

After dinner, a long, leisurely affair beside the darkening harbor that involved much more chatter, the rest of the bottle of wine, two coffees each, a shared wedge of key lime pie, and a good-natured argument about who would pick up the tab—we split it; her maintaining that she had asked me out, not the other way around, and me rebutting that I *would* have, if I'd been given the chance—I waved at one of the drivers of the horse-drawn carriages parked outside.

"You've got to be kidding," Kelsie said, as the rig clip-clopped over the pavement towards us.

"I'm *stuffed*," I told her. "The place I want to take you now is at least three blocks from here, and I need to walk."

"What about your jeep?" she asked.

I told her we could walk back over to get it later, that it was too nice a night to be wasted rattling around in a jeep.

"I see," she said, taking my hand to let me help her up into the carriage, "it's *much* better rattling around in this thing."

She nestled beside me—owing to the smallness of the seat, not to any amorous inclination—and the driver tapped at the horse with a long crop.

We moved off into the soft summer night. The little shops that filled up the first floors of the nineteenth-century buildings in the Stand had closed for the day, but a few tourists still milled around in the hazy glow of streetlights. A sad trumpet solo floated out of a jazz bar that we passed, then was replaced by a lively country tune blasting out of another place a little further on. The big wheels of the buggy creaked along beneath us; a night full of stars hung over the ornate tops of the Victorian era buildings. The horse farted.

Kelsie laughed.

"Now, *that's* romantic," she said, leaning nicely against me. "You should have to pay extra for *that*."

• • •

In my favorite booth at Max's, among all the red leather and all the oak paneling, the brass fixtures and the hundreds of bottles of wine and spirits behind the bar, I told her that this was my home away from home.

"Is that right? So I take it you're an alcoholic?"

"Not yet. But any more smart remarks from you and I might have to give it a whirl."

Max came over and I made the introductions.

"It's a nice place," she said. "I've never been here."

He thanked her, said he'd expect to see her back again, said he knew what I would be having, and asked what she'd like.

She looked at me.

"And what *will* he be having?"

When she heard Max's inspired description of the quintessential Bombay shake she said she'd try one also.

"Do you *like* martinis?," I asked.

She tilted her head. Maybe she tossed some of that dark hair a little. Maybe she worked the pretty smile into something a tad cocky.

"I like adventure. Maybe this will turn out to be an adventure."

When Max had gone, I asked her how she'd come to work at the fitness center.

Over the first drink I learned that she'd seen a help wanted sign at a gym in Fort Worth when she was in college. She reminded me of that big family, how she'd had to chip in financially. They'd started her out at the counter, then she'd joined an aerobics class that she'd ended up teaching. She'd gone on to get her personal trainer's certification and, when she'd come down to Galveston to go to graduate school, she'd found work quickly, and at a place with a manager flexible enough to schedule her hours around her classes.

By the second martini, she had worked her way through a blessedly short giggly phase, then had become serious when she got around to what must have been on her mind. To what I was surprised she hadn't asked already.

"So, what is it that *you* do?"

I shrugged.

"I drink here pretty often. Swim at your gym. That's about it."

Then, when she rolled her eyes, I fed her the old line about being a clerk typist in the army for the two decades necessary for me to retire with full benefits.

And she bought it. Lock, stock, and barrel. As everyone always did.

Nearly a week later, when we'd had one hurried lunch together at a burger place near the fitness center, chatty dialogues after four of my swims, and a lengthy, late-night telephone visit, we ended up in the same booth at Max's, after dinner at the same restaurant.

I told her some more about Gull Cottage, some more about the sailboat that I was still piddling with. Yet another story about Tucker.

The drinks, on top of the wine at dinner, were doing their work. She slumped comfortably in the booth. The pretty eyes had gone narrow. She ran the tip of a slender, dark finger around the rim of her martini glass.

Those eyes, that made me think of Homer's wine-dark sea, were looking at me.

"You've got pretty eyelashes, Just Rafferty," she said, pulling the olive from her toothpick with her teeth.

"Well, Pilgrim," I said, in my best John Wayne swaggering brogue, "yours aren't so bad themselves."

I appreciated it when she didn't ask who it was supposed to be. Which happened more often than not.

"I think it's time we talked about that exercise regimen," she said.

She leaned over the table and dragged the toothpick slowly along my arm.

"I couldn't help but notice," she said," that you had oysters for dinner. Again."

She bit her lower lip softly. I love it when that happens.

"So, when we leave your home away from home, and go out to your home *at* home," she whispered, downing the last of her drink, then delicately lowering the glass to the table by its narrow stem, "let's hope they prove effective."

• • •

Somewhere around three, I left her sleeping, tried to be quiet while slipping on a pair of shorts, and went out to the front deck.

I left all the lights off, plopped myself down in my Adirondack chair, stretched my feet out on its slanted ottoman, and watched starlight twinkle on the churning surface of the gulf. The houses on either side of me were in total darkness also. Tucker would have been sawing logs for hours, and Joyce and Holly had pulled out the afternoon of Joyce's outburst after our walk.

The weatherman on television had said that heavy rain was on its way, that a blustery, wet day was almost a certainty. In my short time living beside her, I'd learned that the wise old gulf always knew things first. Even then, under a cloudless sky, bigger than average white-capped waves worked their frothy way in toward the beach ahead of whatever was pushing them. I could hear them gurgling and splashing just past the dunes.

By every measurable indicator, Kelsie was a keeper. By any sane man's standards, she would rate awfully high on the scale. She was fun. She was intelligent. Witty. Tall, dark, and stunningly beautiful. She was in possession of that smile that I could happily gawk at forever.

And she was in my bed at three o'clock in the morning and would be there when I went back inside.

These were all indisputable facts. But there was one more.

I couldn't have her.

Even if the relationship continued to cement itself after this first, perfect week. Even if it put down roots like an oak tree, it was doomed from the outset.

Because the unwritten rule that I rigidly adhered to was still very much in place. The rule that prohibited bringing anyone into a life that was founded on secrets, on the constant lies that must be kept tended. The cold, awful code that protected the skeleton in the closet. The turd in the family silver.

The old, unrelenting Hemingwayan rule that the General and I had discussed more than a few times, usually right after I had to give somebody up. Don't get involved for the long haul, the rule mandated. Don't bring anything in that you can't afford to lose. Don't put others at risk. Because, who knew? Who knew when some government or terrorist outfit might figure something out, or when some pissed off brother or son somewhere in Outer Slovenia might come calling? Wanting payback. Wanting blood. And the most satisfying blood might spill from a wife, or a lover.

I gazed out at the sea that was changing its mood in the night. And I wondered, not for the first time by a long shot, and almost certainly not for the last, what kind of monster a man must be that had to continually walk away from the normal way of things. From possibilities. I could have made a list of my losses right then, on that dark deck.

And it wouldn't have been a particularly short list.

It was, the General once told me over a few too many drinks in Teheran, the heaviest price that had to be paid by people like me.

People like me.

I had to wonder, in the empty blustery night, how many people there *were* like me. How many islands?

Not too many, I had to hope.

Fifteen

It had taken the army a cluster of fist fights, each more spirited than the last, and a solid month—a frigid, gray Kentucky January in the mid-1980s—of my acerbic attitude to recognize an untapped reservoir that might prove potentially useful.

It rained the first four days I was at Fort Knox. A cold, hard rain at times, driving straight down into wide, frothy puddles that swelled wider between the hundreds of old Beetle Bailey style wooden barracks. A slow drizzle at other times. But always rain. And always cold.

I was eighteen, cocky, and pissed off at the system that had sent me there and at my uncle Donald for arranging it. I was pissed off, in fact, at everybody and everything.

The first altercation occurred when I was barely a half-hour out of the Reception Station. Where all of us new recruits were issued combat boots, helmets, two sets of loose-fitting fatigues, and a pile of olive-drab boxer shorts and wool socks. Then, when all of it was stuffed down into duffle bags, we stripped out of our civilian clothes and were herded like cattle between a group of medics who lunged inoculation guns against our bare arms, each shot poofing out its contents, the tiny needles slicing away at their moving targets. Then, blood dripping down our arms, we were plopped into barber chairs only long enough to have electric trimmers buzzed quickly over our heads, leaving our domes as white and naked as sheep after spring sheering.

That's when our drill sergeant exploded into the room. A short, loud, stocky fire hydrant of a man named Hogan, his chiseled face, neck, and arms a mixture of sun-baked bronze and high blood pressure red, pushing the rim of his Smokey the Bear hat hard against the bridges of our noses, spitting out *shitbag* and *shithole* and *dipshit*—his repertoire of degradations was shallow, but vibrant—literally spitting, so that our faces were as wet as our arms. When we'd gotten quickly into the strange clothing we had been given—*Hurry up, shitheads; I ain't got all fuckin' DAY!*—he walked us—no marching yet; we were still too green to know which foot to start on or how to follow a sung-out cadence—in the wintry rain up to our barracks. Where we all sat quiet as mutes on unmade bunks or on the floor, rubbing our hands over our bald noggins like a bunch of monkeys.

The fellow I tied up with, after the drill sergeant left, had crawled up on my nerves the first time on the flight from Oklahoma City to Louisville. He was a mountain of a guy, more fat than muscle, with a big mouth that seemed built to stay open all the time.

He'd been in his seat, and a good bit of the one next to it, when I'd come on board. One of a group of recruits from Chicago who'd already completed the first leg of their journey.

"Fote Knox," he'd said, after we took off, rocking up and back in the seat, his flabby lower lip hanging as loosely as if a spring had broken somewhere in his face.

"Fote Knox. That's where they keep the *gold.*" He'd looked around then, twisting that head, as big as a basketball, on his porcine shoulders. Slapping his huge palms against the seatback in front of him, like a bongo player.

"Dat's where they keep all the *loot.*"

He'd bobbed the basketball head up and down then, laughing at himself, since no one else did. He looked across the aisle at me.

"How bout you, farm boy? You gonna go afta soma that gold?"

The possibility that he knew the nature of my enlistment—time in the army or time in the clink owing to my failed attempt at armed robbery—was beyond remote, I figured. But I just didn't like him. His looks. His volume. His sass.

That, and the fact that I was trying to look out the window. It was my first airplane ride.

He rocked again. Slapped at the head of the guy in front of him.

"He gonna go after soma that *gold,*" he'd said. Then he'd erupted into a high-pitched cackle.

I'd stared at him. Knowing, all the while, that it was just a matter of time before I went after a piece of his fat ass.

When the drill sergeant left—*Sleep well, shitpiles: you got no fuckin' clue what you're in for in the mornin'!*— I threw the two sheets, a pillowcase, and the green blanket I'd been issued on the closest bunk. When I started stretching one of the sheets across the thin mattress, the big guy let out one of his distinctive cackles.

"Hold on there, farmboy," he said. "Ain't nobody said you get no bottom bed." He bobbed his head once or twice. "And that be *my* bed. That's *my* shit."

He pointed a fat hand at a duffel bag that had been tossed on the floor between two bunks, then he slumped confidently against the wall, one huge leg propped up, the other stretched out straight.

I pulled the sheet tight at its corners, tucked it in, and spread the other one over it.

The barracks was quiet, even quieter than it had been when the only sound had been the scraping of palms over the stubble left on the thirty or so scalps.

I didn't look over at Big Boy, but I knew what he was doing. I'd had ample opportunity on the plane to learn his limited range of mannerisms. Right now he would be bobbing his head again, then he would be looking at several of his cohorts. Then back at me.

"You got trouble wit yo *ears*?" he finally said. "I said that be *my* bed."

I still didn't look in his direction, but kept my attention on pulling the light blanket tight and tucking it in.

"In the first place," I said, putting the pillow beneath my chin so I could pull on the pillowcase, "this is not a bed." I dropped the dressed pillow into place. Patted it. "It's a bunk."

A couple of tugs on the corners of the blanket confirmed that it was a good job. Not tight enough to bounce a quarter—which was a myth anyway—but as tight as it was likely to get.

"I don't know where you come from," I said. "But where *I* come from, beds don't look like these goddamned things. Because these are *bunks*, and this one is *mine*. "

Then I turned around and looked at him, still on the floor.

There was a glazed look on his big face, something between amazement and confusion. He watched me for a moment, then brought himself slowly up to his feet, like a bulging sack of potatoes being hoisted unto a truck.

When he stood in all his massive glory before me, he bobbed his big head a couple of times.

"That be *my* bed," he said. He nodded toward it. "So *yo* shit be on *my* bed."

One of his confederates, the guy who had been in the seat in front of him on the plane, emitted a low, knowing laugh.

"And that gonna haveta change," Big Boy said.

I took one step toward him. It was still early days in the development of my intimidation technique, so I didn't move quickly up into his face. Or give him the glare that would serve me often and well in the future. This time I just stepped toward him.

He didn't back up. Maybe because of some south Chicago grit, or maybe just the logistics involved in moving that much bulk backward wasn't worth it.

What he *did* do was reach down and pull my blanket half way off my bunk.

But only half way. Because that was as far as he got before I plowed my right fist deep into his globular belly. Which took his breath away. Or, more correctly, it sent it blasting out of that flap-jawed mouth.

He wobbled. Swayed. Then doubled over toward me, his arms cradling his great stomach. So that, when I delivered the next punch, this time a left to his jowl, the connection was a perfect marriage of his forward motion and mine. Like a Louisville slugger meeting a fastball in one rare, blissful *thwack*.

And that was the end of it. At the conclusion Big Boy was in the same pile on the floor that he had been in at the commencement. Only bloodier. And moaning.

He had to be attended to by a doctor, owing to a busted lip and the general nausea that a haymaker to the breadbasket often causes. Especially to a breadbasket the size of his. And, since we were not yet officially a company, with no appointed corporal or platoon and row leaders, Drill Sergeant Hogan had to be called back from his quarters to take him down there.

Which meant, when the sergeant returned, having left Big Boy in the base hospital for the night, I was the only thing on his agenda.

He plowed right in with full force. Spitting out a rifle-fire lambasting—replete with every expletive beginning or ending with *shit* that he could locate—which foretold miles and miles of running with full packs. Hundreds of crappers and sinks to be shined to glistening perfection. Thousands and thousands of pushups and sit-ups and crab walks.

The many windows of the long, overly heated room had already been fogged up when he had returned. But I could have sworn that they were even more so when he was done.

Then, when he'd pretty much exhausted his vocabulary and his punishments, he made me drop and do a hundred pushups to get the program rolling. Then he told me I'd pull the first shift as fire guard after lights out. And the second, to replace the guy I had put out of commission for a few days.

When he was gone, the other guys stood around and looked in my direction, then went on about their business. Most of them took out the cheap stationary they'd bought at the base PX and wrote letters home. Some of them got their showers and laid down on their bunks. All of them kept their distance from me.

Except for one.

A skinny, doe-eyed boy was suddenly standing beside me, having appeared out of nowhere. His bald head looked so natural on his Sad Sack frame that I tried to recall if he'd had any hair before our mass cropping a few hours earlier.

"I'm Walter," he said. I shook his limp hand. "Walter Siminsky. From Pocatello, Idaho."

That's all he said. And I said nothing.

He climbed up on to his upper bunk and wrote a letter to somebody. I lay down until lights out and didn't write to my Uncle Donald, the only somebody I had to write to.

Over the next few weeks I paid my dues for pummeling Big Boy, who returned two days into our training and was promptly made a road guard. Drill sergeants always chose recruits who needed to drop pounds quickly to be road guards, since they, outfitted in striped black and orange vests, had to run ahead of the marching platoon at intersections to stop traffic, and then double time it to catch up again. Big Boy, whose name was Harris, would hear our sergeant sing out "Road Guards, *Post*" and "Road Guards, *Recover*" pretty often. There were a hell of a lot of intersections on Fort Knox.

My name was on every KP roster and every guard duty list. I scrubbed toilets and swept floors and then mopped them. This, in addition to the full days of training and late nights of forced marches and night firing on the rifle ranges. And surprise inspections. And all the other bullshit that the sergeants could come up with to intimidate, ridicule, and break us.

Harris was the first to break. One particularly frosty, damp morning, after a three-mile forced march with our M16s held out in front of us, he heard "Road Guard, Post" one too many times. Whereupon, he stopped in the middle of the intersection of two muddy roads, tore off his plastic vest, threw it down, and told Sergeant Hogan to fuck himself.

For a moment, watching him stand there with his flabby lower lip outstretched, defiant eyes blazing in his huge face, I actually almost took a liking to him.

But, even if I had, it wouldn't have mattered. Because he was gone before nightfall. Back to Chicago, we guessed.

Truth be told, I was as pissed off as Harris. But smarter. I never gave any real thought to chucking it in. To saying to hell with it. Because the consequences of *my* doing it were considerably steeper than a dishonorable discharge. Which Harris probably didn't even get. More than likely, the army was glad enough to be rid of his fat ass that they tore up his enlistment paper and bought him a ticket home.

The other reason I dug in my heels was less pragmatic. And, frankly, a little unsettling at the time.

I *liked* the training.

Sometimes I think I even liked the extra crap that Hogan made me do. And I definitely liked what my body quickly became: hard and tight and confident.

At the end of every long day, after physical training and classes and more physical training and then whatever crap Hogan had planned for me, when I'd finally gotten a shower and lay still in my dark lower bunk after lights out, I closed my eyes and enjoyed the heady realization that I was *doing* it.

Moreover, I was damned good at it.

And I had never been any good at anything.

Over the next few weeks I got into scrapes—decidedly of the minor as opposed to the major variety—with a couple of Harris' buddies who wanted payback. And one with a guy that got mouthy when I was tired and on edge.

My final fight was an all-out brawl that was worthy of the designation, and was entirely the fault of Private Siminsky. Mr. Pocatello, Idaho, himself.

It had taken no time at all for him to establish himself as the platoon fuck-up. It wasn't due to lack of effort; he was no sloucher. Siminsky did everything the rest of us did. Or, at least, he tried to.

But his big feet got tangled in the vertical rope course as naturally as the hooves of a cow stupid enough to negotiate a cattle guard will fall through the open spaces. He consistently turned to his left when the sergeant sang out "Platoon, *right*," And vise versa. He couldn't any more execute an about face than he could fly. And he came off as just gut-level stupid when Drill Sergeant Hogan asked him the simplest questions. In fact, he got so flustered one day that, when ordered to name the Commander-in-Chief of the Armed Forces of the United States, he said it was Second Lieutenant Fuller, our straight from college ROTC, pimple-faced company executive officer who was twenty-three and looked like the red-headed kid on *Happy Days*.

In short, Siminsky slowed us down in third platoon. One afternoon, he stopped us altogether.

The company's four units were in competition with each other on the obstacle course. And Staff Sergeant Jefferson, the senior drill sergeant, announced in morning formation that every soldier in the platoon with the best time would get a weekend off-base pass.

"Every swingin' dick in the unit," he shouted, his Mississippi twang forming little white clouds in the cold air. "From Friday afternoon after the last formation till Sunday evening mess."

It would be the first furlough, which meant real hamburgers and fries, real drinks in real bars, and even the possibility of free sex from local girls or procured sex from prostitutes.

We wanted that pass pretty bad.

Our platoon was the odds-on favorite, because of two Hawaiian guys, brothers who had enlisted on the buddy plan and could out-climb and outrun Tarzan. And because of Telmundson, a looming giant from Pittsburgh who had the shoulders and strength of a bull. And because of me. Who, by that time, had located and perfected the rhythm and stamina and confidence that let me be successful at any task that was thrown at me.

It was a cold, clear afternoon. The first one completely devoid of rain since our arrival. We took that as a good omen; but, of course, so did the other three platoons.

We maintained a healthy lead until Siminky fainted at the top of one of the walls. Right there at the zenith, with one skinny leg over the top, he just fainted dead away.

I was behind him, so I caught him as he fell. And then back-tracked all the way down past three other guys, where I laid him on the ground. Where he woke up, blinked his doe eyes, and looked confused.

I left him there, rescaled the wall, and finished the course. But enough time had been lost for us to come in second. So first platoon got the weekend pass, by a margin of less than a minute.

As if on cue, dark clouds rose up slowly in the northern sky. A little thunder rumbled off in the distance. And it was raining by the time we had marched back to our barracks.

At supper, there was a lot of carping. The Hawaiian brothers wanted to know why I hadn't just let Siminsky fall.

"Hell," one of them said, "he falls off that goddamned wall every time he tries to climb it."

"Every fucking time," his brother chimed in. "Nobody had to take him back down before."

I ran my fork around in whatever we were eating. Whatever it was, it wasn't any good.

"He never fell off the top before," I said. "He'd have hurt himself this time."

Siminsky sat at a table by himself. Looking sadder than he usually looked. Shoveling down the bad food as if it was the best he'd ever had.

One day he had been excited enough about lunch to tell me it was going to be hot dogs.

"I *love* hot dogs!" he'd proclaimed.

When I hadn't responded—I usually didn't—he'd said that he could barf down six or seven at a time.

The guys around us had laughed, and I'd told him the word was *scarf*, not *barf*.

I watched him over at his lonely table, one thin leg curled up under him, attentive only to his supper.

Telmundson, the giant from Pittsburgh, made a grunting noise across our table.

"Who'd give a fuck if he hurt himself?"

We all knew that his girlfriend had been all set to drive down from Pennsylvania for the weekend if our platoon had won.

He tossed his fork unto his food and pushed his metal tray away from him.

"Who'd give a fuck if he *died*?"

It got quiet then, and everybody looked at me. Everyone except Telmundson, who had gotten to his feet.

"Well," I said, "I guess *I* would."

He glared down at me from his great height, his wide forehead furled tight over beady eyes. He lifted up his tray to go.

"Yeah," he mumbled. "I guess you would."

His disposition didn't get any better between then and just before lights out. In fact, that few hours served to let his anger simmer into a fine rage.

He popped off at Siminsky a few times, but so did some of the other guys. All of it was wasted effort, of course, since most things went right over his oddly shaped bald head.

When I was done with whatever chore Sergeant Hogan had

dreamed up for that night—my punishments had slacked off and then picked up again with every new fight—I went in to take a long, steamy shower. When I came out, the entire barracks was quiet as a tomb.

I walked, with my shaving kit in one hand and a towel in the other, clad only in my GI boxer shorts and a pair of shower shoes, down the long middle aisle between the bunks.

I heard the whimpering before I got to Siminsky.

He was huddled at the end of his upper bunk, hugging his knees. A little blood dribbled down his chin. His left eye was wider than usual, the right one was already starting to swell shut. A purple splotch was emerging on his narrow, snow-white chest. His soiled boxers and a pervasive stench left no doubt as to his reaction to the beating he'd received.

And he was sobbing.

I said his name. Patted his shoulder.

"Come on," I said.

He looked down, away from me.

"Come on, buddy." I pulled him forward gently. "Let's get you cleaned up."

Nobody said a word as I led him down the aisle to the latrine. Nor when we came back again.

When Siminsky was under his covers, curled up and shivering, I walked slowly down to Telmundson's bunk.

He was propped up, reading a hot rod magazine.

"Get up," I told him.

He made a point of finishing a sentence or a paragraph.

"What?" he said, finally looking up.

"I said get up."

He grinned. Lifted up the magazine again.

"Fuck you," he said.

So I had to *help* him up. By grabbing his T-shirt by the sleeves and dragging him to his feet.

The ensuing fracas clattered down the length of the long room, displacing a couple of footlockers and upending a set of bunk beds. The accompanying shouts—and the inevitable betting that always broke out quickly—were sufficiently loud and boisterous to bring the guys from fourth platoon tumbling down the steps from upstairs.

Telmundson and I both gave as well as we got, each of us landing a few good punches and missing others. We were locked in a double headlock when we got to the door, so the whole business spilled noisily out into the bitter, rainy night. It ended up in a big puddle of mud and filthy water that was in the process of solidifying into ice.

We were bloody and torn and pretty much spent by the time the MP's arrived. And, as we were being prodded into a paddy wagon, the odds-maker officially called it a draw. So nobody lost any money and nobody made any. Except for the odds-maker himself, who would surely end up with more than a few of the unaccounted-for bills that had been floating around like confetti.

The last thing I saw, before one eye closed completely and the doors were shut, was a tall man standing at the edge of the crowd. I could tell he was an officer of some exalted rank by his stature and his demeanor, rather than by any hardware he would be wearing on his collar that it was too dark for me to see anyway.

Before the paddy wagon's doors were slammed together, I saw that the man was leisurely smoking what was, quite possibly, the largest cigar I had ever seen.

• • •

Drill sergeant Hogan stood up for me. But nobody else did.

Not my company commander. Not the senior drill sergeant.

The officer in charge at the military police unit took one look at my file, at the six fights that I had been in, and tossed me in the brig to await formal charges in the morning. Charges that could, I figured, put me in line for a dishonorable discharge. If Telmundson had been detained, he was in another row of cells.

Sometime in the middle of the long night, I was unceremoniously called out and led down to a small room that held exactly one metal table, two metal chairs, a trash can, and an overhead florescent light that emitted a constant, eerie buzzing not unlike a sound effect from an old flying saucer movie.

In a little while the door opened and a tall lieutenant colonel came in, slapped my file down on the tabletop, pulled the chair around backwards and straddled it. He pointed at me. He gazed at the long gash over my eye that a medic had clamped together with a couple of butterfly bandages.

"I'm guessing you were the number one stud in high school," he said.

I just sat on the other side of the table, watching him. One of the big cigars, like the one he had been smoking earlier, was in the pocket of his khaki uniform shirt, protruding over several neat rows of ribbons.

"The top rooster in the hen yard. Lots of cheerleader pussy. Lots of write-ups in the hometown paper."

He leaned forward. Clasped his big hands on top of the metal table.

"Quarterback, right? Or the star running back?"

I glared at him.

"Never played. I never finished high school. I got my G.E.D. right before I came here."

He broke out into a wide, knowing smile. Nodded.

"*Thaaat's* right. You were too busy knocking over stores."

We both sat quietly for a long moment.

I shrugged. Tried to look nonchalant.

"So you know about that."

"Son," he said, leaning back. "I know about every crap you ever took."

He watched me watch him for a long moment.

"That big bastard had thirty pounds on you. And you kept tearing into him like a pissed off cur dog." He watched me some more.

"Why?" he asked.

I kept quiet.

"It just so happens that I *know* why," he said. He pointed back over his shoulder in the general direction of my barracks. "He's big. And mean. But he's probably whipped a puppy or two. He'd rather fight an easy fight than a hard one." He nodded at his own appraisal. "He's a bully. And that gets your hackles up."

He sat waiting for me to respond for long enough to know that I wasn't going to. Then he opened the file and lifted out the top sheet.

"There's a man out there who wants your nuts on a plate. He's an adjutant—that's army talk for a lawyer—and he's got a cob up his ass about this. Thinks the military runs on rules and discipline and all that shit."

He pushed the typed page toward me. I glanced down and spotted the word *recommendation* and then the words *immediate discharge*.

Then the major pulled the sheet back over to him. He looked at his watch. Rubbed his eyes.

"You go on back to your cell and get yourself an hour or so of sleep, soldier. You'll be out in the morning, and back in your unit."

He took out the cigar, glanced at the sign on the wall that said *No Smoking,* and began undoing the cellophane wrapper.

"Then what?" I asked, looking at the document on the table.

"Then," he said, "you finish your last two weeks of training without getting yourself beat to death. Or beating somebody *else* to death."

He took a Swiss Army pocketknife out of his trousers pocket and used the tiny scissors to cut off the tip of the stogie.

"Then you'll march down the parade ground with flags a-flying and the band a-playing and you will graduate with your company. You'll salute some general or other and get yourself on a bus to Fort Benning, Georgia. Where they'll see if you have what it takes to be an Airborne Ranger."

He flicked open a silver lighter and held its flame to the cigar.

"Then, if it turns out that you *do* have what it takes, you and I might just have ourselves another little talk."

The muscles that Telmundson had pummeled were going stiff. My eye hurt. And my busted lip. I had one hell of a throbbing headache.

"I thought you couldn't get ordered to Airborne," I said. "I thought you had to volunteer to be a Ranger."

He took a long, obviously satisfying draw on the cigar. Then he slowly blew out a thick column of smoke.

"That's true enough, Old Son."

He picked up the typed sheet, ripped it carefully in half, crumpled it up, and lobbed it into the wastepaper basket. Then he closed the file and stood up.

"And you just volunteered."

Sixteen

As I saw more of Kelsie, I pushed the Rule conveniently aside for a time.

And not for the first time. Once, on the Isle of Capri, I nudged it completely out of the way for an entire month's leave.

It was the spring of 1991, and I had just finished my first British Lit course, which had left me impressed with, and intrigued by Graham Greene. And, since the General, Gomez, and I had to be in the Mediterranean for a few days on some of our unique business, I had decided to stretch out my stay and blow my entire year's furlough at the place where the famous author had lived off and on as an expatriate for years. I figured that, if I employed several of the stealthy tricks that I had become damned good at by then, the chances were better than average that I might at least catch a glimpse of him on the small island. Or—the best-case scenario—run him to ground at a café or a bar and actually strike up a conversation. Maybe buy him a couple of drinks and tell him how much I'd liked *Brighton Rock*, *Our Man in Havana,* and *The Power and the Glory.*

I wanted, specifically, to ask him about a quote of his that had popped up in my reading about him and then again in one of my philosophy courses. He'd once said that he had converted to Roman Catholicism because he needed a religion that he could measure his evil against. It had lodged in my thinking, like a pebble wedged tightly into a crack in a sidewalk.

Maybe, I thought, over a few stiff shots of the local hooch, he might tell me just what the hell he meant. The horse's mouth, and all that.

As it turned out the horse was not available, since Mr. Greene was away from Capri. He was in fact, I would learn later, in the process of dying at a villa on the shores of Lake Geneva in Switzerland.

But all was not lost. At least in regards to me, if not Graham Greene.

Her name was Katherine, a young beauty from Rome taking a holiday on the craggy island where Romans had been taking holidays since before the days of Caesar.

Katherine of the dark, shiny hair, the mysterious and magical eyes, and the long, tanned body. Katherine of the Anglophile name—her mother was English—and the purely Italian appetite for living.

After a couple of days of the ritualistic dance of getting acquainted, we'd spent the rest of our time together—until she had to go back home to begin the Italian equivalent of graduate school—swimming in the dark Mediterranean, having late dinners on the terraces of hillside restaurants under spreading trees, making the steep journey, three times, up the narrow path that twisted and turned constantly back on itself up to the top of Mount Solaro, pulling cheese, olives, and Chianti from a knapsack for our lunches up there gazing out at the Gulf of Naples.

We spent our nights making love and then sleeping and then making love again in my room under a tall, open window full of stars that seemed altogether brighter than Oklahoma or Kentucky or Georgia stars.

She spilled everything as we snuggled under that window. About her childhood in Rome, her family, her life's ambitions and heart's desires. I, of course, told her lies and lies and more lies. To her I was David Anderson of Sioux Falls, South Dakota, twenty-six years old and spending some of a windfall inheritance left by my recently deceased rich grandmother.

At the end of it all, after promising to be in touch as soon as I returned to America, she left. And I did my drinking alone, in bars other than the ones we had been to together. Then I'd lay awake, and alone, under the tall window whose stars had dimmed considerably.

I missed her for the last few days I was on Capri. Then I—already a seasoned adherent to the Rule—fell in lockstep with its constraints and commenced the slow, old process of forgetting. Remembering, all the while, Katherine's wine-dark eyes and haunting smile.

Fifteen years later, on another island, I spent much of my time thinking of those eyes and that smile, reborn completely— phoenixlike—in Kelsie.

Knowing, as I did it, that the circumvention of the Rule was nothing more than a temporary abeyance. And knowing that I was being just as unfair to Kelsie as I had been to Katherine, who was, by then, probably a mother of teenaged daughters, warning them constantly about foreign men, probably not sharing the tale of the heartless bastard who had fallen out of her life as conveniently as he had fallen into it.

Assessing the fairness of such behavior had already become a futile enterprise for me. For, unlike Graham Greene, I had no religion to measure my evil against.

My brand of evil stood absolutely untethered. And unmeasured.

• • •

Kelsie became enough of a fan of my martinis to share a batch with me on the nights that she didn't have to work. She was between semesters at the university, so she worked mostly day shifts at the gym. Some nights she showed up at Gull Cottage, sprinting up my steps and blowing in with the gulf breeze, wanting not a martini, but me.

And that was fine, indeed. That was, as C. S. Lewis would have said, red meat and strong beer.

In the several days that followed that first good night there were others just as good. And enough hours stolen around her shifts at work and my final preparations for my trip to Bermuda to allow good meals, good walks, and good conversations.

I introduced her to Tucker, who liked her. And who, most likely, was relieved to see that I wasn't a monk after all. She helped me apply the final coat of varnish to the little sailboat. She made buttery scrambled eggs and toast for me in the mornings.

Those days and nights were full of sun and laughter and martinis and fine, healthy frolicking.

Then Joyce and Holly returned.

• • •

It was a sunny day at the beginning of September.

In other parts of the world—in New England and Old England and other northern climes—the first scents and touches of autumn would be teasing their way in.

But not in Galveston. It was still as hot as hell, with no indication that it would cool off anytime soon.

Joyce's Impala came to a rattling stop between our houses about noon. Kelsie had spent the night but had left before daylight; she had the early shift, the one for exercisers who preferred getting their sweating and groaning out of the way before the workday began.

Tucker had gone off to wherever he went every Wednesday morning. I'd hinted around it often enough, knowing that it was none of my business but knowing that I wanted to know anyway. But he was closemouthed about it. So I figured it had to be long established thing in town, maybe brunch with old faculty friends or some charitable doings that he obviously didn't want to talk about.

Mother and daughter couldn't have spilled out of the car any quicker if there had been a snake inside it. So they were pissed. And just wanted to get away from each other.

Holly didn't even look in my direction as she bounded up the steps, making a quick business of unlocking the door and a damned loud one of slamming it shut behind her. In a few seconds, the air-conditioning unit mounted on the side of the house coughed itself awake and the stereo exploded to life and blared out rock music.

Joyce stood in the yard smoking a cigarette and squinting at the sun. I leaned on the railing of my deck and watched her. Finally, after a minute or two of her looking out to sea, she glanced up in my direction.

"Welcome home," I called down.

She watched me.

"It's not home," she said. "And I doubt you mean it about the welcome."

She'd stormed off in a huff the last time I'd seen her, after our walk on the beach.

"Come on up. I'll put on a fresh pot of coffee."

She considered it. Shook her head.

"Maybe later. And not coffee."

Then she walked through the dunes out to the beach.

• • •

That afternoon, after laps at the pool followed by a few playful words with Kelsie at the front desk with her perpetually unhappy coworker frowning in the background, I drove home to find Joyce sitting on one of my bottom steps.

Her eyes were red and swollen. Not from any sort of violence this time—those bruises were healing nicely—but from worry, I suspected. I'm pretty adept at determining people's looks. It's come in handy more than once.

I said hello, lifted up the small bag of groceries I'd picked up on the way home to show her I was headed upstairs to put them away, and came back down with a couple of icy bottles of beer. I sat down on the step beside her.

She drank half of hers in one long pull.

I waited. Watched her dig her toes in the sand. Then I waited some more.

"They didn't count the credits for the classes Holly took at the place they sent her to when she screwed up last semester. That alternative school." She took another drink, a smaller one this time. "So, she won't graduate this year."

She leaned back against the step behind us.

"Shit, she says she's not even going back. So now she won't graduate at *all*."

I asked if she was old enough to quit.

She shrugged.

"I guess so. I was her age when I dropped out."

We both watched a group of pelicans make their way slowly down the shoreline, a few feet above the water. The beach was nearly empty; schools had started back. One of the pelicans dropped out of formation, plowed down through the surface for whatever he was after—a mullet, probably—then reemerged and caught up with his squadron.

"The thing is," Joyce said, not looking at me or even at the pelicans any longer, but at nothing in particular, "Holly is smart. So it's a hell of a bigger waste than it was with me. You see?"

I told her I didn't think anything about her was a waste.

"Then you don't *think*, Rafferty."

She had Holly's mouth and nose and eyes. She had the same small frame and tiny, tanned feet and hands. In fact, I'd have bet that seventeen years before she'd have been a dead ringer for her daughter. But it had been enough time for the eyes to go sad and dull, and for worry lines to wander in delicate, tiny trails away from them.

"Everything I touch turns to shit." She paused, assembling the list. "My kid. My whole pathetic life. Even you, who I barely *know*. You got the crap kicked out of you because of me."

"Not all of it," I said. "There's plenty left."

She leaned her head down. Closed her eyes. I reached over with one hand and rubbed her small collarbone. It felt like tightly pulled cables were under the smooth skin.

I asked her what else was wrong.

Then I pushed my thumb hard against the besieged muscles and rubbed. Her head tilted back up and she hunched her shoulders up a bit.

"Something," I said.

"Nothing. Just Holly."

She lifted up the pack of smokes that lay beside her, fished one out, and lit it up.

What the hell, I figured. One more stab.

"Those guys . . ."

The explosion was fast and furious. She shot straight up, my arm that had been administering the massage falling away like a walkway scaffold on a launching pad at lift off.

"Jesus *Christ!*," she blurted out, spinning around in the sand to face me. "You just won't get off that shit, will you?"

"That's it, isn't it? Those gorillas are putting the clamps on again, aren't they? For whoever their boss is."

She searched for some words, didn't find them, shook her head in exasperation.

The drama of the moment was such that neither of us heard the car pull up behind the house nor its driver walk up to where we were.

"Just stay out of it," She said. Then she turned up the volume. "I'm warning you. Just stay the *fuck* out of it!"

At which point the new arrival, in her fitness center garb, must have wondered if she was addressing her or me.

"This is Kelsie," I offered, standing up. "My . . ."

Since I had no idea where to go with that sentence I just shut up.

"Whatever," Joyce said, and tromped off to her house. Her standard departure of late.

Seventeen

"Joyce?" Kelsie said.

She sat on my couch and sipped the beer I'd given her.

"It's odd that you've never mentioned a Joyce."

I could have told her that I hadn't mentioned lots of people and things in my life in the short time we'd known each other. Which might have made some sort of sense coming from a normal person. But from a guy like me, who trafficked mostly in lies and secrets, it would just sound too damned ludicrous to say out loud.

"And what does she want you to stay out *of*?"

I told her it was complicated. Which, in retrospect, might not have been the best response.

She leaned up over the mile and a half of perfectly dark, smooth legs and sat the bottle on the coffee table.

It was unquestionably not the most opportune time for a teenaged girl in a tight, tissue-thin white T-shirt and a pair of abbreviated blue jean shorts to march uninvited through my open front door.

Holly and Kelsie took a good long gander at each other. Then Holly saved me the awkwardness of another aborted introduction.

"I'm Holly."

Kelsie might have said "Nice to meet you" or "I'm Kelsie." Or "Who cares?" for all I know. The afternoon was getting way too strange for me to keep up with every detail.

Kelsie finished her beer, looked at her watch, stood up and said she had to work an extra shift for somebody who was sick. Which might or might not have been true; what she wanted was *out*.

On the way downstairs, I told her that Holly was Joyce's daughter and they had some problems. At her car, she leaned against the open door.

"And you're helping them with their problems?" she said. "Is that it?"

I stopped, shook my head, and felt my blood pressure start to climb. I felt like a guy who'd somehow landed in a crossfire. And the thing about being in a crossfire is that, whatever you did or didn't do to get there, it's no less dangerous. I opened my mouth to say something, but didn't get the chance.

"Because, you know," she said, "when somebody tells *me* to stay the fuck out of something, I don't usually feel real helpful anymore."

She got in and fiddled with her keys, looking for the right one.

"And if you really want to be helpful, you might suggest to Gidget in there that she should put on some clothes."

"I'll do that," I leaned over the open door. "There're things going on here that you don't understand, Kelsie."

She found the key and slammed it into the ignition. Then she glared up at me, the first glare I'd received from those dark eyes.

"Oh, I'll just bet that's right. I'll bet there's a hell of a lot going on here that I don't *want* to understand."

"Fine," I said.

"Fine!" she said.

Then she slammed the door on both her car and on our schoolyard drama and executed the second hasty exit by an irate female from my presence in a span of fifteen minutes. It had to be a personal record.

Holly was stretched out on the couch when I got back upstairs, drinking the last of my bottle of beer.

I snatched it away from her, took it to the kitchen and threw it away, and came back in. I told her she should learn to knock.

"The door was open," she said, readjusting a pillow behind her head.

"It's still a door. It's still got a frame."

She smiled. Then she winked.

"Did I interrupt something?"

I made sweeping motions toward the door.

"Come on, get out of here. I've got things to do."

She stayed put, still smiling.

"Not any more, Rafferty, thanks to me." She bit her bottom lip softly.

Which is when Tucker strolled in, and when I made a mental note to adopt a new policy regarding keeping my door closed. And locked.

He was in a festive Hawaiian shirt covered with gigantic blossoms and vines, his standard khaki shorts that came to below his bony knees, and leather sandals. He was, no doubt, there for his afternoon martini, a ritual that had become so commonplace in our relationship that he had insisted on buying the gin on every other run to the Sand-n-Sea Liquor Hut.

"I'm sorry," he said quickly, his eyes wider than usual, "I saw Kelsie drive off so I thought you were . . ."

"Come in, come in," I said, much too energetically.

Holly continued to spread herself out on my sofa. One small bare foot worked its way along the edge of the coffee table that still held Joyce's empty beer bottle.

Tucker looked at the bottle. Looked at Holly. Then he looked at me.

I needed that batch of martinis pretty badly.

• • •

It didn't take long, once I'd sent Holly home, to explain things to Tucker, who sipped his drink and listened carefully to the series of events I put forth. When I was done, he mulled it all over and, after raising his glass to indicate he wanted a refill, he honed in on the part that apparently interested him the most.

"Tell me again," he said, chewing on an olive, "about why the girl was denied the credits from the alternative school."

I poured him a new portion from the shaker.

"I don't have a clue. Joyce didn't say. She never finished high school, herself. And I guess she didn't know the right questions to ask."

Tucker looked at his watch, took another sip of his martini, and stood up.

"Come with me," he said, when he was already through the door that had seen altogether too much activity that afternoon.

I followed him down my steps and then up Joyce's. He rapped three hard knocks on the door.

When Joyce opened it, he asked if he could speak to Holly.

"Why," Joyce said, "what did she do?"

Tucker tapped the face of his wristwatch with his finger.

"Look, we don't have much time. The school will close in a few minutes and I need to ask her a couple of questions."

"What school? What questions?"

Then Holly appeared behind her. Tucker looked over her mother's head and spoke directly to her.

"Why did they say you wouldn't get the credits for the courses you took at the alternative school?" he asked her. "What reason did they give?"

Holly stepped up past her mom and come out on the porch.

"They said I didn't do all the assignments. But I did. That bi—, the woman that runs it never sent them over to the high school. She didn't like me."

"I'll bet," Tucker said.

Then Joyce came out.

"What's this all abo..."

Tucker ignored her and kept his attention on Holly.

"You're telling the truth now? You completed all the assignments?"

"I said I did . . ."

"I know what you said. I have to *know* that you did them?"

She nodded.

"I swear to God I did."

Tucker took out his cell phone. He looked at his watch again.

"I don't guess you know the number to the high school, so I'll have to get it from . . ."

"*I* know it," Joyce said. "Hell, I ought to. I had to call up there enough times." She looked over at her daughter, who rolled her pretty eyes.

Tucker asked for Holly's last name and the name of the principal, punched the number into his phone, and leaned back against the railing.

"This is Mr. Tucker with the Galveston School District," he said, in the crisp, matter-of-fact voice of someone who expected to get what he asked for. "I'd like to speak to Mr. Daniels, please."

We all stood quietly until a faint voice came through Tucker's phone.

"Mr. Daniels," Tucker said, "I'm a retired principal with Galveston ISD, and a member of a blue-ribbon panel on accreditation appointed by the state board of education."

We could hear the little cackling voice trying to break in but Tucker didn't slow down.

"I know how busy you are right here at the first of the school year and I won't keep you but a minute. It seems that one of your students, Holly Weaver, was denied certain credits that she was certain she'd earned at the alternative school you assigned her to last semester. She has convinced me, Mr. Daniels, that she completed all of the assignments that were sent over to her by her teachers there at your school, and that, for whatever reason, they either weren't sent back to your people or weren't graded when they got there."

The little voice chirped up then, and rattled on for a few seconds.

"I understand the situation," Tucker said. "I dealt with it every day for a good many years. But what we both know is that state statute mandates that work that is successfully completed in an assigned alternative placement situation must be counted as credits earned toward graduation."

The little voice said some more things.

"Well now," Tucker said, "we both know that the student's responsibility ends when they've done the work and turned it in, which the young lady assures me she did, and in the presence of several other students. Whether or not it makes it back to your campus is out of the student's hands, and she can't very well be held responsible for that, can she?"

The little voice was very nearly singing now.

"Of course, the statute provides for a hearing, as you are of course aware. And, several class days of Holly's senior year already having passed, we'd certainly push for one this week. With her teachers and the principal of the alternative school, and yourself, in attendance."

The voice said something. Then it was quiet. Then it said something else. Then it was quiet for a long while.

"Yes," Tucker said, after the pause. He smiled. "Well, that's fine. Yes, I'll tell her. And thank you for your help."

He snapped the phone shut and looked at Holly.

"They miraculously found your work, and he glanced over it and said it looks to be complete. You start school tomorrow, with all those credits in place. So, if you behave yourself, you'll graduate in May."

She didn't look as happy about the turn of events as Joyce, who managed to thank Tucker with sufficient sincerity to show she meant it. She even gave him a quick hug. But nothing for me, other than a cold stare.

Back at my house, I asked him if they had really located Holly's missing assignments.

He laughed.

"There's about as much chance of finding them as finding Glenn Miller in the English Channel. Whoever runs the alternative school couldn't stomach Holly's attitude so she trashed the work. I guarantee it. And the principal at the high school doesn't want a big hearing because he knows damned well what happened and because he goes to about thirty meetings a week, usually with angry parents or lawyers or welfare advocates, and I knew he would jump at any chance to avoid one."

I asked him if it was true about the state panel, or just additional leverage.

"That was the truth," he said. "We meet in Austin every three months." He flashed one of his broad grins. "One of the other members is a retired superintendent from the panhandle, and she's a little sweet on me." He winked.

"So it always proves to be a nice trip."

He winked again.

• • •

Later, when we'd finished a second batch of martinis and Tucker had gone home, I watched, from my favorite chair, as the late afternoon transformed itself into dusk out over the Gulf. The last light of the day spilled down in pale ribbons through low clouds that were making their snail's progress across the broad horizon.

Holly skipped up my stairs and plopped herself down in her usual place on my porch swing. She curled one foot under her and pushed the other one against the deck to commence a slow rocking.

"I'm sorry I made your girlfriend mad," she said. "She's pretty."

I told her not to worry about it. I told her it had nothing to do with her.

"Why is Joyce so pissed at you?" she asked.

I didn't say anything.

"She's pissed at *me* about my grades and about Jimmy." She leaned way up, and reached over and brushed her fingers lightly through my hair. I pulled away and she smiled. "But what I can't figure out is why she's so mad at *you*?"

I watched the shadows of the clouds move across the surface of the Gulf. Then I watched some of the very last sunlight as it lay on Holly's bare shoulder. The nest of tiny light brown freckles twinkled.

"She's not happy about me wanting to go after the men that came here that night."

I watched her close for a reaction, but didn't get one.

"She won't tell me where they are. And I keep after her about it."

Holly stared at me, then out at the sea, then back at me. When she spoke, her soft little girl's voice was even softer.

"I'll tell you where they are."

Eighteen

The next morning, Joyce and Holly pulled out before daylight for the hour or so trip up to Channelview and Holly's first day at school.

After my morning run, I made coffee and toast, and thought about calling Kelsie.

But I didn't.

Let the ball be in her court, I figured. Let the Rule prevail, and maybe let circumstances hasten the inevitable.

Then I got on the computer and pulled up the website for Southwest Airlines.

My flight was shorter than the last one I'd taken, the return leg of my one-day trip to Washington with the General. And considerably less grandiose. Instead of a leather recliner in first class and filet of sole, this time it was a narrow middle seat and a miniscule bag of peanuts.

From Love Field, the older of the two Dallas airports, it was a short drive in a rental over to the seedy neighborhood beside the state fair grounds to Bonilla Plumbing Supply. Thanks to the map that my computer had sent out for me, I located it with no problem.

I had booked a mid-afternoon flight, so I could arrive at the warehouse about closing time. I'd dealt with businesses that were fronts for more lucrative—and less legal—enterprises, like this one. And one thing they all had in common was that the legit workers left at quitting time, and the crooks stuck around a while.

So I parked down the street in front of a pawnshop and waited for the small parking lot to clear out. When it had, I drove around to the back and found the alley that I figured would be there and spotted the couple of vehicles that I figured would be parked in it. One of them, a pickup, looked distinctly familiar. I stopped near the corner, grabbed the Louisville Slugger I'd just purchased at a sporting goods store on the way from the airport, and strolled down to the loading dock. The sounds of traffic worked their way over from the busy street out front; a train whistle blew a few times in the distance.

The door was unlocked and the warehouse I walked through was filled with commodes and pipe fittings and water heaters. The lighting was dim and the air musty, exactly like about a zillion other warehouses all over the planet. The brightest light came from a little office at the end of a row of disembodied urinals.

The two thugs that I had last seen on the island looked up from their card game when I leaned against the door.

"Mr. Bonilla around?"

One of them looked back at his cards and mumbled that he had gone down to the liquor store and would be back in a minute. The other one kept his eyes on me; I saw the recognition in his eyes.

"What the fuck do *you* want?" he said.

This was the one that had bonked me from behind, then held Holly while his cohort worked me over.

The other one—the bigger of the two with a look on his face that might indicate either severe indigestion or just plain meanness—was the one who'd yanked my shoulder out of joint and planted his boot, several times, in my side.

He'd be first.

"I want to speak to you gentlemen about our last meeting. Down in Galveston."

The bigger one turned toward the desk, but the baseball bat I lifted up from behind me stopped him in his tracks.

"Both of you stand over there together." I pointed the bat to where I wanted them to stand just outside the office. They complied.

Big boy laughed a little.

"You can't take both of us. Not with no fucking *bat*."

I moved closer.

"Now that's where you're mistaken," I said. "In a fair fight—unlike the one you two sleaze buckets pulled off last time—I don't anticipate any problem whatsoever."

I was close enough now to pick up a heady presence of body odor from one or both of them.

"The two ladies you fellows visited that night send their . . ."

Before I came to the end of the sentence I swung the bat around wide and low and as fast as I could and connected with the bigger guy's knees. Which took put him down for long enough for me to ram the handle into the other guy's gut. Hard.

When they were both on the floor, I tossed the bat aside and gave them enough kicks to ensure that they would stay put for the rest of their treatment. Sort of like a little shot of novacaine before the dentist revs up the drill.

Several pummeling blows to their faces and ribcages later, I lifted up the bat and tossed it over where they lay docile enough in the half-light of the big room.

I went into the little office only long enough to get a feel for the operation. If Bonilla had any brains at all, which he obviously did, there wouldn't be anything in there to link him to anything other than plumbing. So I'd be wasting my time rummaging around.

The top, right-hand desk drawer had a pistol in it. Bad guys are pretty consistent when it comes to guns in desks. The top right drawer is almost always a winner.

I waited on the loading dock for the kingpin to return from his errand. Soon, a Lincoln town car made a fast, wide turn into the alley, stopped abruptly, and the big man in the driver's seat watched me over the steering wheel.

I walked over to give him a better look, making sure he didn't make any sudden moves, or reach for a cell phone or anything else that might prove useful at the moment.

"Are you Mr. Bonilla?" I asked, in my best business voice, brimming with cordiality and warmth.

He looked a little confused; probably he had me pegged as either a cop or a lucrative client and he was in the process of choosing which way to take things.

"Yeah, but . . ."

I had the back door open in the time it took him to say just the two words. People like this scumbag really should keep their car doors locked; it should be one of their basic rules. When I was directly behind him in the back seat I leaned forward and watched his eyes go narrow in the rearview mirror.

"What the hell is this?" he mumbled, in what was definitely not a native Texan dialect. More like Brooklyn or Queens. Maybe New Jersey.

I took out the pistol I'd borrowed from his desk so he could get a good look. Then I took a good one, too.

If this guy wasn't a devotee of the whole Tony Soprano style, then HBO must have used him as the prototype. A good many extra pounds on an already stout frame. Muscles in the shoulders and neck. Balding. A prominent gut. An ugly bowling shirt with two buttons left undone at the top to display one of the gaudiest gold chains I'd ever seen. A good tan. Mean eyes. Between forty-five and fifty years old. The last few inches of a stogie as thick as the ones the General smoked protruded out of his big face like the final link of sausage still in the grinder.

Before he could ask the obvious question, I answered it.

"I'm the guy from Galveston who lives next door to Joyce—an associate of yours, as best I can figure—who ran afoul of your two goons in there." I pointed the pistol at the warehouse. "After they had beaten Joyce up and scared and manhandled her teenaged daughter they laid into me."

He sat quietly. Maybe he was processing it.

"I don't know nothin' about any uh that," he said, taking the cigar butt out and inspecting it. It hadn't been lit in a while, so the ashes were dark and brittle and crumbling a little as he turned it in his big hand like some trinket he'd found. Now he looked at the warehouse, too.

"Where *are* those guys, by the way?" He smiled.

Then it was my turn to smile.

"They're getting a little rest. It seems that this time they ran afoul of *me*."

He nodded. Then he lodged the cigar back in the corner of his mouth.

"So justice is done?" he said, tapping the steering wheel of his fancy car with a ham of a hand sporting no less than three diamond rings. "And you wanted to gloat a little to those guys' boss?"

I leaned way up then, so that my words were delivered within an inch of his right ear.

"Nope. What I have to say to you is short and sweet and then we'll both go our separate ways." His cologne reeked pretty badly; you'd think a guy who almost certainly turned millions on the importation and distribution of illegal substances would spring for a bottle of Armani. "Your business with Joyce is done," I told him. "It's over with. I am a man of considerable talent when it comes to fixing this sort of thing, Mr. Bonilla. Both officially and unofficially. And with connections that would greatly impress you, if I chose to make use of them."

He tried to look impressed. But I've found that that particular look is almost impossible to achieve for an out-and-out asshole.

"That's easy enough," he finally said.

We were both quiet for a long moment.

"So you go on back down to Galveston and tell Joyce that whoever has been hasslin' her—not *me*, you understand—will likely stop now. And the two of you can splash away in the ocean and not worry about a thing."

He looked down the alley, then he looked at his diamond-encrusted Rolex.

"Gotta be nice, livin' on the beach."

He smiled. One of those smiles with plenty of attitude worked in.

"And the kid is easy to look at, I guess," he said.

I gripped the pistol a little tighter. The metal was cold on my fingers.

"The kid?"

"Joyce's kid."

He let the fact that he knew Joyce's situation sink in. I watched him closer now, and listened for any movement that might mean he was pressing a switch or a button that would bring the cavalry over the hilltop.

"The guys tell me she's a hot little number these days."

His eyes met mine, again, in the mirror.

"Course, I ain't seen her in a coupla years or more. But even back then she had this a natural talent for . . . showin' off the merchandise.

And sort of—you know?—movin' around in just the right way to make men pay attention."

I tried not to think of her splayed out on my sofa the day before. I didn't want to give this son of a bitch credit for being right about one damned thing.

He took out the stub of the cigar, reinspected it, and replaced it.

"She still got that . . . charm?"

I told him I hadn't noticed.

He continued to smile. He damned near laughed.

"Oh, yeah," he said, scratching his wide chin, "you noticed, all right. If it's Joyce's kid."

He looked outside into the empty alley. Probably he wished for the seventh or eighth time this afternoon that he had splurged and hired a bodyguard. Probably his wife or whoever he was currently shacked up with had hounded him about it and he'd brushed the whole idea away with one of those ham hands and said *Nah, he could take care of himself.* If he needed any muscle work done, like beating the shit out of a small woman and her smaller daughter, he could send Step and Fetchit. After they had some time, of course, to recover from their recent injuries.

"Her right next door there," he said, "and at the *beach*, no less. Struttin' that tight little ass around. I bet she's had you fevered up like a dog in heat."

I lifted the gun higher, so he could see it again.

"Let me remind you of the situation here," I said.

He nodded his head. Smirked. Rolled the stogie around with his tongue.

"You ain't gonna use that," he said, with the obvious confidence of a guy who believed what he was saying. "You'da already used it if that was the deal."

He twisted his big head around on the stout neck, and took his first good look at me.

"So here's the *situation*, as you call it. The situation is that you want me to lay off of Joyce and the kid or you're gonna . . . what? Kick my ass? Kill me?"

I noticed he didn't say "turn me in?" or "call the cops" or "arrest me." He was being particularly careful not to bring any business dealings of the nonplumbing variety into the mix.

"I don't know who you are," he said, not smiling now. He breathed out the words slowly. "Or who you work for. I don't know if you got some kinda badge in your pocket or if you're just a sad case of a dumb shit who's got a hard-on for your neighbor or her kid or both of them. And I don't really give a fuck." His eyes were animallike. Cold and dark, and almost completely hidden between narrow slits. "You said what you come here to say, you settled up with the guys you wanted to settle up with, and I gotta take a crap."

He slammed the cigar stub into the ashtray.

"So, can we bring this interview to—what the hell is the new word—closure?"

I got out, put the pistol in the pocket of my sports coat, but kept my finger near the trigger.

His automatic window whirred down half way.

"Be sure to give my regards to your neighbors," he said. Then he laughed, dug out a crisp hundred-dollar bill, and tossed it at my feet.

"Give that to Holly."

It was the first time either of us had used her name.

"Tell her it's for her birthday." He churned the word out. *Burth*day.

I let the bill stay on the pavement. He laughed again, louder this time.

"It'd be a sorry son of a bitch who didn't remember his daughter on her birthday."

Then, obviously unconcerned about the two thugs lying indisposed inside the building or that I was still holding a gun that belonged to him, he lurched the big Lincoln toward the end of the alley, throwing gravel up on my pants legs and on the bill that still lay on the street.

Nineteen

Back in Houston, I collected my jeep from the airport parking garage and drove the fifteen or so miles out to Channelview.

By the time I'd tried four bars in close proximity to the ship channel, a light rain had begun to fall. Just enough of a slow, dirty, infrequent sprinkle to keep the wipers on the intermittent speed. A pissy rain. Exactly like the mood I was in.

The fifth place was pretty much like the others. A dark, low-ceilinged dive with too much cracked and faded imitation leather, too many cigarette butts in cheap plastic ashtrays advertising brands of beer, and way too many rednecks. A twangy country-western ballad blasted its way through the smoky fog, and the women perched on stools at the bar were carbon copies of the women I'd seen in the other four dumps: past their prime, past their limit, and past any degree of moderation when it came to the application of cosmetics. Each was smoking, and loud, and had at least one of the rednecks held in rapt, boozy adoration.

I nudged my way up to the bar. Joyce didn't look at me when she said, "What'll it be?"

I pushed the crumpled hundred-dollar bill toward her.

"Holly's dad sends his regards." I said, loud enough for her to hear it over the cry-in-my-beer lament throbbing out of the jukebox. "He said to give her this for her birthday."

Then I turned and left. In a few minutes I was on the Sam Houston tollway and the rain had picked up. By the time I got around to Interstate 45 and was on my way down to the island, it was pouring.

• • •

I slept in the next morning. Till six-thirty, a real slugabed adventure for a guy who always rolled out no later than five. I jogged a couple of miles up the beach then back again, showered, and settled into the Adirondack on my front deck with a mug of strong black coffee and watched what the weatherman on television had said would be a blustery washout of a day take shape out over the Gulf.

What I needed to be doing was checking and double-checking some of the finer points pertaining to Bermuda. In the old days, that's *all* I would have been doing on the day before a job.

But this time was different. And it had nothing to do with my being a civilian, I knew. A well-planned operation was a well-planned operation, any way you looked at it. Period. Whether it was planned in an army uniform or in cut-offs and flip-flops.

And this one—like all the others before it—*was* well-planned. No doubt about it.

But I wasn't as mired in every aspect of it as I had always been before. I wasn't funneling every microfiber of my attention in its direction. My having flown, just two days before a mission, to another city to tend to business of a completely unrelated sort was proof positive of that.

The fact was, I just didn't want to do it again.

Which was something altogether new for me. And, when it came to that particular line of work, it was an incredibly dangerous perspective to have.

• • •

When Tucker whistled from downstairs around midmorning I yelled for him to come on up. He sauntered in and asked if I needed anything from town. I told him I was going in myself later, to swim laps at the fitness center.

He rested his angular frame against my bedroom door and looked at the open tote on my bed.

"Look," I said, stuffing socks and underwear into the bag, "I'm out of here for the next week or so. You think you could bring my mail up and dump it on the table? Toss the newspapers in the garbage for me? Keep an eye on things?"

He mumbled something about it not being a problem.

"Where you off to?" he asked. "A little R and R?"

I was ready for the question.

"I've got this army buddy in Wyoming. I thought I'd spend a little time up there."

He picked up a much dog-eared and highlighted Frommer's guide to Bermuda from a stack of paperbacks on the bed. He flipped through it.

"Wyoming should be nice about now," he said. "Cooler."

Then he surveyed the things I'd laid out to be packed. Three pairs of walking shorts, one pair of lightweight dress slacks. Three short-sleeved knit shirts.

He put the guidebook back where he got it.

"It's a shame, though. Andy and I were hoping you'd tag along for another one of our adventures in Huntsville on Wednesday."

"Can't make it this time." I clamped the collar of one of the knit shirts between my chin and my chest and folded it.

"There'll be other times," he said.

I'd folded all three shirts and stacked them neatly in the grip before I responded.

"I don't know, Tucker. I doubt I'll be making any more of those trips. It's not really my thing. You know?"

He nodded. Thought.

"I just asked you for the company, you understand. No other reason. I'm not trying to recruit you. Neither is Andy."

"I know." I said, too quickly. "I know." I held the slacks out in front of me, keeping the crease straight and sharp, then laid them on the bed and closed them into a trifold. I packed them down into the close confines of the one bag—small enough to be stowed in an airliner's overhead compartment or to be scuttled entirely in a pinch—that would be my only luggage of any sort.

"The food's good." I tried for a smile. "And the company. But the death penalty just isn't something that I'm going to change my mind about. So I'm sort of flying under a false flag when I attend a candlelight vigil, don't you think?"

He smiled, too, an altogether better effort than mine.

"What I think is you stole that false flag line from John Wayne in *In Harm's Way*."

The easy rain that seemed to have taken up permanent residence tapped lightly against the windows.

"And, like I said, I wasn't trying to change your mind. I just liked having you along."

He nodded. A fainthearted nod that was barely a wobble, followed by a rumble deep in his throat that might have been a good-natured snicker. Then again, it might have been a smirk.

Whichever it had been, it was enough—on that dreary morning—to flip a switch.

"Look," I said, tossing the Frommer's guide and the two paperbacks in the bag. "Just because I won't fall in behind you and your buddy on this issue doesn't make you right and me wrong."

He nodded again. And I discovered I wasn't finished.

"It must be nice to take such a lofty stand, while the rest of the world has to tend to its business the best way it sees fit."

Another nod. I slammed the canvas flap of the bag shut, jerked the zipper up until it caught on something, pulled on it twice more with not luck, then unzipped it and flung the flap open again.

Tucker watched me.

"What are you so pissed off about?"

I turned quickly, moving my hands slightly up and down in a "let's just settle down" motion. But he was leaning against my dresser with his arms folded, just about as settled as he could get.

"It's just . . ." I started. Then I listened to the rain pelting on the window for a few seconds. "It's just that you don't allow for any gray area. It's either all right or all wrong with you, with no place for the two to bleed over into. Some things . . ."

I pointed at him.

"Some ends . . . *do* justify the means. For the greater good."

An awkward silence fell heavily into place, more than likely the first one ever to have landed between us.

It was Tucker who finally broke it.

"Could *you* do it?"

As I stood staring at him, I thought I knew how a defendant in a trial must feel when asked the one question that, if answered truthfully, would irrevocably convict him.

"Yeah," I said. "I could. Because it's the law, Tucker. It's a constitutionally sound law and, beyond that, it's self-preservation. It's looking out for the rest of us. So, yeah, you bet your ass if I was that guy in Huntsville in that little room who starts the fluids flowing, I could do it without any qualms. Because I didn't condemn the guy on the gurney. A judge and jury did. I'd just be following orders. I'd just be doing my job."

He thought about it for a moment. Unfolded his arms. Scratched his scrubby chin.

"All right," he said, turning toward the door. "Points taken."

I handed him the extra key to Gull Cottage, and thanked him for looking after the place.

When he'd gone out, he leaned back in.

"By the way, that 'just doing my job' bit has been used all down through history. The National Guardsmen at Kent State. Lieutenant Calley in Nam. All those good Germans who fired up the ovens and shoved in the Jews."

I kept working at the zipper, finally pulling hard enough to send bag sliding off the bed to the floor.

"It's not your best argument," he said. "You'd do better sticking to the 'for the greater good' slant. Now *that* was impressive."

He looked down at the bag and its contents.

"And, if you really are going to Wyoming, you better throw in a jacket and some trousers that have a little more fabric in them than those. It's September, you know. That actually means something in places like Wyoming."

• • •

Later, Kelsie checked me in at the counter of the fitness center.

She was every bit as fetching as usual in the dark blue shirt and khaki shorts outfit. Her skin was as honey-dark and her eyes as deep and pretty. But she was curt. Chilly. Noncommittal. The ball, it would seem, was now entirely in *my* court. If the ball had any air left in it at all.

Before I could say anything, she turned to help another customer and I went back to change into my trunks.

I swam with a vengeance that afternoon, plowing through my lane like a juggernaut, pulling through strong, fast stretches alternated, every few laps, with propelling myself underwater to the point where I felt like my lungs would explode. Churning up my section of the big pool with the vigor of a summer tempest.

Then, after a couple of cool down laps, barely more than treading water, I spent a half hour in the sauna. To loosen the muscles that were still tender from the pounding that was nearly a month old. To ease the tension that had moved into my shoulders and back like a bunch of bad neighbors.

Kelsie was by herself at the counter when I came out.

This time, I provided zero opportunity for her to give me the cold shoulder, but nodded nonchalantly in her general direction and walked past her and out the front door. Feeling, with every step, like a high school jock teaching a cheerleader a lesson. Feeling, in point of fact, not a little ridiculous.

Outside, I threw the jeep into gear and shot out of the parking lot, cutting it a mite close in front of a minivan on Seawall Boulevard. The driver honked, shot me the bird, and mouthed a few sweet words. On another day—on damned near *any* other day—I'd have held my hand up in a gesture of *mea culpa*. On that day I flipped the bird back at him, found the next gear, and sped toward home beside the gray gulf and the gray beach, under low gray clouds that sent down a constant peppering of tepid, gray rain.

Back at Gull Cottage, I changed into a pair of cutoffs, grabbed a six-pack of beer out of the fridge, glanced at the packed bag on my bed, and went down the steps, through the dunes, and out onto the deserted beach. I lowered myself down at the surf's edge, leaned up over my knees, popped open one of the brews and drank more than half of it in one long swallow. Warm, frothy water sloshed around me like a hot tub set to the lowest speed.

By the last of the third beer, I'd determined that I probably just wasn't cut out for home and hearth and friendship.

I'd never, after all, had any need for people or permanence before moving to Galveston, beyond the natural and fundamental biological urges felt by all members of the animal kingdom and just enough in the way of roof and walls to keep out weather and intruders. Now, all of a sudden, there were too many damned people in my life. And I was planting deep roots at the edge of the sea, where roots aren't supposed to go in the first place. Even the likes of me, with little to no experience in the religion department, knew that Scripture was adamantly cautionary about building a house upon the sand.

I had, I realized, wandered far, far afield of the Rule. The very rule that the General had long ago convinced me was essential, important, and totally unforgiving.

I had let people that I had no responsibility for and events that I had no control over have way too much of me, I thought, as the alcohol established its warm, comforting parameters. And, I realized, I had done exactly what the Rule was in place to prevent, and put those people in the path of possible danger.

Because of me.

Scarier, still, was the fact that I'd let Tucker lead me into an ethical shadowland that I had no business being in on the literal eve of a mission.

I tossed the empty beer can up on the beach with its four companions, popped the fifth one open, drank deeply, and belched.

I could do without Tucker, I told myself. And without Kelsie and anybody else. I could do without Gull Cottage and Galveston. The world was wide.

The problem was, I knew, that of all the people I was put out with at that moment, on that beach, in that messy rain, I was mostly put out with myself. And I hadn't yet found a way to move away from *myself*.

Off to my left, a huge oil tanker lumbered out from the island, making a slow progress from Galveston toward the nearly invisible horizon.

"You could get yourself a ticket for drinking beer on the beach," a familiar voice said behind me.

The ship was disappearing slowly into the gray nothingness, like a shadow being swallowed by a darker shadow.

"You working for the sheriff's department now?" I asked, not turning around.

Then the ship was just a smudge in the distance.

Joyce sat down beside me in the foaming, swirling tide. Her blue jeans turned a darker shade of blue as water bled into them; she tossed what was left of a cigarette into the surf.

I handed her the last of the beers.

Then we both watched raindrops splatter into the sea for a while.

"You're pissed off, I guess," she finally said.

I let that one go unanswered for a good minute or two.

"Nobody asked you to go up there, you know," she said. "Nobody asked you to dig around."

Still nothing from me.

"You going up there. That won't stop him from coming after me, or Holly. It won't stop him from sending Buster and Bubba again."

I squinted. Then I looked over at her for the first time.

"Their names are Buster and *Bubba*?"

The tanker was gone now, over the edge of the world. The rain picked up.

"Well, Buster and Bubba"—it was all I could do to say the names with a straight face—"needed to be taught some manners. And I had a much more pleasant visit with their boss, about the advisability of leaving things alone. He said he would."

She sighed.

"But that doesn't mean anything, Rafferty. Don't you see?" She spoke quietly, softly. As someone might explain something to a child. "You've crossed him now. That's the only way he'll see it."

The gulf slapped at us. The soft rain, not much more than mist now, blew into our faces from the sea.

"So you married this creep?"

She shook her head, and managed to actually get a cigarette lit in the breeze.

"I worked for him at the plumbing supply, when I was just a kid. About Holly's age now. It was for a co-op class in high school and, when I dropped out, I just kept on working for him. I filed things, did the invoices. Then, when I'd been there a while, he started having me do some things for his . . . other business. Running errands. Calling contacts."

She stopped. I waited.

"So how . . ." I started.

"He was like—what do you call it?—forbidden fruit, you know. Like some of the other girls were about some of the coaches and teachers. He wasn't much younger than my dad, but he paid *attention* to me. He joked around. He called me Sweetie."

We had the entire stretch of beach to ourselves. Even the gulls had found somewhere else to wait out the rain.

"By the time he got around to getting into my pants, I was pretty involved in his dope business. Even selling some on the streets. "

I asked if she'd used it. Knowing the answer full well.

She made a grunting noise.

"Hell, Rafferty. I was *eighteen*. I'd quit school, I was fighting with my dad every minute, and I was screwing a guy that gave me the stuff for free. What do *you* think?"

"And then there was Holly," I ventured, after the ensuing pause.

"And then there was Holly," she said. "I was on the pill—every girl I knew was—but, shit, I was taking one hell of a lot of pills in those days. And I got mixed up and missed every once in a while."

"And Bonilla? Just what part did the Joey Buttafuoco of Dallas play in all of this? Other than stud service."

She sloshed the last of the beer around in the can. Watched the gulf. Finished off the beer.

"He was married . . . a couple of times while I was there. Not that it mattered any; the wives—and the others he didn't get around to marrying—were bimbos or strung out or both, who didn't care who he was sleeping with, as long as the money and the drugs didn't stop."

She leaned back on her elbows, tilted her head back, let rainwater drip off the back of her hair.

"He'd have paid for an abortion. Or I could have paid for it myself. But . . . I don't know. I just never even considered it. Who knows why?" She gave a perplexed look. "I damn sure never have been able to explain it."

"Did he support you and Holly?"

She laughed.

"He didn't have to. I was selling dope as fast as I could get my hands on it, and taking a good cut off the deals I set up for him with suppliers. Then, when Holly got a little older and we started coming down here, I took over the import part of the business when stuff came in offshore. That's when I started making some *real* money."

"And you were hooked on the stuff?"

"Bad." She nodded. She lit the next cigarette· from the last one, and blew smoke out into the breeze. "*Real* bad. When it got so bad that I knew I was about to lose Holly, I went to my dad and he got me into rehab. He took care of her while I was in there. He wasn't any too happy about it, but he did it. My mom was dead. I was his only kid. And . . . he did it. It took three times, a month to six weeks every time, for me to get clean."

"And you're still clean?"

"Damn right. If you don't count having a kid that's smarter than I am who screws around and screws up and runs me *crazy*." She circled her small hand over her head. "And a jackass who keeps putting the squeeze on me to come back into the business. Not to mention a job pouring watered-down booze for men who actually think they have a shot at screwing me. Assholes who can barely string five intelligent words together."

She peeled the drenched T-shirt away from her drenched skin, then let it plop back into place.

"So sometimes I don't feel so clean."

"That's why he sends his hoods around? He needs the money you brought in?"

She kicked at the water, lost a flip-flop, retrieved it as it floated past.

"He's got plenty of money. He needs *me*. Not in any physical way; I was just one notch on a pistol that was filled up with notches. He needs my contacts. He needs me to set up the deals from South America." She almost smiled then, the first attempt at it since she'd sat down beside me. "I was good at it, you see. Hell, it was probably the only thing I was ever any good at. And those guys down there trusted me. Jerry's business took a big hit when I cut loose."

She leaned forward and hugged her knees.

"But the main thing." She nodded her head at the certainty of it. "The *main* reason he won't let go of us doesn't have anything to do with money. He just wants Holly and me to know that he's . . . the boss. You know? That he's still in control."

I thought of the old car she drove, and of the dump of a bar she worked in.

"What happened to all the money you made?"

"He invested it for me, or so he said. He'd dole out cash, a couple of hundred every once in a while, for spending money. When I got clean and told him I was done with the business he hit the ceiling. Shit, he hit *me*. When I asked him about my investments, he said they'd gone bad. That nothing was left. I knew he was lying, but what could I do? Go to the *police*? Take him to *court*?"

The afternoon slid slowly over into dusk. The rain kept falling.

"We get by," she said. "My dad's had this beach house forever, but he never came down after Mom got sick. So he pays me to keep it clean and keep it rented. We've got a one-bedroom apartment in a complex that's not too bad. And I've got the job at the bar."

She flipped the butt of her cigarette into the water.

"The drunker I can get the assholes, the better the tips."

• • •

Inside, after darkness and heavier rain had pushed us in, I offered coffee but she said she wanted something stronger. So, straight scotches all around. I brought up short sections of wood from the stack by the firebox downstairs and ignited my inaugural blaze in Gull Cottage's fireplace. To take the damp chill out of the room, I told Joyce, and to give the flue a test run to see if it drew as well as the realtor had said it did.

We sat on the floor by the hearth in white terrycloth robes I'd bought because I'd long ago decided that one of the best indicators of inviting and comfortable abodes is white terrycloth robes in bedroom closets.

When the glasses were splashed with refills of Glenlivet I rubbed my hair dry with a big towel, then she leaned over so I could do hers.

Then, in just the flickering light of the fire, she leaned closer and I held her small, pretty head in both hands and I kissed her.

Then, she sighed and rested her head against my damp neck and the soft shoulder of my robe.

Then, she closed her eyes and slowly breathed out a pair of syllables.

"Oh, shit," she sighed.

Which might, of course, have been a pronouncement of bliss. But which, I knew, was, rather, a simple confirmation of yet one more bad road being taken in a lifetime that had been traveled entirely along bad roads.

• • •

Later.

I stood knee-deep in the swirling tide at just about the exact place where Joyce and I had sat the afternoon before.

It was early, early morning. Long before daylight, earlier even than I usually started my run along the beach, the daily jog that I would not be making that day.

Joyce was gone, back up to Channelview to make sure Holly got up and went to school. She hadn't awakened me when she left. Hadn't leaned down to kiss me or tell me anything of the sweet nothings variety. Hadn't left a note.

The rain had moved inland about the same time that she had, and now silver moonlight spilled out over the uneventful surface of the gulf.

Soon, I'd go in and make coffee and shower and dress and leave for the Houston airport.

But I needed, just then, to be still. And quiet. And completely, resolutely, and unashamedly uncluttered and unfocused. I needed, for just a few minutes, to stand with my bare feet planted firmly, the warm water churning past my legs, my toes sunk firmly into the sand. I needed anchorage, for whatever infinitesimal span of time it would take the planet to rotate a few fractions of degrees toward wherever it was taking all of its passengers.

The onshore breeze was salty and brisk and clean after the long bout of rain. The eerie moonlight caught the slick fins of several dolphins—a family, maybe; I hoped so—heading gracefully westward just beyond the sand bars.

I watched the fins rise and fall slightly, in an almost imperceptible and surely an effortless undulation, until they were gone, too.

Twenty

Long ago.

The Greyhound bus that took me from Fort Knox to Fort Benning wound its way through endless miles of dark forests, along high ridges, and through more than a few tunnels chiseled through the sporadic, undersized mountains west of the Appalachians. Farmhouses and towns and small cities in Kentucky and Tennessee were closed up tight against a pesky cold snap that was the last onslaught of a determined winter. Light snow flurries swirled, a couple of times, among trees and hills and bluffs and into the countless steep indentions—called hollers thereabouts—that fell unexpectedly away beside the highway.

Once in Georgia, the weather grew a little warmer and the terrain flatter. Fort Benning was much like Fort Knox. Inside the gates and chain-link parameters of army reservations, one is pretty much like any other; flags snap and pop in the breeze, cadence-chanting training platoons march or double-time trot, and one hell of a lot of saluting gets done. The buildings common to bases—post exchanges, bowling alleys, NCO and officer clubs, chapels and mess halls and hospitals—are so completely interchangeable that, twenty years and thirteen camps after that bus ride, I wouldn't any more be able to distinguish one from another than I would be able to levitate.

When the bus's air brakes finally hissed and its door whooshed open at Benning, I was locked so completely into an inner zone that I had put every emotion aside, like furniture and clothing from one world that had no use whatsoever in a new one, and so had been packed away for the duration. Or forever.

Eight weeks of boot camp had left me hard as a slab of granite and as narrowly focused as any mule that ever wore blinders. All I could see was the training; my mind was a compendium of precise executions of dozens of soldierly maneuvers, calibrations of weapons, and the slowly ascending plateaus of the sacred chain of command. I could rattle off regulations and procedures like a Holy Roller preacher spitting out platitudes. There was not one thing they could throw at me that I couldn't handle, not a single thing in the manual or out of it that I couldn't excel at.

That was a given. A lead-pipe cinch.

I was the perfect soldier. I didn't question, didn't hesitate, didn't bitch, didn't—other than when it was essential to the performance of some soldierly thing—*think*. Putting thinking off the agenda for the foreseeable future was the keystone of my survival plan. Which was, of course, fueled entirely by a rich mixture of pure anger and spite. But the army didn't care about that. My trainers didn't give one whistling shit about *why* I was the way I was.

They just liked what they saw.

The cigar-wielding colonel who had sent me to Benning in the first place was nowhere to be seen. I looked for him at the edge of parade grounds, at the firing ranges and obstacle courses. I expected him to pop up at airborne training—first on the tall towers that we dropped from on cables, floating down to the red Georgia dirt, learning to hit and roll and gather up the chute and disappear quickly—and then in the planes themselves, before we fell away into nothingness, day and night, in all weathers, again and again and again. The wide, hovering domes of fabric exploding above us like the massive wings of fortuitous giants.

I half expected the colonel to pop up in the grueling survival drills, when they bounced us along in deuce-and-a-half trucks or dropped us out of airplanes into the vast backwoods of the big post, into the many square miles of wilderness without so much as a compass. In the last part of it—a two-day trek out by myself, with a couple of roots and a clutch of wild onions I found for nourishment and a little water from a tiny joke of a stream—the colonel would have been a welcomed sight.

But he never showed. And, in spite of the fact that I was better at the bullshit that was the business of that place than anyone else in my platoon or my company, I had, by the end of it, become convinced that I wouldn't see him again.

Which was fine by me. Let me, I figured, do my court-ordered sentence and then slide back into my life. Whatever it would turn out to be.

During the final week of training—when I was as dark and chiseled and brainwashed as anyone was likely to get—and the duty guard woke me out of a sound sleep to tell me I had an emergency phone call in the captain's office, I figured that it had to be the colonel.

But the slight, careful voice that came tenuously over the line was nowhere close to his curt, gravelly tone. In fact, it took me a couple of minutes to adjust to the softness of the words.

". . . difficulty finding you," he was saying, when I'd tweaked some inner dial to pick up his delicate frequency. "Even though he didn't *want* me to call you."

Whoever he was, he sounded tired.

"He said *don't* call you, in fact. You know how he is about not wanting to be a nuisance to anybody. But I thought you'd want to know." He paused. "I know he really wants you to come."

I broke in only long enough to ask him who he was talking about.

"Donald," he said, obviously surprised. He'd probably said his name at the first of the call, when I was just waking up, just finding my feet in the conversation.

"Your uncle. Donald."

"Tell me *what?*"

And then he did tell me, this soft-voiced, exhausted fellow who I eventually learned was named Morgan, only stumbling over the words once or twice. This fellow whose heart was breaking, and who no doubt expected mine to break a little, too.

I mumbled something about not having seen Donald in over a year. About not being able to come because of my training. What I didn't say was that I didn't want to see him, didn't care about whatever was going on. But he got the message. After another long pause, he slowly trooped out exactly ten words.

"You need to come," he said, his voice finally cracking.

"You need to come right away."

• • •

The First Sergeant, a short, stocky veteran of two tours in Viet Nam, cut me orders for a forty-eight-hour emergency leave and arranged for a covey of military hops on civilian airlines from Columbus to Atlanta to Dallas to Oklahoma City.

Ten hours, four airports, a bad hamburger, and about fifteen Styrofoam cups of coffee later, I looked out the dirty window of the cab that was taking me from Will Rogers airport to the hospital. The afternoon sky was filled with low, heavy clouds that hadn't decided just yet to send more of their cargo down. The downtown streets glistened, with long, dark puddles along their curbs. The cab's window was covered with filthy streaks and spots, so the streets and alleys that I had spent much of my youth running through slid by like a grainy black and white movie that had been shot through a filter.

The man who slowly stood up from the couch in the waiting room on the eighth floor of the big downtown hospital had to be Morgan. He was slender, and in spite of the fact that he wore nicely tailored slacks and a starched, light blue dress shirt, he looked like he had been dragged through hell.

He might have slept in the last forty-eight hours, but I wouldn't have put any real money on it.

His handshake was firmer than I had anticipated, and he cupped his other hand over mine while he shook it.

"I'm sorry for this," he said, realizing that no introductions were necessary. I was in my Class A uniform and he was the only other person in the room.

"I'm not sorry I called you, because in spite of what he said, he wanted you to know. But I'm sorry you had to come all that way, and on such short notice."

I asked how long he'd been sick.

"Since before you left." Which was news to me; and why wouldn't it have been? He hadn't been anything more to me in those days than a convenient provider of a roof, a bed, food, and spending money, some of which I had stolen outright from his wallet. "He was diagnosed as HIV positive in eighty-three, then he became ill about a year before you left."

I'd no doubt heard the phrase HIV positive somewhere—probably in a joke in the barracks; certainly not in a serious discussion—but it didn't ring any bells.

"I was a little groggy when you called, and didn't really understand some of the stuff you told me."

He smiled at that.

"I could tell. The doctor's in with him now; he'll talk to you about it."

He had a pleasant smile, a somehow reassuring one. His salt-and-pepper hair was cut short like Donald's had always been. They were lovers, of course. It had never occurred to me that Donald might be a homosexual. None of the usual clues had been in place. He might not have been John Wayne, but he wasn't effeminate—in his speech or his clothing or his demeanor—and I didn't recall seeing any Liza Minelli or Barbara Streisand cassettes lying around. But, as I believe has been established, I hadn't made a habit of snapping to anything that didn't directly benefit me. So, Donald could have been running a meth lab in the kitchen and I probably wouldn't have noticed.

The doctor came out, said a word or two to Morgan, then came over and introduced himself. He looked down, once or twice, at the open file he was holding while he talked to me. The wide, empty hallway that smelled of Lysol sprawled off away from us on both sides; his words were punctuated often by the swooshing of elevator doors and the quiet dings that must be the common heartbeat of all hospitals.

I had so effectively buried myself in things that only pertained to me—first my dance with delinquency in the city, then getting my GED in jail, then my training in Kentucky and Georgia—that I'd never paid any attention whatsoever to the news. So, when the doctor was telling me about the new plague that had smitten the land he might as well have been talking to a Martian, fresh off the flying saucer.

"So," I said, when he was done, " . . . he's going to . . . *die*?"

He watched me for a moment. Then he closed Donald's file and took off his glasses.

"That's correct," he said. "And fairly soon, I imagine. A week or two, maybe."

In the room, Donald looked thirty years older than when I'd last seen him, a little more than a year earlier, in a courtroom just down the street. His eyes were still blue, but they resided now in gray craters in his narrow face; his skin was pale and seemingly paper-thin, and he might have weighed a hundred pounds, if you left the bedclothes on. He could barely lift his hand to touch mine. He must have read my hesitance.

"The doctor says you can't catch this," he said, his voice barely more than a raspy whisper, "by touching."

"No," I said, "it's not that. I just didn't want to ..."

He smiled.

"You look handsome in your uniform."

Then the smile was gone.

"Has it been horrible?"

From there we wandered into the first real conversation we'd ever had. And the last. Morgan had gone home to bathe and change and get a little rest, and we had the room to ourselves. The effort it took for him to keep up his end of the exchange was evident. But he soldiered on.

"I wanted to be a teacher. Did you know that?" he said, nearly an hour into our visit.

"I remember you slinging Shakespeare quotes all over the place." I dug around deep enough to come up with one, then hoisted my index finger dramatically. "To be or not to be!"

He laughed. A sad, short sputtering of a laugh. He fiddled with the plastic ID bracelet that engulfed his narrow wrist. It probably didn't have enough notches for his skeletal forearm.

"I wanted to learn all about literature, and then to teach English," he said. "I've always loved to read, you see, even when I was a kid."

His voice scraped a little; I picked up the cup of juice and held the bent straw to his dry lips. He took a sip.

"But there wasn't any money for me to go to college. Your father never wanted to go—he went to work at the air base right out of high school—and my father, your grandfather, never saw any need for me to go either."

He looked at me.

"You never knew your grandparents. Your grandfather died about the time you were born. Your grandmother a long time before that; I barely remember her myself. There was absolutely no way my father could have sent me to college, even if he'd wanted to. He owed too many people."

He gazed out the small window into a day that was slipping slowly into evening. The rain had moved on, and the sound of the city crept in through the glass.

"I promised to pay a few of his friends back some of what he owed them, so I had to keep my job." He looked back at me and smiled. "At an *IHOP*! Can you imagine? Then I got my realtor's license and went to work, selling mortgages to people who couldn't afford them. It took a few years, but I paid off my dad's debts."

I asked him if my father had helped. He would have been married by then, with a steady job.

"Your father ..." he started, then shut his eyes and let his brother drift away.

He was quiet for long enough for me to think he might have fallen asleep. Then he opened his eyes and looked at me.

"Maybe you shouldn't talk for a little while," I said.

He smiled again.

"I think I'd better talk while I can. Don't you?"

I put my hand on his arm.

"Because I've got something to tell you now."

I waited while he organized his thoughts.

"I want to apologize to you," he said.

I stuttered out something about not worrying about the army deal, but he cut me off.

"Not that. That had to be done, to keep you out of jail. You'll just have to see that through to the end, and make the best of it. Just ..." I watched him make the necessary calculation.

I told him he didn't have anything to apologize to me for.

"I *do*," he said. He tried to sit up, felt the futility of it, and rested back against the pillow. "I . . . resented you when your parents died. I tried to never show it, but I . . . resented you coming in and changing my life. I mean, having a cat was one thing, but having a *boy*. That changed things all together."

I tried to say something, but he touched my hand to stop me.

"You see, I never wanted you to know about my . . . lifestyle."

I told him I never did. Then I told him he hadn't needed to keep it from me.

"I didn't know what you'd think about it," he said. "I didn't know what you'd think about *me*." He waved his hand, to summon us back to where he wanted us to be.

"Anyway, I was gone a lot. I had to work long days and nights to get my real estate business going. And that meant you had all that time to . . ."

"Fuck up . . ." I finished for him. Which made him laugh.

"So," he said, nearly worn out now, "there it is. I was away too much, and I didn't want you at the start. And I apologize."

I leaned down closer to him, and tried again to say something. This time he stopped me by holding one frail finger up.

"But, more than that, I wanted to tell you something else. I wanted you to know that I came to love you very much, and I wouldn't have had it any other way than for you to have lived with me." He took a long look at my uniform, then at me.

"I'm so proud of you. I've kept up with your progress; the judge made sure I could do that. I botched it up when you were in school so, this time, I kept up."

He patted my hand, and relaxed. He was obviously done now. He'd said what he wanted to say, and he was done.

Later, after Morgan had returned, after Donald had slept through two short naps, I told him I had to go. That my plane would be leaving in a little while.

He asked Morgan to hand me the canvas bag full of hardback books that I had noticed in the corner.

"They're some of my favorites," Donald said. "I enjoyed all of them several times. And I'd like to think that you might, too."

Morgan went into the hall so we could say our goodbyes.

I held his hands in mine.

"You're a good man, Donald Rafferty," I told him.

He thought about it, and nodded. A tear worked its way down his sallow face.

"Yes," he agreed, nodding once more. "We're a couple of good men. Finally."

He squeezed my hands.

"Isn't that fine?" he said.

And I left, stopping in the hallway to ask Morgan to call me when I needed to return.

On the plane, I lifted the top book out of the canvas bag. It was *The Heart of the Matter*, by Graham Greene. On the title page, a short inscription had been carefully written in a wobbly hand.

To thine own self be true, it said.

Twenty-One

Back at Fort Benning, everything was winding its way frantically toward graduation.

Orders had been cut for most of the company to report, after the ceremony, to various infantry outfits around the country and the world. There wasn't a war on at present, so there wasn't a hell of a lot for Airborne Rangers to do, other than keep training.

I checked with the first sergeant. Nothing yet for me.

Later that week, I marched with my unit in another parade, and saluted another general, and graduated again. Then all I could do was wait. Then, when all of the company had packed up their duffle bags and shipped off, I reported in at the company office every morning, picked up cigarette butts outside the barracks, ran countless miles, worked out in the post gym, arm-wrestled and wrestled and boxed any and all takers, and sat alone in the empty barracks night after night and read Donald's novels.

"Hell if I know what's up," the first sergeant said every day, after he told me there was nothing yet in the way of orders. "Maybe Uncle Sam fucking forgot about you." *Fucking* was the universally utilitarian adjective in his vocabulary.

When a new training platoon moved into the barracks, I bunked in one of the small cadre rooms at the end of the building.

And I waited.

Finally, one morning when I was sitting outside in the sunshine reading, the wait came to an end. The branches of the tree I was leaning against sprawled out against the blue, almost summer sky into which a familiar face suddenly loomed over me.

"You got a minute?" the colonel asked.

I closed *Great Expectations* and stood up. Snapped a salute, which he snapped back.

"I have a hell of a lot of minutes here lately, Sir."

He grunted, and looked around.

"I guess you figured out I held up your orders till we could have that little talk."

I was still at attention, so he told me to be at ease.

"So," he said, "let's talk."

• • •

"They started kicking this idea around back in the early sixties," he said, as we strode briskly beside a wide parade ground. "They, meaning the joint chiefs and maybe the Secretary of Defense. And maybe not. The chiefs sometimes have their own agenda wherein they don't appreciate some political appointee's opinion. After the Bay of Pigs, which the CIA fucked up gloriously, they decided it would have to be a military operation, soup to nuts. "

He picked up his already rapid pace, getting comfortable in the story. One of his big cigars magically materialized.

"They leaned toward the Marines first, then all the attention went to the Navy Seals. It rocked on over at Annapolis for a few years, without any great success."

He made a small production of unwrapping the cigar, clipping its end, lighting it, and puffing it to life.

"Then they finally put two and two together, and figured their best resource was already there, right under their noses." He came to an abrupt halt, bringing me to one also. "Draftees." He blew the single word out with a white puff of smoke.

"You see, they clicked to the fact that men who signed up, who wanted to *serve*, might be gallant and brave and committed and all that happy horseshit. But they'd never be what they needed them to be."

He looked over at me then.

"They wouldn't be *pissed off*."

We started walking, very nearly trotting, again.

"And one hell of a lot of draftees were."

He fired off returns to the salutes of nearly everybody we passed, jerking his big hand up to his brow and then back down in one brisk motion, like a gunslinger.

"Since the army had damned near all the guys who'd been

drafted, that's where I came in. I found some of the angriest ones—the monumental fuckups that spent more time in the brig than on duty—and I tried to channel some of that acid into something I could use. And it worked okay. Sometimes. Then they stopped the draft after Viet Nam. And I had to fold up my tent."

"After a couple of years, during which a few hairy situations came and went where my particular style of closure would have come in handy, the chiefs ordered me to put something back together. And I wondered, who are the pissed off grunts now?"

He smiled.

"And you know the answer, Private Rafferty. Guys just like *you*, who—courtesy of the courts—arrive angry and stay angry and every great once in a while one of you hides himself in the army and festers into exactly the kind of machine that I need."

"That you need to do *what*?" I asked him.

And that is when I first experienced just how blunt this man could be. He didn't slow down, or change the level of his voice, or even blink.

"To kill people."

• • •

"How will this work, if we do it?" I wanted to know, after another hour of hearing him out. We'd walked. Stopped for lunch in a mess hall. Walked again.

He shot me a look then that I would come to know, over the next two decades, extremely well. A hard stare that said that this, whatever *this* happened to be, would damned well work if he intended it to.

"I'll bury you. You and a kid named Gomez I've got my eye on and maybe one other guy."

He turned the big cigar in his big hand.

"I'll bury you so fucking deep in this man's army that you will be completely invisible. Gomez will be a supply clerk. You, I'm thinking, will be a clerk-typist. Or some other MOS that any prick can qualify for."

He blew some ashes off the end of the stogie.

"By the way, can you type?"

I told him no.

"Not a problem. We'll cook up a short course for you. Hell, you'll probably never have to type anyway. Most of the guys I've seen manning typewriters are hardly speed demons. Most of 'em hunt and peck."

"So, it would just be three men," I said. "Maybe just two. And you?"

He didn't answer.

He went on, for another quarter of an hour or so, about what he had in mind. When he was finished, I told him that when my hitch was up, I'd be gone.

"You'll be gone," he said. "If you still want to be. But I'm betting you'll re-up."

I damned near laughed out loud at that.

"How you figure that?"

The colonel stretched. Then he tossed away what was left of the cigar that had long since gone cold.

"Simple," he said, stopping on the sidewalk to watch a platoon of trainees double-time down the street.

We watched the two road guards post themselves in the inter-section, and listened to the cadence the platoon sang out to the drill sergeant and to the slow, heavy rhythm of their combat boots pounding down, like the shuffling of perfectly aligned gears in some huge motor. The platoon was almost to the next crossing before the colonel continued.

"Where the hell would somebody like you *go*?"

He looked over at me with something new in his steely eyes. Sadness, maybe. Regret, maybe.

"What the hell would somebody like us *do*?"

• • •

The next day Morgan called and told me that it was time for me to come.

I found the colonel at the officer's bachelor's quarters and he said to go on. To say my goodbyes and tie up my loose ends.

"Then," he said, "we can start. When you get back we'll go to Fort Bragg and you'll meet Gomez, and maybe that other guy. And we'll start."

He took out his wallet and pressed a wad of bills into my hand.

"Get yourself a round trip ticket. Direct flights. Get your personal business taken care of and get your ass back here. ASAP."

Back at the hospital in Oklahoma, I sat for a long, long time with Morgan at Donald's bedside. He hadn't waked up since my return, so we just sat and watched him sleep, or whatever he was doing. Nurses came in every little while to look at the monitors and check the IVs and smile at us, and then they left and we sat and watched him some more.

Morgan held his hand much of the time. But he was gone from us, we both realized. Gone, maybe, already to wherever he was headed. A good place, I hoped. He, more than anyone I had ever known or ever would know, deserved to go to a damned good place.

If there is a place at all.

After the sixth or seventh hour, all I could think of was the time the cat died. This was the cat that I had vowed, when Donald brought me to live with him when I was a little boy, to not care anything about. It was a gray cat named Stormcloud and I had spent most of my first two weeks there shooing her away from me and closing doors between us. But she was persistent, and never gave up on the notion of us becoming friends.

Which we finally did. By the end of the third week, Stormcloud was completely my cat, and no longer Donald's. She slept beside me at night. She watched me eat and get ready for school every morning. When I came home in the afternoons she was sitting in the window waiting for me. Then, when I took up my nefarious lifestyle, she gave me long, accusing glares when I snuck back in from my shenanigans. Knowing my black heart completely, even when the trusting Donald did not.

By the time I was fifteen, Stormcloud had gotten so old and feeble that she couldn't get herself up onto my bed at night. So I had to lift her up, like a loose bag of dry sticks, and place her gently next to the pillow beside mine. Where she would wheeze for a few minutes before falling asleep.

Finally, when she was nearly blind, completely deaf, and unable to walk for more than a few steps before collapsing, Donald said it was time.

At the veterinarian's office I realized, as I stood holding her as the doctor pushed the contents of a syringe home, that I was too old to be crying about anything. Especially a cat. But when she looked up at me one last time with those totally devoted eyes that had watched me like a hawk since I'd first come into the house five years before, I sobbed so uncontrollably that Donald had put his arm around me. He'd had to help the doctor pry her body away from my embrace.

About midnight, I told Morgan I was going out to the waiting area to see if there was any coffee made.

There wasn't. So I walked over to the big window and stretched. Outside, the lights of downtown Oklahoma City sparkled in the darkness. Several stories below, the mean streets where I'd tried hard to be a tough guy crisscrossed each other under dim streetlamps and in the low beams of a few cars creeping along between stoplights. Those were the streets and alleys where the cocky little bastard that had been me had unceremoniously crashed and burned. Only to be scooped up and saved by the man who lay dying in the room down the hall.

Just before dawn, Donald slipped back into the world for just a few minutes. He smiled when Morgan squeezed his hand. Then, after Morgan whispered some words to him and kissed him on his forehead, he opened his eyes and looked at me.

I touched the side of his face and let my hand stay there.

He tried to say something, so I leaned down close.

"It's like . . ." he started, his voice barely there at all, like the transmission of a faraway signal over a weak radio, ". . . it's like . . ." He reached harder, but couldn't locate it. "Like . . ."

I took a stab in the darkness, and ventured a guess.

"Like those porpoises? At Sea Arama?" I whispered it into his ear.

I'll never know if my guess was right or wrong. But it satisfied him.

He closed his eyes, nodded his head against my hand, and, a few minutes later, he left us again. This time for good.

• • •

Two days later I straddled a comfortable stool in a bar at the airport and motioned for the bartender, a lady in late middle age who might have been a real looker in her day. But this wasn't her day.

I ordered a draft beer, took a long pull, wiped the foam away, and sloshed the remaining brew around in the tall pilsner glass.

I'd gone straight to the airport from Donald's funeral, a nice affair held in a big church across the street from the Federal Building that would, a few years later, become the first ground zero in our terrorism saga.

The preacher had said nice things about Donald, about his involvement in community affairs, his devotion to his friends—he stopped obviously short of mentioning Morgan, who sat stoically on the front row with me—and about how he had raised me after the death of my parents. There was nothing mentioned, of course, about how he made the many phone calls and hounded the judge until he finally cut the difficult deal that delivered me into the army instead of prison. Not one word was uttered about that singular, heroic act of salvation, when the first stages of his illness had already laid claim to him, emotionally and physically.

A few of Oklahoma City's movers and shakers showed up, and a couple of them spoke. The preacher had asked me if I wanted to say a few words, but I said no. Donald died knowing how I finally felt about him. And I figured it wasn't any of those peoples' business. Except for Morgan, who already knew.

The body had been cremated, so there wasn't any burying to be done. After the service, I asked Morgan if he would be okay. Then I asked him if he wanted to go for a drink. Yes to the first. No to the second. He gave me his phone number and mailing address and held out his hand. Instead, I pulled him close and hugged him. He hadn't told me if he was sick, also. And I hadn't asked. A little over a year later, one of the nurses who had stood vigil over Donald with us wrote to me that he had died.

On the way to my rental car, one of the honorary pallbearers, a lawyer, stopped me and told me I'd be hearing from him soon about Donald's estate. He'd done extremely well in real estate in the City, the guy told me, and had left some money to several charities. But one fat portfolio, wisely invested and generously bearing fruit, was for me. He gave me his card.

The draft beer wasn't doing the trick, so I motioned the bartender back over.

"I want to try something new," I told her. She wiped her hands with a bar towel and waited. "I guess my life is about to change."

She listened with the feigned interest that all good bartenders can conjure up when confronted with information they could care less about.

"I always order beer, or whiskey. But I want to try something different." I leaned forward, and pushed the half empty glass toward her. "Something that's . . . true, I guess. And dependable." The words would have been fine in dialogue penned by Hemingway, but they felt completely wrong and inadequate when babbled out by a nineteen-year-old who'd failed high school English. I took one final stab at making some sort of sense.

"Something that means more than just having a drink."

She could have laughed then, this peroxided, overly made-up, slightly over the hill matron in a dark bar in an airport in Middle America. But she didn't.

She nodded.

"What you want," she said, reaching behind her for a silver shaker, "is a martini."

Part III
The Dark Side of the Moon

Twenty-Two

Now I had to focus.

The stuffy cabin of the 737 was packed tight with vacationers, the dark Atlantic glittered under swatches of pillowy clouds outside the window beside my seat, and the two kids in front of me—who should have been in school somewhere, as best I could figure, it being early September now—were having a belching competition. The fatter of the two was definitely winning. The woman beside them, probably the one who spawned them, thumbed through a magazine and seemed to have effectively tuned the little bastards out.

Which was exactly what I needed to do.

I needed to put everything and everybody other than the matter at hand—conflicts and emotions and relationships and memories—completely aside. Like cramming things into a drawer or a closet to be sorted out and dealt with later.

It was essential that, for several days, maybe as long as a week, I concentrate only on what I had planned down to the minutest degree. For, in spite of that detailed preparation, there would be surprises. Things would go wrong. And things wouldn't be as I expected them to be. Inconsistencies, improbabilities, and incongruities would pop up. And inconsistencies, improbabilities, and incongruities were the lions and tigers and bears in that line of work.

My mind was a veritable smorgasbord of things that screamed out to be mulled over. But not then. Not then. So I rammed the plastic stethoscope into my ears and dialed the control on my armrest to jazz. I kicked up the volume. Closed my eyes.

Someday, I thought, as Herbie Hancock pounded away in my head, I might just bite the bullet and stretch myself out on some psychiatrist's couch and a tale unfold that would provide him fodder for a batch of journal articles. More likely a whole textbook.

The steward who had already brought two refills of soda for the burping lads in front of me brought one more, though it was obvious he wasn't any too pleased about it. He told them to drink up quickly, that we would be landing soon. The aircraft had already groaned and heaved its way through the contortions required to line up for its descent. Somewhere beneath us, the landing gear whirred heavily into place.

Whoever that lucky shrink on whose couch I might someday recline might turn out to be, he'd have a field day with this particular one-man circus of quirkiness, all three rings frantic with activity. He'd scratch his chin—a goateed chin, surely—and opine that I'd had no choice but to give up my chances with any number of women, one of whom was Kelsie, because of the possibility of them becoming victims. On the other hand, I could, he'd reason, have somebody like Joyce, who was already a victim before I had the opportunity to taint her. He'd figure I needed to be a father to Holly—in spite of the fact that I didn't turn away when she traipsed around in her dental floss bikini, which would be a whole separate slice of fruitcake that would require another session—and that I needed to be a son to Tucker and/or the General, in spite of the fact that they were polar opposites on almost every issue. And the entire morality/ethical issue—that had only recently *become* an issue—would blot out multiple boxes on his appointment calendar, and probably provide him a new wing on his summer home.

A bell dinged. The ends of seatbelts clicked into their sockets all around me like an entire platoon cocking rifles. The fatter of the two children emitted one final, resounding belch.

I opened my eyes and reminded myself, not for the first time by any means, that I needed to get my mind off of the psychiatrist that I would never actually meet, since a fundamental tenet of the Rule forbade it.

I had to push him away with everything else, I realized, as the clawlike outline of the Bermuda Islands emerged through the wispy clouds.

I had to focus.

• • •

I stepped out of the airport terminal into the bright sunshine of a cloudless, nearly eighty-degree afternoon. My passport had been stamped—bearing a photograph of me and the name of Mr. Jeffery S. (for Scott) Whitten of Tacoma, Washington, the authenticity of whom could be verified in all the usual ways—driver's license, library and credit cards, even a summons for jury duty—since the alias had been established by the General's people two years previously for an altogether different adventure that had never actually materialized and recently updated. My wallet was full of a little over ten thousand American dollars and several hundred Bermuda dollars that I could exchange for exactly the same number of U.S. greenbacks.

I took a cab over to St. George, one of the islands' two largest burgs, because it was close, and because it was at the opposite end of Bermuda than The Outrigger, the exclusive private resort where Jacques Deminille would, if all was working according to schedule, be arriving the next day.

I checked into a relatively inexpensive inn—relative, that is, when considering this was one of the trendiest and priciest tourist destinations in the world—threw my tote on the double bed, and headed out in search of dinner.

There were numerous transportation possibilities. Rental cars were nonexistent, but I could take a cab, a bus, a rented bike, a horse-drawn carriage, or a motorized contraption called a "putt-putt." What I really needed, however, after the lengthy and circuitous route I'd intentionally booked on three airlines as three different people, was to reenergize my legs after all that sitting. So I opted for hoofing it on my dependable size elevens.

The late afternoon pink-streaked, pale blue sky made a fine backdrop for palm trees flanking two-story houses with latticework balconies. Everything put up by man that could be painted had been, with every color of tropical pastel imaginable. Lush plants—some flowering, some not bothering to—sent their delicate aromas into the moist, overriding scent of the sea. A mammoth cruise ship, a real behemoth, loomed up ten or so stories in the harbor, dwarfing the tiny, centuries-old buildings beneath it like the vessel that might have delivered Gulliver to the Lilliputians.

I strolled along a tree-lined street called Duke of York as far as Barber's Alley, turned toward the harbor, and stopped beside an attractive mansion called Tucker House. Its handsome iron tablet proclaimed it to be the ancestral home of an important colonial family. Now it was a museum. A coffee cup from its gift shop would have made a dandy souvenir for Tucker, except for the fact that I was supposed to be in Wyoming.

A little backtracking along Water Street took me to King's Square and, after a pint of pilsner and a plate of shepherd's pie at a place called the White Horse Tavern—after all, who could pass up libation and pub grub at a place called the White Horse Tavern?—I crossed a bridge to something called Ordinance Island. Which was composed of a small, tree-thick park at either end and one hell of a big open plaza in the middle, in which sat a full-sized replica of a tall ship called *Deliverance*. Its iron tablet told me the original had plied these waters in the early seventeenth century, taking English settlers to Virginia and hauling the disillusioned ones back again.

I'd had enough of iron tablets for one day. Enough of touristing. So I wandered out to the end of one of two piers that jutted out into the harbor and watched the sun drop over the edge of the ocean. Burning its way down toward a repeat performance, several hours later, behind Gull Cottage.

Bermuda was attractive enough; at least the tiny portion of it that I had seen was. It was full of small, obviously old yet well-maintained stucco cottages and buildings decked out in every festive hue imaginable. And abundant tropical plants and interesting things and clever names of places, like Mullet Bay and Convict's Bay and Nonsuch Island. A wider array of bodies of water than I would have thought possible was represented, in spades. There were cuts, harbors, sounds, bays, lagoons, shallows, deeps, and holes absolutely everywhere—each of them christened and most of them of some historical significance—with towns and villages along their banks, and sometimes just clusters of tea shops, bakeries, book dealers, and pubs. Then, beyond it all, in every direction, there was the slowly approaching surf, the darker water that swirled over the reefs, and then the deep purple, brooding Atlantic stretching out to infinity.

Ghosts ran thick here, I knew.

They ran thick on Galveston too. With somewhere between six and seven thousand islanders cashing it in on one night in the 1900 storm. Long before that had been the Karankawa tribe, cannibals who had several of the first Spanish settlers for dinner, literally. Not to mention influenza epidemics, sundry other fatal disasters, and the normal mortal attrition that a city will chalk up over a couple of centuries.

But here, they'd had a half a millennium of pirates, puritans, persecution, plagues, pestilence, and too many maritime misfortunes to recall. Reefs and the seabed just beyond them were cluttered with wrecks. From sloops to frigates to oil tankers to liners, the victims of cannonballs, torpedoes, lightening bolts, drunkard pilots, foggy nights, and countless hurricanes that the curled string of islands had caught like fastballs in a mitt.

Quiet dusk fell slowly into quiet night. Tennyson's deep moaned round with many voices.

It was a beautiful place, and no denying it. Travelogue material, every inch. Full of one vista after another that would splash out nicely across double-page spreads in *Conde Nast* and *National Geographic*.

But, I figured, as I leaned over a rope-draped handrail at the edge of the pier, I'd take Galveston. With her beaches and surf that were only slightly different shades of brown. With her mosquitoes and humidity and loud revelers along the seawall.

Of course, I had only been in Bermuda a couple of hours, and hadn't seen enough of the place to make a fair comparison. And, if the comparison used beauty as its sole criteria, then Bermuda would win hands down.

But I had a hard thing to do there, among all the palm trees and tea shops and British gents in their starched Bermuda shorts.

Plus, I missed my own island and my house. I missed my friends, who I'd left in various stages of discord.

I was homesick.

Which was an altogether new emotion for me.

...

The next morning, I took a bus from St. George back toward the airport, across a tall causeway bridge spanning the northern mouth of Castle Harbor, then along the beach at the top of Hamilton Sound and across another bridge at Flatt's Village. Then we had a long stretch—long, that is, for a small cluster of islands—into the capitol city of Hamilton.

Stately government buildings, museums, large churches and a cathedral sat old and well-kempt among tall trees, manicured lawns and hedges, and enough iron tablets to keep a history-minded traveler occupied for a long time.

In Hamilton, I changed buses, watched more pastel-colored houses and profusely overachieving vegetation slide by outside and in a few minutes we—the other three passengers, the sleepy driver, and myself—had left the little city behind and were bending around the end of Hamilton Harbor and heading out toward the westernmost narrow strip of connected islands that curled themselves up like the tail of a giant scorpion. The road twisted and turned through four parishes before the bus rattled across the world's smallest drawbridge—literally; my well-thumbed Frommer's guide locked away in a cabinet in Galveston had made much of the fact—before, a few minutes later, letting me off at Somerset Village, a hamlet stretched out along the highway that the bus was already pulling away on, making its way toward Ireland Island, the end of the world in Bermuda.

Though small, Somerset was a place I could happily spend some time in, given other circumstances. Everything was neat and tidy and perfectly picturesque and it seemed to have not changed one iota since Cary Grant and Doris Day had filmed *That Touch of Mink* there before I was born. Which, film buff that I am, was practically the only thing I'd known about these islands before the General had come calling.

It had not, however, been the reason I'd debussed there.

The Outrigger was just up the beach. I could just make out the steep pitch of its pink-tiled roof above a wide oasis of palms swaying in the sea breeze. And sometime later that day Jacques Deminille would be there.

That, and the fact that the complimentary continental breakfast at my inn must have hailed from some continent given to eating only dry rolls in the morning. I was hungry.

So I chose one of the little eateries, and settled myself down to a steaming bowl of fish chowder with crusty homemade bread and a tall glass of dark ale. In a snug booth beside a wide window that looked out over Mangrove Bay and, beyond it, nothing but endless square miles of cold, briny deep all the way to Newfoundland.

Twenty-Three

Powell's Dive Shop was a short walk from the village, just up the highway toward The Outrigger.

It was tiny, as most businesses there seemed to be, and done up entirely in bamboo and thatch. More like places I'd seen down in the Caribbean. Which, by all accounts, the proper Brits of this aristocratic kingdom by the sea considered hedonistic and superficial. Powell, himself—if the lean, well-tanned fellow in his late twenties or early thirties was indeed Powell—even looked out of place. He wore baggy shorts a size or two too large, flip-flops, a rumpled Hawaiian shirt unbuttoned half way, a necklace of large coral beads, and a smile broad enough to set his white teeth to gleaming in the midst of his bronzed face.

"Fancy a dive, do you?" he asked, in a friendly brogue that landed somewhere between Michael Caine and Hugh Grant, a smooth blend of Cockney and Queen's English.

"Never tried it," I said, stepping up to a big scuba rig and wetsuit laid out like a deboned cadaver on the table in the center of the room. "I always wanted to."

He put down the regulator hose clamp he was adjusting at the workbench and came over.

"So," I said, "how involved a process would it be to learn how to do this? Just well enough to still be alive at the end of the day?"

His smile grew, almost impossibly, even wider.

"We can have you trained and certified in a couple of days."

He wiped his hands with the rag he was holding.

"I'm Timothy Powell."

He had a dead fish handshake that would have failed the General's test for both masculinity and sincerity.

"Jeff Whitten."

I asked a few questions as he showed me the pressure and depth gauges on the outfit, then the air tank and regulator and a few other gadgets. I put the mouthpiece over my mouth and nose and tried to look bewildered.

I could have taken the entire apparatus apart and put it back together again blindfolded. Had done it, in fact, more than a few times.

A single ceiling fan turned so slowly overhead that I couldn't tell if the breeze through the open door and windows was powering it or if it was actually turned on. The walls were covered with hoses and flippers and masks, interspersed with a couple of framed photos of Powell with a pretty girl, the same one in each shot, and of underwater shots of divers exploring reefs and wrecks.

I thumbed through a brochure. Then wandered over to the door and looked up the road.

"You get much business from that swanky joint up the beach?" I asked him.

"The Outrigger? Some." His eyes narrowed. "That where you're staying?"

I laughed.

"Hardly. I just tried to go in to get a look around, maybe have a drink at the bar. Didn't get past the gate."

He nodded.

"It's private. And, like you said, quite snobbish. That lot generally doesn't rent gear. They either bring it with them or the resort furnishes it."

He looked at his wristwatch, a gigantic, obviously waterproof, monstrosity.

"Listen, I was just about to pop down to Molly's for a pint myself. Since you didn't get that drink, you could come along."

• • •

Molly's was one of the countless watering holes of Bermuda. Like most of the other establishments, it sat beside the sea—which would be difficult for an establishment not to do on this last slender spit of terra firma—and Powell climbed onto a stool at a tall table on the patio and motioned through the open door for the proprietress.

I asked if she was Molly. Which brought a laugh from both of them.

"Molly could have served drinks to my great, great grandmother," the girl said. "That's how long this place has been here. My name's Ellen." Which might have been Helen and might actually have been Ellen.

Powell ordered us a couple of beers.

"Your great, great grandmum was a rummy then, was she?" he asked.

"Could 'ave likely drunk your ancestors under the table," she shot back, smiling all the while. She turned to pull the bottles up from a huge reach-in cooler. "You bein' . . . delicate and all."

She was closer to my age than Powell's. And considerably shy of being attractive enough to make the smiles and banter that zapped between them amount to anything. She was probably American, or had started out as such; unless I missed my guess, the accent was a polished affectation of what she thought a publican on a British island was expected to sound like.

When Helen or Ellen had opened the bottles and gone inside, I took a long, icy drink of one of the local brews.

"I thought the English went in for beer at room temperature," I said.

Powell lifted up his bottle and swirled the dark contents around.

"This close to America, which we lovingly refer to no longer as the fallen colonies but as Bread and Butter—we go in for pretty much whatever you Yanks want."

The conversation wandered through two bottles of beer for each of us, hitting on the local economy, the weather, Mr. Bush's war, the Prime Minister's support of Mr. Bush's war, and finally to what I did for a living.

"I'm a writer. Actually, I'm an English teacher *trying* to be a writer. I'm working on a novel, some of it set out here, so I splurged and bought a ticket. Thought I'd better get a good look at the place."

He looked surprised.

"No shit. My . . ."

Then Ellen or Helen was back, carrying on what was apparently a daily flirtation with the tanned and toned Brit that she most likely dreamed about every night.

A stretch limo, with two vans close behind it, sped along the highway a few yards from us, heading for The Outrigger.

I drained my beer, and pointed the bottle at the parade.

"More rich folks, looks like," I said, "ready to supplement the island's economy."

Powell finished his own brew.

"That'll be Deminelle," he said.

I gave a bewildered look. It seemed to be my day for giving bewildered looks.

"Jacques Deminelle. Surely you've heard of him. Jetsetter and all that. He's due in today."

I fished more Bermuda dollars out of my shirt pocket than was necessary to pay our tab, folded them, and put them under the bottle. Powell lifted his hand in protest. I lifted mine to refute it. I asked if the guy in the limo came all that often.

"Couple of times a year. Maybe three. He's a diver, damned good one."

Outside, he asked if I wanted to come back up to the shop and register for the next day's class.

"I'll walk with you," I told him, "but let me sleep on it about the lessons. I might be getting cold feet. I'm not all that good a swimmer, and I probably saw *The Deep* one too many times. You have many giant, head-snapping Moray eels hereabouts?"

He laughed, and took a pair of Ray-Ban Wayfarers out of his shirt pocket. An exact duplicate of the pair in the console of my jeep at the Houston airport. I never took them on missions; a hundred-dollar pair of sunglasses usually broadcast the wrong signal for whoever I was supposed to be.

"Not all that many," he said, wiping the shades clean with a handkerchief before putting them on. "And we keep them well-fed on fat, rich Yanks. Since you're not fat, and—being a writer—probably not rich, you're safe, I reckon."

We started walking toward the shop.

"Listen," he said when we got there, "my girlfriend and I live just over there." He pointed toward some stucco cottages a few hundred yards up the highway. "I'd like to buy *you* a drink later on, if you'll join us. We might even get lucky and persuade her to cook."

He caught my surprised look.

"I have an ulterior motive. I'll bet you and Sammy could strike up a hell of a conversation." He grinned. "Thing is, you see, she's writing a novel as well."

Which I already knew. Having scanned the walls of his shop and determined that the attractive girl in the framed photos with him was also the attractive girl whose photo appeared above the byline of several articles thumb-tacked to his bamboo wall. And almost all of the young journalists I'd ever come across—be they freelance or in bondage to a local paper—had novels in various stages of completion in the bottoms of desk drawers or in shoe boxes in the tops of closets.

Twenty-Four

Sammy, it turned out, was short for Samantha, which had been her grandmother's name.

She'd grown up in South Africa, where her parents still lived. And had come out to the islands often to visit her grandparents— her mother had been raised there—and, after completing her journalism degree in Cape Town, had returned to work for the *Bermuda Sun* as a features writer and as a stringer for a couple of publications in the states.

Her accent was softer than Powell's, and she was as strikingly attractive as the photos of her on the dive shop wall had shown her to be. Full-bodied brunette hair, cut short, that framed a smooth, tanned face. Twenty-five, I'd have bet, give or take a couple of years. Pretty eyes. She was slender, and surely not the sort to fool with any more jewelry than the occasional necklace or anklet of small coral beads. Or makeup. Her beauty radiated naturally, and she drank her wine in big gulps. I liked her immediately.

I'd spent the afternoon browsing through the shops in Summerset—I'd found a little blue Wedgewood plate with the definitive white cameo for a gift for my hosts—and then had met Powell at his business at closing time and walked with him to a nearby market. There we'd bought groceries and several bottles of wine. He'd insisted on paying for everything, but I'd held forth and bought the wine. Then we'd hiked the short distance to their bungalow overlooking Mangrove Bay.

We sat outside for a while, in big metal lawn chairs that were starting to rust through their most recent application of paint. The wine flowed. The conversation zipped along, first about Sammy's job as a journalist, then about the novels we were writing. Hers a historical piece concerning a young Irish immigrant who loses her virginity and her life's savings—in which order was not made clear—in eighteenth-century Boston. Mine involved a dissatisfied podiatrist—I'd seen a podiatry clinic from the bus that afternoon—who inherits some money and goes to interesting places looking for more meaning to life than handling peoples' feet every day.

When they moved into the little kitchen to start the supper, I insisted on helping. So I was given the salad chopping and tossing duties while the tanned, lean couple tended to the grilling of lamb chops and roasting of potatoes.

Sammy set four places at the table.

"My grandfather lives with us," she explained. Then she flashed one of her fetching smiles. "Actually, we live with *him*. Since it's his house."

When everything was ready, and the scent of the sea came in through the open windows and mingled nicely with aromas of rosemary, garlic, and peppery broiled lamb, Sammy went into the back of the house. I could barely hear a faint tapping at a door, then her low voice.

She came back in.

"He watches the BBC world news every afternoon. And reads the London papers."

In a few minutes, when we were already seated, a tall gentleman came in who probably had been mistaken a few times, at long range or in a dimly lit room, for the actor Max Von Sydow. An unruly thatch of white hair topped a long, much lived in face. He wore slacks, dress shoes, and a button-down white shirt with one of the open sweaters that old men seem to like. And he was, indeed, old. Early-eighties, surely.

I stood, shook his dry hand, and we were introduced. He said something pleasant and sat down.

"*Wine*," he said, lifting the glass in front of him and turning it. "You must be quite an important guest, Mr. Whitten." His voice was deep, dignified, and precise.

"He's a novelist, Popi," Sammy said.

The big, serious face managed a smile.

"I *see*. A man of letters. Would I know any of your work?"

I told him I was at work on my first novel.

"Well then," he said, turning his attention to his dinner, "I'll look forward to reading it."

He lifted up his knife and fork and considered them a moment, as if the entire concept was new to him. Then he skillfully sliced the meat away from the bone, dipped a piece in mint jelly, and brought it to his mouth.

"Samantha's novel is quite good," he said.

"Popi . . ." she protested.

"No, no," he said, chewing the lamb, "I read constantly. And it's fine. Fine."

Generic dinner conversation floated along, among the clinking of wine glasses, the sliding of silverware on porcelain plates, and the ticking of a clock from another room. I had to do some fabrication on demand, regarding a few insignificant junior colleges where I had taught literature before winning the grant that made it possible for me to take a year's sabbatical to research and write my novel.

The old man listened politely, speaking only when asked a question.

When there was a lull, I broached the topic that I'd come about.

"Tell me about diving," I said, as Sammy served the mango tart that Powell and I had selected that afternoon.

The old man might have rolled his eyes slightly. Maybe not. He took a couple of small bites of the tart and stood slowly up.

"If you'll excuse me," he said. "I'll go out and have a smoke."

I stood up, too. He waved me down with his big Max Von Sydow hand, like Father Damien shooing away a minor demon. Then he went outside.

Powell leaned over his plate. Locked his long fingers together. Gave a deep, philosophical sigh. He'd had a lot of wine.

"Diving . . ." he began. He reworked the words in his mind. "Diving is the perfect . . ." then he rambled on for a few minutes. About nirvana, bliss, and something else I missed altogether.

"So," I said, when he was finally done, "the rich guy we saw arriving today."

"Jacques Deminelle."

"Yes. You said he was a hell of a diver. What makes him so good?"

He leaned back, scooped up the last of his slice of tart with his thumb, and sucked it dry.

"In his case, it's that he dives all over the world. Deep water, dangerous reefs. Everywhere."

Outside, beyond the open windows in the next room, the old man coughed a couple of times.

"So, if he goes wherever he wants," I asked, "why does he come to Bermuda several times every year? I mean, is the diving here that spectacular that it keeps drawing him back?"

Powell grinned.

"As the owner of a dive shop, I wish I could say yes. But the answer is absolutely not. It's *good*; I'll even go so far as to say it's excellent. With plenty of good, healthy reefs and oodles of shipwrecks. But there are plenty of other locations just as good, and many better."

"So," I said, "back to my original question . . ."

"Which doesn't have a satisfactory answer, I'm afraid," he said, standing up and helping Sammy clear the plates away. "Deminelle has been coming here for as long as I've been here, and long before that. He's famous, of course, a jetsetter and all. Sometimes media from Europe and the states shows up; you know, the society news people for the telley and the rags you see at pay-out counters. But, in spite of the huge splash his arrival always makes—with his young girls and . . . everything—he's really quite a predictable sod."

I asked him what he meant.

"For instance, he *always* stays at The Outrigger. That never varies. Which isn't that surprising really, since he's mega wealthy and it's the most exclusive place here. It's something of a local conundrum, really, as to what exactly goes on behind those high walls and that pink roof."

I'd dug up what little I could about the private resort, but it had proven to be a chore. There'd been one blurb in an issue of *Travel & Leisure* some years back, but it had been more speculation than fact. More of a "what's this place about?" sidebar, with only a photograph taken from the highway and another from a plane or a helicopter. There was no website. No promotional materials. And no explanation as to how to become a member.

"But," Powell continued, "what's really perplexing is that he always, *always*, dives on just the one site. The *Cristobal Colon.*"

I tried for a blank look.

"A huge Spanish liner that went down in the reefs," he said, "in 1939, I think."

I wasn't surprised.

I'd done considerable research about the wrecks in Bermuda's waters that Deminille might dive on, and the *Cristobal Colon* had settled at the top of my list. Because it was the largest—one foot short of five hundred feet long—which would offer an experienced diver any number of nooks and crannies to poke around in. And because it lay in significantly deeper water than any of the others, almost ten miles due north of St. George's Island, Bermuda's northernmost tip.

"Why only that one, do you think?" I asked.

Powell lifted both hands in the age-old symbol for beats-the-hell-out-of-me.

"That's the great mystery. Here's a guy that dives everywhere. And he keeps coming back, time and again, for *years,* to explore that old hulk."

He drained the last of his wine.

"And the only person who can provide the answer doesn't *give* answers."

I asked more questions about Deminelle, about the sections of the ship that were his favorites, about the condition of the wreck itself, the accessibility of cabins and holds and passageways. About the strength of the current out there, and the depth. Timothy shared what he knew but, overall, I didn't learn anything I didn't already know. Then Sammy, done with the dishes, sat down with us and said that that would be all about diving. So the topic was our novels again until the old man came back in and walked slowly over to me.

"Mr. Whitten," he said, in his precise slow delivery, "it's been a great pleasure."

I got to my feet and shook his hand for the second time.

"By the way, Timothy," he said. "The *Cristobal Colon* sank in 1936. Not 1939. October 25, 1936."

Powell nodded. Not smiling, not looking at Sammy's grandfather.

Then the old man said good night, accepted a kiss on his cheek from Sammy, and went back to his room.

My hosts—both of whom had to go to work the next morning—were wearing down, and I got up and thanked them for a wonderful evening and a delicious meal.

Powell waved his hand at the prospect of my departure.

"It's too late for a bus, too bloody far away for a taxi, and I'm a bit too tipsy to drive you. We have, it so happens"—he lifted one tanned hand dramatically, proof of his tipsiness—"a relatively comfortable guest room. And you, sir, are our *guest*."

"Absolutely," Sammy agreed, putting her arms around his neck from behind, nuzzling her nose in his hair.

"Brilliant!" Powell said, tapping the tabletop and concluding the issue.

A few minutes later, when my host had already fallen into his bed, my hostess put forth the ritualistic litany of logistics that must be common to all cultures in all places: the location of the bathroom and clean towels and the blanket in the closet in case the night went nippy.

Then she, too, was off to bed and, after a trip to the toilet to dispense of the two glasses of wine that I had nursed along while they plowed through something like a bottle and a half each, I went into the dark little guest room.

I saw the man sitting in the armchair by the window before I turned on the light, so it was no great surprise when he was illuminated.

"So," Sammy's grandfather asked me, nearly whispering. "How do you intend to do it?"

I didn't ask the obvious question, but let it hang silently in the still room. He answered it anyway, in the same quiet voice.

"How do you intend to kill Jacques Deminille?"

Twenty-Five

"Underwater," I finally got around to telling him, in answer to his question.

We had relocated to the front yard—called a garden there—in the squeaky, uncomfortable metal furniture that I'd spent time in that afternoon. Midnight darkness fell all around us. Crickets, or their Bermudian counterparts, chirped now and then. An occasional car passed by on the road just beyond a low hedge.

"On a dive. Inside the *Cristobal Colon*, it looks like."

I saw no benefit in denying it. It was abort or go-ahead time. It was time to, as the General would have said, fish or cut bait. Or, if he were in a fouler mood, shit or get off the pot. And, though I had hoped—and even *looked*—for a way to avoid this mission, for a legitimate reason to scrap it altogether and call the General and tell him to tell the government to go to hell, there was, surprisingly, enough professionalism—or pure stubbornness—left in me to avoid forfeiting this close to the big game.

The old man took a pack of English smokes out of his sweater pocket, didn't offer me one, and stabbed one between his thin lips, pale even in the faint moonlight.

"So," he said, around the cigarette, "the plan is to separate him from the security fellows who shadow his every move, swim up behind him, tap him politely on the shoulder, and dispatch him."

It wasn't a question, so I didn't answer it. He took out a slender silver lighter and set the long cigarette aglow.

"I suspect you aren't so daft as to have risked bringing a firearm through customs." He blew a line of smoke out into the dark night. "And trying to buy one here would be even riskier, not to mention very nearly impossible."

He was quiet then. Considering.

"And spear guns are outlawed in Bermuda."

He took a long pull on his smoke, leaned back in his chair, and watched me.

"Did you know that, Mr. Whitten? Or whatever your name is."

Then I watched *him*.

"Yes, sir. I did know that."

Several metal chimes hanging under the eves of the cottage and in the sprawling tree beside us caught a sudden spurt of wind off the water. They erupted into a small cacophony of tinks and dings.

"Who are you?" I asked.

It was possible, of course, that he was some sort of operative. Or had been. Maybe British. Maybe even CIA. The likelihood that he had been sent here to check up on me was remote, and bordering on impossible. In the first place, the General would never have done it. In all our years and all our missions, he had never had Gomez or me shadowed. The man in the big office in Washington who hadn't given us lunch could have planted him, without the General's knowledge. Him sending a man this old was unlikely, but if he lived out here—if he had retired from his cloak and dagger days to a quiet life full of sand and sea—he might have given him a call and asked him to pop in.

But—and this was the determining factor—he *hadn't* popped in. I had. The possibility of my stumbling into the household of the one man in the islands who had been instructed to find *me* was beyond the realm of happenstance. It was preposterous.

He'd smoked quietly while considering his answer.

"I'm an old man," he finally said. "Who lives in a little house by a big ocean."

A few lines of verse bubbled up from the vault.

" 'I have circled every possibility to come to this: a low house by gray water, with windows always open to the stale sea.' "

He laughed quietly. A small, dry laugh that fell into the soft breeze and floated away.

"I don't recognize it," he said.

I told him it was Derek Walcott. He sat quietly for a while, whether considering me or the poet I couldn't know.

"Well," he finally said, softly, "I've seen many things in a long life. Most of it here on this island, in low houses by water, always with windows open to the sea." He stared off into the darkness over the low hedge, where Mangrove Bay lay still and quiet. "I'm more content, and more adept, at listening and watching than speaking and doing. And I've been watching *you*. And listening to you."

The wind died enough so that the chimes went quiet again. He crossed one leg carefully over the other.

"When you put the plot of your supposed novel—the doctor's quest for truth and beauty—up against Samantha's finely planned tale, yours came up rather sparse—didn't you think?—for a man who supposedly has been at work on it for a year."

He nodded, obviously agreeing with himself.

"Then, you asked question after question about Jacques Deminelle. About his habits. And the exact nature of his dives. Far too many questions, in fact, for someone who never knew of his existence before this afternoon. "

He might have looked like Max von Sydow, but his voice was pure James Mason. Soft, crisp, exact, and stabbed through with the confident echoes of old school and upper class. He flicked an ash away from his cigarette.

"I'd have thought you'd be better at that sort of thing. But, to be fair, you were dealing with the pair of inebriates at the table, and saw no reason to heed the ancient dragon outside the window."

Then he held what was left of the cigarette upright between his thumb and index finger, like a German in an old movie.

"And you've got a look about you." He paused. Thought. "I do so wish I knew your name; it would make it much easier to carry this on. Anyway, you've a particular . . . aura. Part of it is physical, of course, and not a little intimidating. You're tall—there's that—and broad shouldered. Obviously strong and almost certainly in possession of quick and dependable reflexes."

He blew on the tip of the cigarette, making it glow brightly in the darkness.

"But, beyond that, there's a . . . confidence. Something in the eyes."

The next came quieter, almost in a whisper.

"You have a hawk's eyes."

He waited a moment before going on.

"You've done this before. Many times, I'd reckon."

He leaned back. Smiled.

"Am I correct?"

I watched him with my hawk's eyes.

"So I knew, you see, why you came here. It's the only reason you *would* have come."

Then he stopped talking, closed his eyes, and seemed to make an effort to breathe in the subtle fragrance of flowers. Or maybe the scent of the sea. He opened his eyes.

"You're not a big believer in coincidence, are you?" he asked.

Maybe I shook my head a little. Maybe my gaze was answer enough.

"Then how about providence? Where do you stand on providence?"

"I don't really have an opinion," I said. "I don't get to Rhode Island all that often."

He started to laugh, then reconsidered.

"And witty, as well," he said. "The brave, witty warrior who deals out death, and laughs in its teeth."

He uncrossed his legs, and sat forward.

"Come now, Mr. Whitten. Let's put aside pretending," he said, mashing his cigarette into an ashtray on the table beside his chair, "we both know that neither coincidence nor providence played any great part in our meeting."

I sat quietly, determined to let him do most of the talking.

"You've done your homework, and a sound job of it, by all appearances. You didn't wander into Timothy's dive shop by chance. There are many dive shops in Bermuda."

"Only one of which is so close to The Outrigger Club," I added.

He smiled. I continued.

"And the *only* one on real estate that once was part of the strip of land bought by whoever built The Outrigger in 1940."

"Oh, I *am* impressed," he said, pushing his big hands together in a slow-motion clap. "Top marks, all around!"

I touched the small button on the side of my watch that

illuminated its face. Nearly half past one. In the middle of a dark night, in a dark yard on a tiny island in a gigantic ocean. The old man slumped a little in his chair.

"Unlike you," he said, after a moment, "I *do* believe in providence." He leaned toward me, his hands touching at the fingertips. "I believe you are an instrument of providence, Mr. Whitten. I've waited a long, long time for you. Or someone like you."

He lifted himself slowly up from the low chair. I kept my seat.

"Now, if you'll excuse me, I need a bit of shoring-up to see me through what I'm going to tell you. Things I've never told anyone. And I imagine you do, too. I couldn't help but notice that you spent more time gazing at your glass of inferior hock than drinking it during dinner. Brandy is my poison, but I can clink things around in there to see what else is available."

"Brandy will do," I said. "Be careful not to wake them."

He gave the brittle little laugh again.

"Their room is at the back of the house. And, I don't have to remind you, they lapped up all the wine you kept pouring for them. They'll slumber through any slight commotion I might raise."

In a few minutes he came back outside, with two large snifters and a crystal decanter.

"First off," he said, when he had splashed liberal servings into each glass and settled back into his seat, "I can assure you that I represent no danger to you."

He smiled. Moonlight danced on the amber brandy he swirled around.

"Which sounds ludicrous, really—doesn't it?—what's left of an old man saying that to someone like you. More accurately, I represent no danger to your . . . agenda."

He hesitated, obviously weighing his next words carefully.

"Before I confide certain things," he said, "I need to know if I can trust *you*. Specifically, I need to have your assurance that you won't divulge any of this." He pulled the lapels of the big sweater together, even though it was a warm night. "For a time."

I told him this was beginning to sound like two kids in a tree house.

"Nevertheless . . . ," he said.

I nodded. He'd have to accept that as compliance. I took a sip of the brandy. I'm no connoisseur, but I'd bet this one—warm, full-bodied, and velvety smooth—was a cognac. And a very good one.

"Why don't you tell me what you have to tell me," I suggested.

Whereupon he got comfortable in his chair, lit another cigarette, and did.

Twenty-Six

"In 1936," he said, "when I was twelve years old, the *Cristobal Colon* ran aground out at North Rock. Due north of St. George's. I'll give you the truncated version of the ensuing events, for which you should be grateful, this late at night and with a limited store of brandy."

He lifted the decanter up by its narrow throat and inspected its contents. His gaze didn't move away when he resumed his tale, as if he were watching it come to life in the golden liquid.

"The light out there had been out for a fortnight, for repairs, and all the shipping companies who were expected to have any business in Bermuda's waters had been so informed. But the *Cristobal Colon* wasn't supposed to be anywhere nearby."

He slowly eased the bottle back down on to the table.

"She'd fallen on rather a bad run of luck lately. The Spanish Civil War broke out while she was at sea, and the rebels in control of the Spanish ports wouldn't let her return. Other countries weren't sympathetic. And it turned out that only France let the Spanish shipping company offload their full compliment of passengers, after many more weeks at sea than there had been provisions that a posh lot like that were used to."

He almost smiled.

"No one quite knew what to make of the fact that France had proved so accommodating when no other country had."

I watched him as he told it, his narrow, pale face even paler in the moonlight. He was a gifted yarn spinner, to be sure. But I could tell that this was one that he had long ago worked out to its smallest detail, and I had no doubt that I was being treated to its first performance.

"And I'll just bet," I said, "that *you* know the reason."

He smiled. Then he continued.

"It so happened that a wealthy young Frenchman, whose name will greatly interest you, offered what must have been an irresistible bribe to port officials in St. Nazaire. The Spanish owners of the ship had to do *something* with her; she wouldn't be allowed to remain there for long. So they likely leapt at the opportunity to lease—or sell—her to someone with the cash. I've never known which."

"He was, this Frenchman, already in what you Yanks would call ca*hoots* with a certain German corporal from the first war—you know, the one that was to have ended *all* wars. And he needed to remove himself and certain documents to a safer, calmer harbor than his homeland was likely to become very soon, when it would be made strikingly apparent that the world was not yet done with wars after all."

Now I was damned interested.

"Deminelle's . . ." I did the math in my head, ". . . grandfather?"

"His father. Henri." He gave it the Frenchified pronunciation: *Aunree.* "He was not yet thirty then, and his only child wouldn't come along for almost thirty *more* years. Henri's father had made the first fortune, in vineyards and exporting. The old man was dead by then, and his wealth had fallen to Henri, his only surviving child, who proved to be dissatisfied with merely a windfall, albeit a considerable one. He yearned for *power.* And he saw the grand opera just tuning up in Germany as a means to achieve it. He approached Hitler when it became apparent that the little corporal, now elevated somewhat in the ranks, had France in his grand scheme. There's no telling how much Henri poured into the Nazi coffers, all of it going surely for tanks and planes and shells, it being a bit early on for bricks and pipes for the concentration camp ovens. But he transferred the funds, having no intention of sticking around for the occupation that was imminent."

"So he came to Bermuda on the *Cristobal Colon*," I said. "Whose rendezvous with the reef was, I'm guessing, not part of the script."

"Correct," he said. He used the break in the story to take a generous slug of his brandy and to replenish each of our snifters. "It's always been supposed that the ship was on her way to Mexico to take on arms and ammunition for the war in Spain. And she might well have been headed there after offloading Deminelle and his small cargo; the voyage must have cost him *pots* of money, and he wouldn't have turned up his nose at a bit of convenient gun-running. But the North Rock light was dark, she floundered, and where she might have been off to later will never be known."

He hoisted his snifter and swirled its contents around.

"One passenger on a liner built to comfortably accommodate hundreds. A full crew, all of whom were rescued. You no doubt know that the ship didn't completely sink until your American air corps used her as target practice during the war. They finally pounded her so completely that her back broke on the reef. Half of her lies on one side, half on the other."

In my research about the ship, I'd learned that the crew of over a hundred and fifty men had found less than a friendly welcome in Bermuda. Spain could have cared less about their fate and made no effort to bring them home, and the Bermudians, who couldn't understand them and looked down on the Spanish anyway, refused to provide for them. The government finally put them to work repairing roads and, one by one, they trickled home or to friendlier ports over the next few years.

I put the pertinent question.

"What were the documents Deminelle was carrying?"

The smile on the old man's face told me he'd been expecting it. He rattled off the litany with ease, having done so, I suspected, in his mind hundreds of times.

"Transferrable bonds. Deeds of vast holdings in France that would be protected during the occupation. More importantly, the precise documents of agreement between Henri Deminelle and Adolph Hitler, who by the time the *Cristobal Colon* met her demise, had been Fuhrer for two years."

"Documents of agreement about *what*?" I asked.

"About Deminelle's place in the eventual Valhalla that would come after the war. His reward, for services rendered."

I took as strong a pull on my brandy as he had. It burned its way down. Not as nicely as a jolt of straight Scotch, nor even in the same *ballpark* as a well-built martini. But nicely, nonetheless.

"Okay," I said. Getting as comfortable as I could in the metal chair that had probably been a chair when all of this had been happening.

"I can see that Henri was of some use to Hitler. Money is money, right? But, come on. By then, Adolph controlled the purse strings of a nation, and a damned big one. How much of a difference could one man's wealth, substantial as it might have been, have possibly made in the big plan?"

He sat quietly, nursing his drink.

"None," he said, matter-of-factly. "Absolutely none whatsoever. Hitler took the money, I'm confident, and was glad to have it. But his deal with Deminelle regarding his status after what he saw as an inevitable Teutonic victory had nothing whatsoever to do with finances."

I waited. He leaned forward, put his glass on the little table, and no doubt relished telling me what he had kept to himself for seven decades.

"There was one more document in that case. A relatively short, straightforward covenant that was enormously more important than anything agreed to between Hitler and a well-heeled Frenchman."

He ran the tip of his thin, bony finger around the narrow lip of the snifter.

"Henri Deminelle, you see, was a high society playboy, much like the fruit of his loins, the current object of your affections who is no doubt sleeping soundly now just up there." He pointed toward The Outrigger, which sat just down the road in the dark night. "Entwined, perhaps, with a tender young girl or boy, or both. Or several."

He lifted himself up, and stretched. I thought, at first, that he was probably going in for one of the frequent rest room breaks that old men have to have. But the stretching seemed to have been his only objective.

"He associated with the richest young people in Europe. The elite of the elite. Had done, for years."

He tilted his head up slightly, letting the soft sea breeze wash across his face. Then, after a moment, he turned and faced me.

"One of whom he managed to convince that a . . . mutual understanding with Herr Hitler would prove, in future years, to be most beneficial."

I thought I knew what he was about to tell me, having run the dates and the corresponding world events through my mental calculator. I feared it, would be a better way to put it. But, even so, when he did tell me, I had to convince myself that I'd heard him correctly.

"Henri Deminelle," he said, slowly and succinctly, "was delivering a treaty of alliance, already signed by Adolph Hitler, to Edward VIII, King of England, Scotland. and Ireland, the British dominions beyond the seas, and Emperor of India, who intended to sign it in Bermuda in October of 1936."

Twenty-Seven

When he was again seated, and *I* was on my feet, I bypassed propriety and protocol completely and poured myself some more brandy.

"Now," I said, pacing and scratching the annoying beard that I'd grown over the last month or so, "let me get this right. The Duke of Windsor"—I'd recently read a book about him and his whole *my kingdom for the woman I love* dilemma—"was here when Henri Deminille arrived."

"Yes," the old man said, pointing in the general direction of Hamilton, "at Government House. But he wasn't yet the Duke of Windsor. At the time, he fully intended to marry the American woman, but the parliament was just getting around to delivering its ultimatum. Edward had been king since his father's death in January, even though there'd been no coronation, and would be until his abdication in early December, less than two months after his meeting with Deminelle."

I was probably staring at him. My mouth might very well have been hanging open.

"But surely he realized," I said, when I'd taken a moment to process some of it, "that any agreement he made with Hitler wouldn't be worth the paper it was printed on. Parliament would have never let him get away with it."

The old man slowly fluttered the long, slender fingers of one hand in the air before him, as he might shake crumbs away after eating a scone.

"Who knows? The British devotion to the monarchy runs rather deeper than your American politics. And, believe me, seventy years ago, it ran very deep indeed. If Edward had scuttled the plan to marry the Yank divorcee and been crowned, he could have done great damage, perhaps irreparably so, by signing a pact with Germany. Hitler knew that.

"But, he *did* marry Mrs. Simpson," he continued, "in the end.

And he packed it in, and was exiled, with his black-sheep bride, off to the Bahamas as governor. In name only, of course, since all he did there was drink tea and Champagne and complain about his brother's reign."

I shook my head.

"But he *signed* the thing? Then, in October of thirty six, when Deminelle got here?"

He yawned then, and settled a little lower in his chair. He was wearing down. Just as the adrenalin supplied by his bombshell surged into my system and jolted me wide awake.

"Oh, no." He said, through another yawn. "He never had a chance to. He threw a bit of a snit in the stateroom of the royal yacht, told Deminelle to leave, and the *Britannica* was under way back to England straight away. There's no official record to this day, even at Government House—where he was in residence for several days and nights—that he was here at all."

I sat down on the edge of the low garden table between our chairs.

"Now, wait a minute. If Edward was here, and Deminelle was here, and the document was here, why . . ."

He blinked a few times, trying to shake some of the grogginess away.

"I never said the document was *here*." He pointed to the ground. "It was out *there*." Then he waved off to his extreme right. "On the *Cristobal Colon*."

I looked in its direction, as if I might actually see her there. In spite of the fact that it was dark. In spite of the fact that she was thirty something miles away. And in spite of the fact that she had been totally submerged for nearly three quarters of a century.

"But why . . . ," I started.

He rubbed the sides of his neck with his fingers and thumbs.

"Hitler was every bit as paranoid as history records. He insisted that the documents be kept in a waterproof canister, hidden away deep between bulkheads or in some sufficiently dark, tight space. He didn't want them stolen. Or, in the case of disaster, ever found. Deminelle wasn't carrying the documents himself, of course, like a child sent off to market with a list. One of the ship's crew was, in fact, a stormtrooper, charged with safeguarding the canister and seeing the entire thing through to the end.

"You're wondering now, I imagine, why Hitler sent Deminelle at all, and agreed to his terms. And it's easily explained. Edward, being an old chum—polo, drinking, whoring, and all that—trusted Henri rather more than he did the Austrian usurper. Edward's uncle had been the Kaiser, after all. So Hitler needed Henri to bring the alliance to fruition. But he sent an envoy along to guard the goods.

"That German was, by the way, the only fatality in the accident. It was never clear how he managed to get himself trapped in the depths of the big ship when everyone else got out easily. Only Deminelle would have known the truth; that he perished making a frantic attempt to retrieve the canister, knowing full well that drowning would be preferable to facing his Fuhrer empty-handed.

"Deminelle abandoned ship with everyone else; they thought she was going down and, not being from Bermuda, they didn't know that she didn't have very far to go. Then, in the morning, when he made his way through the crew, he discovered that Hitler's errand boy was missing. It wasn't until later that afternoon that the body was discovered."

"Without the canister, I presume."

"Without the canister."

He rubbed his eyes.

"Perhaps he had wedged it too snugly somewhere," he said. "Or, more likely, it became dislodged when the ship ran aground, and shifted deeper into a bulkhead."

I drank the last of my brandy, saw that we had depleted the decanter, and ran the whole sordid story through my head once more.

By the time I got around to saying something, the old man had probably dropped off for a few minutes.

"So. The plan fell through, due to the missing document. Edward's and England's fortunes changed before another meeting could be set up, Hitler's friendly ideas regarding Great Britain took a nose dive, and . . . Deminelle?"

He frowned. His voice became harsher, more menacing.

"Deminelle stayed on in Bermuda till the war was over. Then he went back to France. There were always rumors about his collaboration with the Germans during the occupation. But his constant defense was that he hadn't *been* in France at the time. And, remember, collaboration rumors ran rampant in those days, and old Henri's finally fell in with the rest and amounted to nothing."

"He just . . . went home?"

"Well. There were no incriminating documents, were there?" he said. "As desperately as he tried to locate them when he believed Germany would win the war, their absence proved entirely beneficial when things went ultimately, and decidedly, the other way.

"He returned to his lavish lifestyle, managed to increase his fortune considerably, fell into one sordid affair after another, and finally married, when he was past sixty, the young starlet who produced his sole heir, Jacques."

"And the documents . . ."

He'd closed his eyes once more. I thought he was sleeping again. So I waited.

"That's where I made my entrance," he finally said, his eyes still closed.

He leaned forward. Yawned. He shook his head, making his white Max von Sydow hair thrash around.

"My parents—my mother, actually—owned some property, mostly out here in Sandy's Parish. *This* property, in fact." He glanced around at the dark yard. "Four cottages, a couple of shops, and the land on which The Outrigger would eventually be built. And much more, then. Including a good bit of prime waterfront acreage down along Little Sound and Granaway Deep."

He pushed himself up from the low chair, which was a longer, more involved process than it had been the last time. When he was on his feet, he wobbled slightly, then put his hands into the pockets of his trousers.

"It's late. I'm very tired. And my story has wandered on far too long, I fear. So allow me to bring it to a swift conclusion. It's hardly the part I wish to linger over, anyway. I can assure you of that."

He paused, and nodded.

"By the end of his first winter on Bermuda, Henri Deminelle managed to lure my entire family into his web. I was his first victim . . . and, quite obviously, his last.

"I was twelve, remember. And when he saw me swimming just out there," he pointed past the hedge toward the bay, "he asked if I would like to make a bit of cash by poking around in the wrecked *Cristobal Colon* with him, searching for something he'd left on board."

"He came to our house, *this* house, and discussed it with my father. He brought whiskey—single-malt Scotch—with which he plied my parents liberally, oozing out his considerable charm. We all three should have seen through the banter and the polish. Believe me, I've had many a long year to ponder that. But our life here was uneventful, routine. Or we saw it as such. And he represented . . . adventure, I suppose. This handsome, mysterious Frenchman."

A little Coleridge emerged. *Beware! Beware! His flashing eyes, his floating hair.* I pushed it away.

"So my parents drank up his whiskey and his blarney and agreed entirely to my spending the summer in his employ."

He told it all in a dull, rapid monotone, as a school boy might rattle off just the pertinent facts of a novel in order to get credit for a report.

"Then, to make an exceedingly long story short, he turned his attention to my mother. Who was young, and beautiful, and, in retrospect, entirely too eager and willing to be led astray.

"She'd inherited everything, remember, from her father, who had gone to his grave believing she'd married beneath her station. So, when she chose to abandon home and hearth and husband and son, which was unfortunate but entirely inevitable, she took the land with her. To Deminelle, who, as you must have determined by now, had only been after it, and it alone. He'd charmed his way in over at the recorder's office, and poured over enough old, dusty ledgers to determine who owned the best property to be had. Over the next few years, as the great war thundered along overseas, and as the Frenchman wined and dined my fallen mother to elegant extremes, she methodically signed over to him every holding excepting this small parcel on which we are sitting. Stupid, I realize. And unforgivable. But . . . there it is."

I kept expecting him to pause. To light a cigarette. To take a breath. But he was like a runner now, sprinting to the end.

"He built The Outrigger in 1940, as a private resort where his European friends, who—like rich gypsies—fluttered between mansions and villas all during the war, could come for visits.

"By then, he had everything from my mother that she had to give. And, instead of just going *away* . . ." He pushed one hand out away from him. "To some other part of the world, as most people here thought she would after her shame and what they saw as her comeuppance, she took . . . the easier path."

Then he did stop. The wind chimes under the eves and in the tree sent out a sad little elegy.

"She came here one day. My father and I still lived here, you see. It was our . . . allowance, I've always believed. Mother had assumed she would be going back to France with Deminelle when the war was finished. They could certainly afford to do without the six lots, including this one, with three other cottages and a couple of shops that he deeded to my father after . . ."

I waited, then helped him along.

"After your mother's death?"

He touched the crystal stopper of the brandy decanter. Maybe wishing, as I did, that there was something left inside.

"She came here one day," he repeated, finally. "I think we both expected her to tell us what a bloody fool she'd been, and how if she could do it all again and, you know, the things people say after they've thrown everything away and have no hope at all of getting any of it back."

He turned now and looked at me.

"But she didn't say any of those things. Either because she knew that they would have been meaningless, or because she'd determined, for once in her capricious, wavering life, to see something all the way through. I don't know."

He shook his head slightly. As if it were an enigma that he had wrestled with before, and never broken.

Then the last part came quickly, as if he couldn't be rid of it fast enough.

"She went back into my father's bedroom—once hers too, and all these eons later, mine—and came out with a framed picture of the three of us that she asked to keep. She took it away in her handbag along with, unknown to us, the big army revolver that my father had brought home from the first war. Which she used, later that day, to bring her part of the whole squalid business to an end in a dreary little room in a cheap hotel in Hamilton."

He forged ahead.

"My father stayed on here, living on the rent the other cottages and two shops brought in. He sold two of the cottages after the war in order to send me to school in England. Then he proceeded to drink himself to death, which he accomplished in short order.

"A better man would have called Deminelle out. Would have thrown his filthy sins in his face and demanded some sort of satisfaction, be it in the street or in the courts. But my father—bless his kind, sweet soul—was hardly the man for that. Surely he saw Henri Deminelle hundreds of times, The Outrigger being just over there. Even after the war, when he had moved back to Europe, Deminelle came back frequently, as his son does now."

Then he was quiet. His eyes were closed. I began to think he was through.

"You said, a little while ago, that you were his first and last victim."

He didn't open his eyes.

"Surely you've guessed that part. Henri saw more, that first morning when I was playing in the surf, than cheap assistance for his search. Oh, to be sure, we spent months scouring the *Cristobol Colon*. This was long before your flyboys sank her, remember. So it was easy going, above the water line and below. But tedious, and time-consuming. By the time he'd given up on finding the canister, he'd found me. Many times. Sometimes in the cottage he rented from my father—where, ironically, he launched his seduction of my mother— sometimes inside the old ship herself. In the cool water, all of our primeval moans and thrashing echoing in those cavernous metal compartments and passageways."

I kept my gaze aimed discreetly at the ground, all the while clinching my fists tightly together. I listened to him lower himself heavily back into the chair.

"Judge me as you will," he said, after a pause. "I was twelve. I was spellbound. But I could have stopped it. Just as easily and as quickly as my mother could have."

The ensuing silence in the dark yard was like the dead quiet that a good defense lawyer hopes for at the conclusion of a summation before a jury.

"So," he said, after a moment, "he ruined all three of us, didn't he?"

He looked out at the pale, silver wash of moonlight on Mangrove bay, just beyond the hedges and across the road.

"My mother is over in the Hamilton cemetery. Alongside my father, by the way. I thought it somehow fitting to finally tie that package up with one neat bow. And here, as Isaiah said to God, am I." He gave a slow theatrical wave with one hand. "Such as you find me. And very close, surely, to journey's end."

"You went to England after the war?"

"My father packed me off to a second-tier school. Where I fell in with a pack of unruly lads who became classmates and lifelong friends, nearly all of whose obituaries I would eventually read in the *Times*."

I asked when he came back to Bermuda.

"Oh, not long after I finished university. I was a barrister; of the distinctly unglamorous ilk, I'm afraid; no courtroom speeches like *Rumpole of the Bailey*. More wills and codicils and deeds; I was a glorified clerk, really. A good, old firm in Hamilton took me on, owing to my maternal grandfather's memory, I always suspected.

"I married. Had a daughter. Had a life. When my wife died, years after our girl had moved away to South Africa with her husband, I sold our house in Hamilton and moved out here. I'd leased this place out occasionally, but it felt . . . right, somehow, for me to wrap things up here. Among the ghosts, you see?"

He looked back at the little cottage that had been a set of bookends for his life, his beginning and his ending.

"Then, Samantha moved in when she hired on at the *Sun*. And Timothy wandered in, like the nice enough but unambitious relative who comes to dinner and puts down roots. When I saw that the relationship might run on indefinitely, I let him have one of the shops in which to exploit the only skill that he seems to possess."

He was exhausted, I could tell. His pale hands rested one under the other on his chest, as if he were already in his casket.

"I've sat out here on countless dark nights and sunny days, wondering how this new Deminelle—the last of the line, thank God—was using his great wealth. Your being here confirms, I'm sure, that he has not applied it or his considerable power to the furthering of world peace."

He nestled in the big sweater, against a chill that I didn't feel.

"You see," he said, "in spite of my dubious start—or perhaps because of it—I believe myself to be something of a fine judge of people's propensities for good and evil. I've sat close range at both extremes."

He leaned forward and put our two empty snifters close together on the table, then carefully placed the empty decanter beside them. Like a priest tidying up at the conclusion of Mass.

"Deminelle is easy to place," he said, his voice nearly spent. "And someone like Timothy who, though he's unmotivated and not, in the admittedly prejudiced eyes of an adoring grandfather, good enough for Samantha, isn't evil. Nor good either, as far as I can tell. So he'd have to go somewhere in the center."

He locked his gaze on me now.

"I'm inclined to think, for no good reason that I can locate, that *you*, Mister whatever your name is, might land rather far out on the *good* end of the register."

I leaned forward in my chair. The quiet, still night had settled into the last hour or so of its ancient vigil before giving itself over yet again, for the billion billionth time, to one more day.

"You might, this once, Mr. Darnell," I realized that it was the first time I had used his name since Sammy had introduced us, "be mistaken, regarding me. But I can tell you something that will confirm Deminelle's location on your register of good and evil."

And I told him—committing more security breaches than I could have counted as I did so—about the primary financial source for the September Eleventh attacks.

At which time he leaned more comfortably back in his chair, took out one of his cigarettes and lit it with his silver lighter.

"Ah," he breathed out. Letting the smoke work its way into the darkness.

"Ah, yes. I see."

Then he looked for a long moment at the moon, which had traveled pretty far along its graceful path during our visit.

"Do your job well," he finally said, so low that I could barely hear him.

Twenty-Eight

By the time I'd found the fourth marina, late the next afternoon, I'd looked—from discreet distances—at nine or ten boats large enough to get me out to the *Cristobal Colon* and back again, but neither too new nor with too many fancy bells and whistles to call unwanted attention to the voyage.

I needed something in the thirty to forty range, in both length and age.

I could charter any number of crafts. But this had to be a solo affair. And it had to be a cash only deal.

Which meant I had to locate not only a boat of the proper vintage and size but an owner who might prove to be willing to hand over the keys to a sizeable investment to a complete stranger. And I didn't spy my first good prospect until I'd strolled down to one of the last slips of the last pier of the last marina I visited. On the southern shore of St. George's Harbor.

I was thirsty. I was hungry. And I was beat. Stiff wind had slapped me in the face all day long on a rented motorbike, not to mention the pounding my posterior and legs took straddling the vibrating contraption.

Darnell and I hadn't gone inside the night before until after three. Then I'd lain awake and worked my way back through everything he'd told me. Which was one hell of a lot.

When I'd asked him, just before we'd gone in, how I'd know when Deminelle would dive on the wreck, he'd told me that was easy. He'd dive every morning that he was in Bermuda, weather permitting. And since he'd just arrived, he'd be here for at least a week, probably two.

That morning, I'd listened to Sammy and Timothy clatter around in the bathroom and the kitchen and go off to work. Then, when I'd rolled out, splashed some water on my face, and pulled on the same clothes I 'd worn the day before, I'd found Darnell already having his coffee in the same chair outside where he had spent most of the night. I'd poured myself a cup and joined him, and agreed to meet him for drinks at his club in Hamilton the next afternoon. Then I'd stopped by the dive shop to thank Timothy and say goodbye and rented, at a shop down the road, one of the famous Putt-Putts that I'd seen zooming all over the place.

Then I'd putt-putted briskly all the way back over to St. George, grabbed a shower and a change of clothes at the inn, had lunch, and remounted the jolting little chariot and began my search for the perfect boat. And the perfect owner.

He sat, all three hundred plus pounds of him, on the deck of his big Chris Craft, both of them—the vessel and her captain—a little heavy, a little old, and a little weather beaten. He wore a splashy Hawaiian shirt that had to have come from a big man's shop, white twill slacks, and topsiders with no socks. Which caused his globular ankles to spill out over the tops of his shoes like red dough rising in baking pans.

"She's a beauty," I said, and watched him drink in the compliment.

She wasn't, in fact, all that much of a beauty. She had enough years on her to make her look past her prime, but not nearly enough to qualify her as a classic. I was certainly no expert—the only boat I'd ever owned was sitting, at the moment, on her little trailer under Gull Cottage, never having touched the water under my command—but I guessed this one to be a mid-seventies model. There was enough blonde woodwork and avocado colored plastic cushion covers to tie her to that polyester and disco decade. She was a forty-footer, with a wide cabin, and a flying bridge. Plenty big enough to make the run out to the *Cristobal Colon* and back seem like a stroll in the park.

"Ya'll fonda boats?" he asked, the sharp Dixie twang coming unexpectedly out of a plump Celtic face that should have sent out something like *Sure, and you're a boatman, I'm thinkin'.*

Central Casting couldn't have dug up a more stereotypical Irish tippler. A huge bulb of a red nose, pink-veined cheeks, tousled wisps of sparse white hair. Big, flabby jowls. Sort of a cross between

Ted Kennedy and Tip O'Neil, with a touch of W. C. Fields in the snout department.

He gave a hospitable look.

"Permission to come aboard?"

He heaved himself slowly up from his deck chair.

"Ya'll climb on up hearah."

So I did.

Three Old-Fashioneds later—glucotic concoctions that I somehow managed to get down and keep down—we had covered the pertinent points. He'd been married three times and divorced twice, the present Mrs. Ralph Rawlston having elected to stay in Valdosta, Georgia, when he decided to sell his five hardware stores to a national chain and move onto the boat he'd owned for years. She was still in Valdosta, was still Mrs. Rawlston, and I got the impression that the long separation was working swimmingly for both of them. He lived on the boat, which was called the *Eloise*. Which was not the name of any of his wives, but of his sainted mother.

I was still Jeff Whitten, neophyte novelist from Tacoma.

By the time he'd had enough highballs to begin slurring his renditions of the many jokes in his repertoire—all of them sexist or racist or just plain crude—I figured it was time to make my pitch.

Five thousand dollars, cash, for the loan of his boat—just three or four hours at a time, and never at night—for a few days proved sufficient to slice through copious amounts of sugared bourbon.

He studied me, then his drink, then me again. Through squinted, bloodshot eyes.

"How the hell do ahh know," he finally said, readjusting his bulk in the deck chair, "that you ain't no drug runnah? Or sumptin' like dat."

At which point I took another sip of my own glass of syrup, and flashed him my most winning smile.

"Do I look like a drug runner to you, Ralph?"

He kept me locked in his narrow vision for another moment, and grinned. His nose seemed to glow a little brighter.

"No suh," he finally allowed, "you don't. But, then again, Ah married a woman one time that didn't look like a bitch. On our first meetin'."

●●●

I ended up leaving my—or rather, Jeff Whitten's—driver's license with Ralph. Which could be verified by a phone call, if he turned off doubtful after the sweet hooch wore off. I'd checked with the General a few weeks before, to make sure that his arrangement for an electronic equivalent of a wild goose chase was still in place. I gave Ralph a five-hundred-dollar deposit and told him I'd need the boat first thing in the morning. Just to make a few runs into the bays and holes and deeps and sounds, with a certain lady I'd met at the hotel who might end up enjoying my unchaperoned company.

I showed up bright and early the next day—another sun-splashed beauty that fate had strung together like yellow beads for my stay—and treated my new friend to the breakfast buffet at the marina restaurant. Raisin Bran and fruit for me; pancakes, sausages, bacon, and hashbrowns for Ralph, all nestled like a thriving village beside a mountain range of scrambled eggs.

Then, I let him take me out into the harbor to give me a little crash course in the operation of the *Eloise*.

"She's fulla gas," he said when we were back in his slip. He somehow made *gas* rhyme with *lice*. "So she'll need to be thataway when you bring her home."

I eased her carefully out of the marina, waved at her still somewhat dubious owner, pushed the throttle forward and churned out into the harbor. She lifted up a little the faster she went, and sent out a fine wake behind us. Her big engine growled away, reverberating up through my feet and legs. The wind felt good as she sliced through it and, in no time, I was bringing her through a wide turn around Hen Island, with two big cruise ships docked at St. George just to the north, and then straight on through the channel.

Gate's Fort and Higgs Island slid by on either side, like Scylla and Charybdis, and then the big Atlantic opened up like the whole wide sky that always used to take my breath away as I fell into it from the hatch of a plane. The night before, in my room, I'd studied the map and navigation chart—that I now had unfolded on the console—like cramming for a test, so when I swung the *Eloise* to port and threw the throttle wide open I was confident that I knew how to negotiate the reefs. I planted my feet wide apart on the flying bridge like an old salt, leaned into the stainless steel wheel, and pushed up past Building's Bay, Warden Hole, and then, finally, Fort St. Catherine, the last piece of Bermuda before North Rock, eight miles out.

The enormity of the open sea, and the islands falling away behind me, worried me just enough to make me check and recheck my headings and the chart, and pay damned close attention to the reef markers along the way. Boats were plentiful, of every size, color, and shape; I was hardly Columbus sailing off toward the edge of the world.

Four vessels were anchored over the wreck site, spread far apart. Two of them were big buslike outfits that obviously hauled tourists out to dive. One was smaller than the *Eloise*. The last would qualify as a bona fide yacht, though a small one. A fifty footer, I'd say, sleek and ebony and shiny. I'd put my money on that one being the prize.

I pulled the engine back to a slow idle far enough away to use the big binoculars I'd located in Ralph's cabin. Which had saved me the trouble of buying a pair. Then I shut her down completely and went dead in the water.

This needed to look like a fishing expedition, so I cast an empty line out with one of the big rigs and jammed it down in its holder. I plopped into the frayed avocado-colored cushions of a deck chair, lifted up the big glasses, and took myself a long gander while the boat rolled slowly in the slight swells.

There was no name on the bow. Only a registration number. Darnell had told me that Deminelle always used The Outrigger's boat, so it didn't surprise me that she wasn't named. Just as there hadn't been any identifying markings on the resort's stretch limo that Timothy and I had seen whisk by us a couple of days before. In fact, I hadn't come across one thing, in my research before arriving or when I'd gazed at the high walls of The Outrigger, to lead me to believe that any effort had ever been made to make the place known to the public. No logo. No catchy slogan. No sign.

In a few minutes a girl came out on the deck and looked around.

She might have been eighteen—probably wasn't—and her deep tan stood out next to a bright yellow bikini every bit as tiny as Holly's. She flicked her long brown hair out of her eyes and adjusted her sunshades. Her slender, oiled body shone brightly in the brilliant sunlight.

I watched her watch the sea for a while, then she dropped down on her belly on one of the lounges. In not too many more minutes, two divers broke the surface of the water just beside the boat and hauled themselves on board. The girl looked over at them for a few seconds, then put her face back down.

The smaller of the men—over two months of research left no doubt as to who he was—took off his mask, tinkered with it, leaned down and kissed the girl on her dark back, and let his hand drift down across her butt. Then he went into the cabin.

The other one—surely a bodyguard: brawny, hairy, and big—said something to the girl, who, if she responded at all, didn't lift her head to do it.

Several minutes later, Deminelle came back out, paid no attention to the girl, strapped his mask and tank back on and slipped gracefully over the side. Followed closely by his resident ape, who made a much bigger splash.

I went inside the cabin, helped myself to one of Ralph's ice-cold Heineken's, and settled back into the deck chair for what I was sure would be a long wait.

But it wasn't.

The ape was back up in less than twenty minutes, exploding out of the sea like the creature from the black lagoon. On deck, he scanned the horizon, then took off his tank, peeled out of his wet suit, and stood in all his furry glory in a sparse Speedo. The girl got up, looked nervously out toward where Deminelle had descended, let the ape grope at her a little and then followed his hairy back into the cabin.

I put the binoculars down and took a long drink of the beer.

So, when the cat is away, I determined, these mice play. I only hoped it was a daily occurrence.

Twenty-Nine

I returned the *Eloise* to Ralph a little before noon, and told him I'd probably only need her for the next two mornings. Then I putt-putted back to St. George, had a plate of curried conch and a pint at the White Horse Tavern, and went back to the inn. In my room, I kicked the A/C down as low as it would go, fell face first onto the king-sized bed and sawed logs for over an hour, waking up in such a groggy haze that it required an extra long shower to wander back out of it. Then, into a pair of slacks and the only button-down shirt I'd brought.

I splurged and took a taxi over to Hamilton, where I told the concierge at Mr. Darnell's club that I was meeting him there.

"Ah yes," he said, nervously inspecting my upper torso, "he's just arrived, and asked me to bring you into the smoking room." He held up a finger, asked me to wait just a moment, and stepped through the door behind him.

He came back out with a blazer and a blue silk tie.

"Our policy, I'm afraid," he mumbled, as he watched me manipulate the tie into a knot and then helped me into the blazer, which was way too big at the bottom and a might tight on my shoulders.

Inside, Darnell stood up from his paisley printed wingback chair and motioned me into its twin.

The big room was exactly as I expected. Tall ceilings. Plush carpet. Large prints of hunting scenes—foxes, hounds, dandies on horseback, cottages at the edge of dark forests sending smoke out of their stone chimneys into drab English skies—in ornate frames. Plenty of dark mahogany paneling and tall brass lamps. A stoic waiter—complete with cummerbund and black cutaway jacket—was immediately at Darnell's side. And in a very few minutes he was back again with our drinks. Gin and tonic for the old man, and, for me, my first Bombay martini in several days. The initial frosty sip was like a homecoming.

I pulled at the necktie and gave him a report of my morning's spying.

"I'll go out again tomorrow, just to make sure of the logistics."

He took out his pack of English cigarettes; before he had one to his lips the waiter was beside him with a silver lighter.

"So," he said, when the man had gone, "the morning of the day after tomorrow . . ."

He let the rest of it trail off. So did I. Then I nodded.

Heavy curtains were pulled apart by wide velvet sashes at the tall windows. Sparkling leaded panes gave a handsome view of Church Street and the harbor beyond it.

"What I don't understand," I said, "is why Deminelle didn't give up a hell of a long time ago. That old wreck must have been dived on a million times. There's no telling how many times he's searched it himself."

"Four hundred and fifty," he said, promptly and conclusively.

I undid the button at my neck; spread the knot wider.

"That's five dives, three times a year, for thirty years," he said.

He gave a mischievous smile, and sipped his brandy.

"Each of the three numbers is too low, so it's a quite conservative estimate. But a fine enough one for me to dwell on when I can't drop off to sleep."

I let the number settle in my thinking.

"You wouldn't have much trouble convincing me that Jacques Deminelle is the devil incarnate," I told him, after another sip of my drink. "But I refuse to believe that he's an idiot. He has to know that the canister isn't *there*. Surely the thing washed out to sea years ago, or is buried under the superstructure of the hull."

The old man inspected his nails. Curling his fingers into his palm to do so, which the General always insisted was the masculine way for one to inspect the nails, not stretching the fingers out at a distance like a woman. He harbored as deep a dislike of that as he did of men who swung both legs around to get out of a car.

"I was . . . helpful there, I imagine." Darnell said. "A few discreet notes over the years, sent along to young Mr. Deminelle at his Paris address. Marked confidential, of course. Just friendly reminders that the family heirloom he sought was still in Bermuda, still on board. Still waiting to be found."

I watched him take a slow sip of his drink and slosh what was left around in the tall glass.

"His father must have told him about the canister early on. Henri died when Jacques was—oh . . .—eighteen or nineteen. Then, shortly thereafter, my discreet promptings must have spurred him on."

I thought it over.

"Even so," I finally said. "Your letters wouldn't have been enough to keep him looking."

"Oh, I shouldn't think so," he said.

He leaned forward.

"You seem to be a bright chap. Well-versed, and all that. Coming up with that appropriate passage from the Caribbean poet. So, tell me. Why did old Ahab pursue Moby Dick across all those oceans and all those years?"

I looked for the trap, and didn't find it.

"To make the kill. And for revenge."

He shook his old head. Smiled his Max von Sydow smile. Spoke in his James Mason voice.

"I disagree."

He carefully placed the glass on the table beside his chair, lifted his cigarette up from a crystal ashtray, and rolled it between his fingers.

"He kept up the chase because of the *chase*. The quest became the totality of his existence."

Then he took a pull on the narrow cigarette.

"And you think that's what drives Deminelle?"

He nodded slowly.

"What other explanation is there? He's obscenely wealthy. Has plenty of willing sexual partners who meet his unique require-ments. Power. Homes in Paris. The Rivera. Switzerland. And yet he shows up out here at least three times a year and scours that old hulk time after time after time."

He was quiet as he looked out the window for a moment. Then he waved the waiter over.

"No," he concluded. "Mr. Deminelle never really expects to find the canister."

He waited for the waiter to scribble something on the thick, cream-colored card he left on the side table.

"But he's allowed the quest itself to shape who he *is*."

He took out an old-fashioned gold pocket watch and flipped open the cover.

"We've just enough time," he said, stubbing out his cigarette in the ashtray and dashing his initials on the card with a silver pen, "to make one more short stop before we have our dinner and bid each other farewell."

He came slowly to his feet and pointed toward the big doors that led to the lobby.

"It's not far, just down the way."

• • •

Outside, Front Street was bustling.

With Bermudians making their way home from the busy city center in the last hour of the workday. And flocks of tourists gawking at store windows, drinking in cafes, and milling around in the shade of old trees along the harbor. Two groups were snapping pictures of an ornate, wrought-iron contraption on a small island in the middle of the busy street.

"What's the thing that looks like a bird cage?" I asked.

"The bird cage, actually," Darnell said, not slowing down. "It's always been called that. Until not too long ago, there would have been a police officer in Bermuda shorts in there directing traffic."

At the corner of two streets, he turned abruptly and I followed him into a handsome and imposing bank whose iron tablet identified it as having been founded some twenty years before the American Revolution.

The lobby we traversed had the required lofty ceiling that all old banks have, and was rich in tropical flora and fauna in gigantic clay pots. Our footsteps blended in with many others, resonating nicely on the marble floor and echoing throughout the cavernous room, whispering *money, money, money.*

The man behind the big desk was already standing when we got to him. He and Darnell greeted each other by name.

We followed the man through a maze of hallways and, finally, through three round, open vault doors and into a room filled, from floor to ceiling on all its walls, with old fashioned safe deposit boxes, each one covered with intricately raised curlicues and flourishes of polished metal. The man went to one of the medium-sized panels, inserted the bank's key, took Darnell's key and inserted it into the adjacent lock, turned both at the same time, and opened the door.

"We've reserved room three for you, Mr. Darnell." He pointed to one of the narrow corridors. "Just down there."

Darnell thanked him, slid the safe deposit box out of its cubicle, and I followed him as he carried it down the hall. Inside the small room—just two leather chairs facing a handsome table, with a strong light overhead—he locked the door, sat down, and tilted up the top of the box up on its hinges.

I had known when I saw that he was taking me to a bank what he was going to show me. But it didn't keep my heart from racing when he carefully lifted out the stainless-steel canister.

I looked across the narrow table at him.

"Oh," he said, "I found it during our second week out there. Henri was in another section of the wreck. She was really quite enormous then, when she was still all in one piece and so much of her still above the waterline. So I stowed it away in the boat and, that night, went back down to the docks and brought it home. Where I hid it."

I asked if he had known what it was.

He smiled.

"I might not have been a genius, at the ripe old age of twelve. But neither was I the village idiot. I couldn't read the French documents, of course. But I could pick out enough of it to know that it was some sort of an agreement between Henri and Hitler. I was just a boy, so the inclination was strong to have some of my chums over and let them have a look at the great villain's scribbling. But somehow wisdom managed to prevail. And has prevailed all these decades."

He lifted a pair of white linen gloves out of the pocket of his coat, pulled them on, and unscrewed the top of the canister. It came away remarkably easily given its age.

I smiled. Probably I beamed.

"You've had it all this time."

He cautiously slipped out the small batch of papers.

"It helped—later, in Henri's and my . . . relationship—to know that I had something that he wanted badly. Very badly, indeed."

The documents on top were new, on thick, crisp stationary with gold embossed letterheads. Underneath, the much older ones had grown brown with the long years. I could tell they would be brittle when he got around to handling them. Like autumn leaves pressed between the pages of fat, old books.

"Then, when he died, and his son started his quest, I must admit to having enjoyed leading him along. Providing his life's work, as it were. That, and the simple fact that I didn't want the world's media hounds on my doorstep. Samantha can deal with that as she sees fit, soon enough. Personally, I hope she tells them all to go to blazes."

He touched the pile softly with his gloved hand. His voice went softer, coming finally as if from somewhere further away.

"But it should be known. It should be told."

Then, remembering the time, he picked up the first paper.

"This is simply my personal instructions to Samantha. Who, as the executor of my estate, shall be the first one allowed to see these papers after my death. There's a brief note here that she shall give to her mother, my daughter. Affectionate regards, and so on. And, of course, there are a few things for Samantha, herself. Instructions about the money she'll be getting, and the deeds to the cottage, the shops, and the property. Along with a heartfelt wish that, should she go on seeing whatever the hell it is she sees in Timothy, that she will *marry* him, and bring a bit of legitimacy to the whole business."

He laughed his dry, crackling laugh.

"Timothy will shine bright as the sun in all the commotion that will come. The *Cristobal Colon* will surely be more popular than ever for divers and documentary producers and historians. And he'll lead the hordes out there, like pilgrims at Lourdes."

Then the old man was serious again. He leaned closer to me over the table.

"There's a long bit here about exactly what Samantha should do with the contents of this box. The next letter, addressed to the Director of the British Museum, is to be delivered as soon after my demise as possible. It's long, since it tells the story that I told to you, and it ends with my giving these documents to the museum, provided they make their contents public and put the pages themselves on permanent display. There are also letters here to be sent to the managing editors of the *Bermuda Sun*, the *New York Times*, and the *Times of London*, informing them of the bequest."

He lifted out two particular documents very carefully by just their edges. One was in English, the other in German. Each bore Adolph Hitler's small and precise signature, and each had a conspicuously empty place where Edward VIII had been expected to sign.

He let me gaze at them for a long moment, then he put them back into the stack.

"I only wish it were possible for there to be one more missive here," he said, deftly returning all of the papers back into the container, "telling the world of the invaluable assistance of a certain tall American who finally put things right."

He screwed the top back on the canister, and placed it back in the lockbox. Then he smiled, and put his pale hand over mine.

It was as close to a blessing that the likes of me could ever have any right to expect.

Thirty

The morning of my third, and last, visit to the wreck was cloudy and cool. The paper had said that a storm system was working its way up from the Caribbean. Not a hurricane, nor much chance of becoming one. But a healthy depression nonetheless, and bringing impressive winds and plenty of rain.

I'd watched—the day before, from the opposite side of the wreck—a repeat performance of the return of the bodyguard for his mid-morning canoodling with the willowy, tanned teenager. Of course I could only guess at what they were up to in there; I was pretty sure it wasn't a Bible study.

Now, as the southern horizon filled with ominous clouds that would soon send Deminelle and company packing, I watched the two divers slip back down into the Atlantic and the girl plop back down on the lounge.

I went into the cabin and changed into a wetsuit, hoisted on a small tank and pulled a mask tight against my face. All of which I'd bought at a second hand shop the afternoon before. The regulator was an old one, but it worked. And, of course, it would only have to work once. Then it and all the diving garb would be weighted down and tossed overboard on the way back in.

I wedged my feet into flippers, and watched out the cabin window for things to develop.

Soon enough, they did.

The bodyguard emerged from the sea, and Beauty and the Beast retired into the cabin of the ebony yacht. I made sure the mask was snug, tested the flow of air through the hose, and dropped backwards over the side of the *Eloise*.

The water was invigorating, and bordering damned close to being cold. "Grabs your attention," the General had said once when he'd watched Gomez and me ease ourselves into the choppy Irish Sea. "Grabs my *cahones*!" Gomez had stuttered back.

It took a few minutes for my body to become somewhat acclimated in the wet suit. Then I followed the anchor rope part of the way down and propelled myself off on the long sprint to the area under the yacht. Now was when all those laps at the fitness center—above water and below—would have to pay off.

Soon the *Cristobal Colon*, the half of it on that had settled on that side of the reef, loomed up ghostlike in front of me. The water was clear enough for me to make out a small group of divers off to my right, inspecting something big—maybe a dislodged boiler or a toppled smokestack—that rested in the debris field. I stayed close to the hull, running my hand along the barnacle-covered metal until I found a porthole large enough for me to make my way inside.

It took only a few minutes of exploring—down eerie passageways, peeking into compartments—before I heard the evenly spaced dinging echoing through the dark place. A few minutes later before I saw the flickering light coming from one of the staterooms. The vessels full of divers that had been anchored near the wreck the last two mornings were absent today, due probably to the bleak weather forecast. Other than the few divers from the only boat in the area, and currently interested in whatever outlying object they had discovered, Deminelle had the wreck pretty much all to himself.

I swam up slowly, looked in the hatchway, and saw exactly what I wanted to see through the particles of debris floating around. Deminelle, his back to me, held the light in one hand and tapped slowly on the bulkhead with a small metal hammer.

Now.

This was the time when things usually went wrong. The critical minute or even a few seconds before, when everything either fell into place and you went ahead. Or everything fell apart.

I looked around, just to make sure.

Usually things fell into place. Almost every time.

The big diver swimming a rapid beeline in my direction down the corridor gave me the distinct impression that this wasn't going to be one of those times.

• • •

Sometimes the providence that Mr. Darnell had put so much stock in does actually make an appearance. At that precise moment it manifested itself in the hatchway that I was already halfway through.

I took the only course of action possible, swimming as quietly as I could completely into the compartment and into the nearest dark corner.

The ape blundered in, making enough of a racket for Deminelle to look back at him.

I sucked in several big gulps of air from the tank. Listened to my heart beating. Felt my blood coursing too swiftly through my veins.

The ape swam up to Deminelle, gave him the thumbs up to see if all was well. Got a nod, looked back at the hatch, and pointed toward the surface.

Deminelle looked at his watch, then at the gauge on his regulator. He held up five fingers.

The ape executed a particularly ungraceful turn, swirling up the water like a whirlwind, and moved back to the hatch.

Then he stopped.

With both big hands on the frame, he slowly turned his big head in my direction.

I stretched my fingers wide and got ready. I'd have to kill them both now, if I could. The ape would be first, and the most difficult. Then, unless Deminelle proved to be made of some heroic timbre that I hadn't bet on, I'd have to chase him down and do away with him before he reached the surface.

Because killing the little girl was not an option.

Then, ironically, it was probably the girl who saved the day.

The ape stopped the rotation of his head just before he would have surely seen me. He pulled himself through the hatch and was gone. Heading surely for the quickest of quickies before the boss got home.

Deminelle went back to his tapping. I waited a couple of minutes to make sure we were finally alone.

Thirty-One

So, I thought, it would be surprisingly easy after all. Most of them were. The deed itself would be swift and clinical, then the wedging of the removed air hose tightly over that piece of pipe there, to make it seem an unquestionable accident.

Jacques Deminelle worked away, unsuspecting, at his task. Like a gazelle so intent on the watering hole that the cheetah could relax, take his time, and savor the moment. Like Claudius on his knees, focused so keenly on his hopeless prayer that Hamlet, standing close behind him, might make short work with his bare bodkin. Like Eden, sinking to grief.

For some reason I sometimes spewed up metaphors at the crucial moments, the literal points of no return. But I pushed them all away as quickly, especially in this case the last part. Shakespeare was very much in his element, but Robert Frost had no business there at all.

What I couldn't push away was the General's cold and unforgiving Rule and Tucker's frequent trips up the freeway to his candlelight vigils and Mr. Darnell—both as a thin shell of an old man, waiting for eternity, and as a twelve-year-old boy, tanned and glistening in the surf, waiting to be ruined—and Donald, finding ultimate perfection in, of all things, a porpoise.

Then, all of those things—and probably Joyce and Holly and Kelsie and Stormcloud the Cat, too—became just the one thing.

Then the thing itself was all that I could see. The swimming slowly up, the jerking around, the ripping away of the mask and the air hose, the short wait while pressing him against the wall and holding the arms tight to the sides, almost like a last embrace.

Finally, the inevitable final look in his eyes that I would add to the long catalogue of others just like it. Surprise. Panic. Anger. A burst of purpose. Confusion. Then desperation. And, at the end, something between amazement and grief.

One more mental snapshot for the collection. Like a page from an old yearbook where all the faces are forever frozen in the bright flash of the photographer's bulb.

It is quite a portfolio to carry through life, this rogue's gallery. Its numerous subjects taking turns jolting me awake, sweating and gasping, on the darkest of nights.

• • •

When I had him twisted around to face me, one look into Deminelle's eyes was all it took to convince me that he would not go easily or quietly into that portfolio. There, in his immediate and frigid recognition of what I was about, I saw the resolute determination of a survivor, the spunky self-confidence of one used to slithering—or fighting—his way out of things. I'd seen it before, lots of times. It clanged out its warning.

I rammed him hard against the bulkhead. Many men, when similarly surprised, would have dropped the hammer that had been the source of all the tapping. But Deminelle not only held on tight, he managed to swing it in a wide arc through the water and land a resounding thwack on the side of my neck.

The force of his assault propelled me away from him, and then we were at it in earnest, pushing ourselves through the fluid atmosphere like a couple of pissed-off vampires flying around in an Anne Rice novel.

We both lunged directly for the goggles and the air hose. He scored first, yanking the gear away from my face. Long years of training had taught me instinctively not to panic when the air source is removed, the only possible chance of survival lying in closing up tight and maintaining a steady heart rate. And, of course, getting your own mask back on quickly; removing your opponent's would have to come later.

In the twirling we were doing I was able to bring one knee up solidly into Deminelle's groin. Then I wrenched my mask out of his grip and pulled it back on. Having to use one hand to do this allowed him to dart away toward the cabin's hatch. My grabbing his ankle slowed him down, but in a matter of not many seconds we were out in the wide passageway, particles of debris and plankton frantically swirling around us, agitated by all of our flailing.

I had to hope that the few other divers would keep to their own business, and leave us to ours. Which had suddenly become mobile; Deminelle had kicked my hand away from his foot and was now leading a merry chase past stateroom after stateroom.

But I was gaining on him. In a few seconds I would either overtake him or he would turn and make his stand.

Being the fighter I had determined him to be, I expected the latter. And soon, I knew, the burly bodyguard would be back to check on why his lord and master hadn't resurfaced. My head was pounding from the wallop with the hammer; I probably wouldn't be up to the pair of them at the same time.

When Deminelle twisted around he had the small knife in his hand that I'd expected sooner or later. He was a world-class diver, and there was no way he wouldn't have had one tucked away somewhere. The fact that he unsheathed it so quickly was impressive; I had to give him that.

The swipe he made with it at my goggles was close. Millimeters, I'd guess. The next one nicked my arm, cutting through the wetsuit and into the flesh. Not deep. By the time I grabbed the wrist conducting all of these assaults we were tumbling along on the floor of the passageway, the clutter there ripping away at us. I felt a sharp puncture at my knee, another on my thigh.

Just as it was about to be advantage, Rafferty—I still had his knife hand locked in my grip and was about to twist it around behind him—he executed an entirely unexpected maneuver.

He twirled in the opposite direction with the agility of a seal, severing my air hose in the process. In less than a second, I shifted from offense to defense, the speedy transition inspired by an equally speedy assessment of the unfortunate turn of events. And, to be fair, by the knife that Deminelle had plunged firmly into my right calf, probably half way up to the hilt.

• • •

The dark, murky water all around us was darker now, with a good bit of my blood weaving its way through it. And some of Demi-nelle's as well, I imagine, given all the scraping we'd been doing along the walls and floor.

The next order of business should rightly have been for him to pull the dagger free from my leg and reinsert it in a more vital territory. My heart being the best candidate.

But that is when an old, old friend popped up. He'd made similar opportune appearances over the years. And I was glad to see him on this, hopefully our final meeting.

Pure adrenalin—the magical, providential, stock in trade of the likes of me—kicked richly in and let me do something that I, by rights, shouldn't have been able to do. The normal, physical order of things is, on some glorious occasions, no match for one sweet rush of adrenalin. Or for a hardscrabble determination that was, I could only hope, stronger than Deminelle's.

Before I had time to plan it, or consciously execute it, or for my worthy adversary to predict it, I had the knife out of his hand, tossed aside, and him wedged tight against the bulkhead. I punched him twice, hard, in the abdomen, jerked his mask off, and watched him first try to hold his breath, then panic, then gasp frantically, reaching for air that wasn't there anymore, sucking in water and more water.

I watched him die. Then I found the knife, swished it venously in the water and wiped it clean of any clinging bits of my blood with my hand, and slipped it back in the narrow scabbard on his arm. Then I leaned him against some protruding pipes, took a long, long pull on his air hose, and hooked it over one of pipes. Then I groped at hatchways and out a porthole and made for the surface, trailing enough blood from my lacerated leg to interest other divers and sharks, all of whom I hoped would not be paying attention.

I hoisted myself up the ladder and over the side of the *Eloise*, lay panting and wheezing on the deck for a couple of minutes, then inspected the nasty gash on my calf. Dropping in for a good scrubbing and stitches at a clinic or hospital was not an option; neither, really, was sewing it up myself. I had done it a couple of times, but I was never as good at it as Gomez had been, and I had the scars to prove it.

So I watched the bodyguard splash over the side of the distant yacht and cranked up the engines and slid away from the *Cristobal Colon*, putting a good five miles between her and me before throttling down to an idle. I hobbled into Ralph's cabin, located plastic bottles of hydrogen peroxide and isopropyl alcohol and some bandages, and made do, pulling the wrapping as tight as I could without cutting off the circulation altogether. I could give it better attention at my room in the inn before heading to the airport.

On the way in, the wound throbbed in sync with the growls of the big outboard engines. I propped myself against the captain's stool and let the oncoming wind, salty and damp, wash over me. The clouds off to the south were darker, meaner, than they had been on the voyage out. My leg hurt like hell. I had a headache. I was beat up and wet and exhausted.

But I had the wind in my face, a fast boat under me, the last job behind me. And I was going home.

Thirty-Two

It was almost five in the morning when I paid the Jeep out of hock at a satellite lot near Hobby Airport. The lanes on I-45 leading out of Houston didn't have much more traffic than country roads that early, and downtown Galveston was just waking up as I drove along streets still wet from an overnight rain. Puddles hugged the curbs, and everything shimmered, scrubbed and fresh, like the opening scene of *Peyton Place,* when the new principal drives into the well-washed little town for the first time.

Getting out of Bermuda after handing the keys of the *Eloise* back to Ralph had been a quick business. I'd already paid him, had returned the putt-putt earlier and had depended on buses, and, after a long, steamy shower, did the best job of cleaning and bandaging my leg that I could before checking out of the inn in St. George and dumping the clothes I wasn't wearing in a lonely looking dumpster—painted pastel pink—at the end of an alley.

I'd scored a standby ticket on the first flight out to New York, using good old American cash and Jeff Whitten's passport and driver's license, which, due to a short call on my cell phone to the General, would only be useable until I was safely home, when the bohemian novelist from Tacoma and all of his substantiating credentials would vaporize completely.

Tucker was already ensconced in a deep canvas chair on his front deck when I pulled up to Gull Cottage. In his oversized bathrobe. In what he called his Jesus sandals. In his half-frames, perched on the tip of his substantial, milk chocolate proboscis.

He held the *Houston Chronicle* out wide in front of him and took his glasses off.

"I borrowed your paper," he called down, as I got out of the jeep. "Actually, I've borrowed it every morning since you've been gone. I used to subscribe to it, but the delivery man pissed me off by throwing it a good bit later than I wanted it."

He put the glasses back on, leaned back in the chair, and held forth.

"I finally called the circulation department in Houston and asked whoever answered if the *Chronicle* was an afternoon publication now. Then I cancelled my subscription."

He rustled the pages.

"Now I've gotten into the habit of reading it again. So I guess I'll have to go on reading yours, since I don't intend to let them win."

I made my slow way up his steps, went inside to pour a big mug of coffee, and plopped down in the other chair.

"It's nice to see you again, too, Tucker."

He folded the paper, and tossed it to me.

"All the others are on your coffee table, along with your mail." He yawned. "Which doesn't amount to anything more interesting than the mail *I* get." He stretched. "We're a couple of pitifully boring sons of bitches, and that's a fact."

He looked over at me.

"How was Wyoming?"

I mumbled something about it being cooler up there. I rubbed my tired eyes and broke into a longer yawn than he had.

"You're plum pooped," he said.

"It was a long flight, with a couple of layovers."

He gazed at me over the tops of the half-rims, as he must have scrutinized thousands of fibbing students in his years as a school principal.

"Your tan sure didn't suffer."

Some of our usual silence ensued.

"The paper said it's been overcast and rainy up that way all week."

We spent the next few moments watching a couple of early wind-surfers glide across the surface of the gulf. Gulls squawked overhead, a tangy breeze swept in off the water, and way out toward the horizon a few shrimp boats lumbered slowly away from the Bolivar Roads.

"I wonder," I said, having nearly fallen asleep in the canvas chair, "if you have the fixings you need for Tuckered Eggs?"

He brightened up then. And ran a silent inventory in his mind.

"Everything but Canadian bacon, I think. We'll have to make do with ham."

In a little while, he came out with two bowls full of the concoction he'd made so often that I'd decided to name it after him. At the bottom of the bowls were halves of English muffins, heavily buttered and toasted to crisp-edged perfection, under big mounds of seared, diced ham and topped off with two eggs poached so softly that, once impaled, the whole assembly became drenched in thick, yellow yoke. Tilted against the edge of each bowl were the other halves of the toasted muffins, slathered with dewberry jam that one of his lady friends put up every season and kept him supplied with.

We didn't do any more talking as we ate, each of us finally using the jam-covered bread to scrape up what was left in the bowls.

"You go get some shuteye now," Tucker said, while he gathered up the empty bowls and coffee mugs.

Which I did. In my own bed, in my own house by gray water, with windows always open to the sea.

• • •

I slept for nearly nine hours.

And found Tucker, looking awfully comfortable on my porch swing reading the newest P. D. James whodunit.

"I'd started to think you were *dead*," he said.

I yawned mightily, scratched at the stubble on my neck and chin, and dropped down into the Adirondack chair that I was happy to see again.

Tucker pointed at the sun, already well into its leisurely descent.

"After five, I make it." He closed the novel and pointed to the side table, where a perfectly round mass of something brownish-yellow sat amid a nest of snack crackers.

"I did my cayenne cheese ball. That ought to help you wake up."

I leaned over, scooped a generous portion on a cracker, and partook.

The several flavors—some subtle, some definitely not—erupted in my mouth like a miniature fireworks extravaganza.

"Good," I managed to get out. "Hot!"

He grinned.

"Makes you thirsty, doesn't it?" he asked.

He watched me blow out some heat, then suck in some air.

"What are we going to do about that?" he asked.

• • •

I left him to another chapter of Inspector Dalgliesh and went in to shower, shave, and put on fresh khaki shorts and a T-shirt before filling the silver shaker with cracked ice.

We were well into our second icy batch when he scooped up yet another glob of cheese on a cracker. The ferocious concoction didn't seem to faze him in the least.

Then we entered into one of our quiet phases, this time—like most of the previous ones—spent looking out at the late afternoon sky spread over the gulf. Two precisely aligned groups of pelicans sailed slowly along just under the horizon; countless gulls looped around haphazardly just above it. Two big tankers were perched in between, so far out that it was difficult to tell if they were moving or sitting still. A man and woman sauntered through the foamy surf, her stopping every few steps to pick up a shell, he, hands behind his back, stopping to watch her. Only one other human was on the beach; he stood waist deep, flicking a heavy rod to send out something that might prove tantalizing to a flounder or a redfish.

His catch, about ten minutes later, was too small to be either.

"Mullet," Tucker and I both said, in unison.

We watched him for another moment or two before Tucker spoke.

"I've got a little news. Now that you've got some gin in you."

He tilted his glass up and drank the last few drops. For reinforcement, maybe.

"Joyce showed up one day." He squinted his eyes. "The day before yesterday, in fact."

He fished the toothpick out of his glass and pulled the fat Spanish Queen olive off with his teeth.

"Looking for you, I guess. She didn't stay long enough to clean up the house. It won't likely rent out any more this season anyway."

He made a loud business of chewing the olive. "I told her you were gone for a few days."

I glanced over at the empty house next door, then turned my attention back to the fisherman.

"She said Holly had taken off with that little dung beetle you had to run off that time. Said they went off somewhere." He waved his hand in the direction of off somewhere. "Joyce doesn't know where. Said Holly had skipped school four or five days before the nitwits up there called her. Then, when they had the showdown, Holly hit the road with the spikey-haired dipshit. That's her term, not mine."

He inspected his empty glass.

"Dung-beetle was mine. In case you missed it."

I said that Joyce must have been purely pissed about the new state of affairs.

He waited a long few seconds before saying not really.

"She's probably at the giving up place," I said. "At the *to hell with it* place. And who could blame her?"

"I don't think that's exactly where she is," Tucker said. "She . . ."

He hesitated. And hesitation was not a common undertaking for Tucker. ". . . wasn't right, Rafferty."

Then I looked over at him.

"What? Was she sick?"

He shook his head. Shook his empty glass. I reloaded it.

"I worked in schoolhouses for forty years. And I saw plenty of sick people, kids *and* adults. And plenty that *said* they were sick, but had something else wrong with them."

The fisherman reeled in and moved further up the beach. The shell-seekers had strolled out of our sight. The two ships still sat on the far horizon.

"Was she high?" I asked.

He gave a sad nod.

"As a long-stringed kite on a blustery day."

"Damn," was all I could think to say.

"Amen," Tucker said.

• • •

Over the next few days, after paying a visit to the doctor to get my wounds cleaned up and an injection of antibiotic, I did some hard thinking about Joyce and Holly.

I almost convinced myself to drive up to Channelview and drop in at the bar Joyce worked in. Then I decided to wait till in the morning, and try to find her apartment, where I could talk to her away from her work. Then I wondered if any of it was my business in the first place. After all, one night with Joyce hardly gave me territorial rights regarding her behavior or her daughter's. And she'd told me to stay out of it—not her exact words, as I recalled—more than once. So why couldn't I just *do* that? Until less than three months earlier, I hadn't had any difficulty whatsoever staying out of everybody's business. In fact, I'd have damn near had to have been walloped in the head and *dragged* into somebody else's business. So I finally decided to sit tight and see if Joyce called or came down.

One night I flipped through the menu on the television remote and found *The Quiet Man* on a movie channel. I figured there was nothing better than watching Duke Wayne fistfight his way through an Irish village and drag Maureen O'Hara up a hill to take a guy's mind off his troubles.

Then the phone rang.

The General's gravelly voice rumbled over the line. The conversation was curt and completely one-sided.

"We debrief tomorrow at zero eleven hundred. Sharp. At Fort Hood. Somebody will meet you at the main gate."

It didn't occur to me to say that this was inconvenient. Or to tell him that I might just have something else to do the next day, or to remind him that I was a civilian now, and would appreciate his *asking* me if that place and time would work. Or to tell him that, rather than making a round trip of over five hundred miles, I could give my report, in precious few words, over this obviously secure line.

I simply said, "Yes sir," put the phone down, and mentally saluted. Then I turned off the television and pulled the copy of *Poems of Yeats* that Donald had given me down from the bookshelves beside the fireplace.

I stood for a long moment or two looking at the ashes in the grate that were the remains of Joyce's and my fire on a rainy night just a week before. Then I sat myself down in my recliner to read a few poems that I could have recited from memory, saving "The Lake Isle of Innisfree," as always, for last.

Thirty-Three

My Texas road map told me I had basically two choices when it came to driving to Killeen, the home of Fort Hood, from Galveston. I could take what looked to be the scenic route, up farm-to-market roads and state highways that wound through towns with names like Hempstead, Brenham, Milano, Buckholts, and Heidenheimer. Or I could shoot straight north up Interstate 45 to Centerville and head west through a twisting maze of country roads over to the base.

Either way, I had rural highways to enjoy—or endure, dependent on my mood at the time—so I opted for the route with a long stretch of freeway.

It was a nice morning in late September, so I put the top down and left the radio turned off. Flatland turned into rolling hills north of Houston; the stench of exhaust fumes and big city was replaced by the more pleasing aroma of pine trees, cedars, hay meadows and, in one place, the pungent tanginess of wild onions that had been mown beside the highway.

The M.P. sergeant at the main gate checked me in at 10:42 A.M., studied my service identification card, took a good, long look to make sure I was the guy in the mug shot, walked me through a metal detector, and asked what my business was on Fort Hood that day.

He was already poised to write down *visit to PX*—which he probably did all day long when retired vets arrived to stock up on tax-fee cigarettes and High-Ho crackers and canned tuna at the base store—when a major came up behind him and read my name on the clipboard.

"Good morning, Staff Sergeant Rafferty," he said. "Come with me, please."

So we left my jeep in the adjoining parking lot and got into his.

• • •

The General was standing in the office of the base commander, looking out a big window at troops marching on a parade ground. The major saluted, did an about-face, and left, closing the heavy doors behind him.

We shook hands. He gave me a pat on my shoulder. Then he inspected my attire.

"Spiffy," he allowed, letting his granite face almost break into a grin.

I had on slacks, a pressed Oxford shirt, and a pair of loafers that weren't yet broken in sufficiently to be anywhere near as comfortable as the sandals I usually wore. When I bothered to wear any shoes at all.

He looked back out the window and I glanced around the big room. The walls were dark panels of rich, grainy wood covered with the crossed flags of regiments and battalions. Behind the commander's football field of a desk, his personal flag—three white stars on a field of dark blue—stood just a little lower than the banners of the three most prominent residents of the base—a corps and two divisions, one cavalry and one infantry—which stood just a bit lower than the stars and stripes. A polished sword rested in its scabbard across the front of the desk, which must have been more than a little off-putting for any wayward privates who'd sufficiently screwed up to be called unto the intricately woven blue and white carpet.

The General was still standing ramrod straight at the window.

"How'd it go?" he asked, still watching the troops.

"No problems. It's done."

He nodded. He lifted up the briefcase at his feet and took out a section of that morning's *New York Times*.

"Page four, in the corner."

There, under *Deaths Elsewhere* was a photo of Jacques Deminelle, along with the news that he had died in a diving accident in Bermuda. There was no mention of any suspicion of foul play, or of an impending investigation. The piece wandered off into his wealth and his notoriety; I stopped there, and handed the paper back to the General. He folded it and dropped it back into the case.

I pointed at a table set with plates, silverware, salt and pepper shakers, and empty glasses by another window.

"Seems like there was one of those in the last office we were in together," I said.

"This time it's for us," he said.

I asked if the base commander would be joining us.

"I don't think Mike's even here. Seems like I remember hearing he was going over to the big rodeo for a couple of weeks."

Which I knew meant only one place. Much of Fort Hood was deployed to Iraq.

When we resumed our quiet contemplation of the soldierly maneuvering on the big parade ground, I tossed the words around that I'd been playing with during the several-hours drive. Words that I never would have thought I'd say to this man. But here we were, at the end of it. And I figured, what the hell. This would be my last chance.

"Do you ever wonder if what we do . . . what we *did* . . . is right?"

He didn't blow up. Didn't curse. Didn't even turn his attention away from the window. And when he responded, after thinking about it, his voice was as soft as mine had been. And he was actually smiling.

"I wondered when you'd get around to that. I guess maybe I'd convinced myself that, after twenty years, you wouldn't even ask. I guess I hoped you wouldn't."

"Did Gomez ask?"

His eyes got narrower. His stern visage got sterner. Then it relaxed a little.

"You know goddamned well he did."

I waited.

"All right," he finally said. "Let's do this the one time. And be done with it."

The several rows of ribbons over the pocket of his uniform jacket caught the morning sun. His grizzled neck rose up from the sharp edge of his shirt collar and the precise knot of his black tie like an old oak growing out of a manicured lawn. Polished gold stars, two on each shoulder, shone brightly.

"The way I always figured it," he said, "was somebody fucking well has to get their hands dirty. And people like you and me—and Gomez—just . . . drew the short straws. You fucked up early and needed to keep your ass out of jail, then you got up enough of a head of steam to be useful to me. Gomez, same story. Me, my wife was dead and my boys were gone and I was just . . . lost. So I went ahead and buried myself in our particular line of work."

One of the platoons on the field executed a nice right face and moved off in another direction, like a blanket being pulled slowly across a floor.

"As to it being *right*, I'll leave that to the preachers and the prophets. But if you're asking me if we did any good, than you'd need to have your goddamned head examined if you thought we didn't."

Outside, flags hung limp in the still morning. Sedans and SUVs moved along the streets. Things had changed since I'd reported to my first post on a cold, rainy day over two decades before. Now there were more civilian vehicles and fewer of the little loud, bouncing jeeps grinding through their gears.

"Speaking of the examination of heads," I said, "how *is* Gomez?"

Then he turned away from the window and looked at me.

"He's getting the best care available."

I thought of the kid I'd first met at Fort Benning, then of the man who went into hell with me time after time.

"Where is he?"

The General rubbed the back of his neck. Closed his eyes.

"You know I can't tell you that. Hell, I don't even know myself, yet. Stashed away somewhere on a psych ward, I guess, in either a very secure military hospital or in the most remote section of some fancy clinic that movie stars and rock singers go to when they flip."

He looked over at me. Put his hand on my shoulder.

"We had no way of knowing that he would ..."

On our last mission before I was scheduled to muster out, Gomez had come up way too short on some of the things that he was best at, putting us both in what old Darnell, back in Bermuda, might have called a sticky wicket. Then he'd cratered altogether, leaving me to get us both out of the area with the job undone.

"*I* should have known," I said.

The ghosts finally got to him, of course. So far, they hadn't made any serious inroads to me. But it was just a matter of time, I figured.

We resumed our quiet perusal of the parade ground.

"We can't afford the luxury of a conscience, Rafferty," the General finally said, obviously having sidestepped the Gomez issue to his satisfaction. "Other people can. And most of them overuse the damned thing. They pick every little thing apart and prod at it and analyze it and then—when they figure they aren't good enough to do it themselves—they pay a shrink a few hundred bucks an hour to get to the root of the problem."

He looked at the canister that held his big cigars in the brief case. I knew he wanted one pretty bad.

"But they don't, you see. They don't know one fucking thing about getting to the root of a problem. But we do. You and I do. And Gomez did."

I would have liked for him to follow that up with "and will again when he gets better." But he didn't.

"*We* know that sometimes the only effective way to get to the root of a bad problem is to rip the root out completely. Sometimes . . ."

There was a knock at the door behind us. The General growled out a "come," and a mess sergeant rolled in a cart laden with domed metallic covers. He removed the biggest two and lifted up plates that were not quite large enough for the enormous sizzling steaks that spilled over their edges.

When the sergeant had everything positioned the way he wanted it on the table, the General thanked him and the man left. Then he sat down, motioned for me to do the same, unfolded a large cloth napkin and tucked it into the collar of his uniform shirt.

"I thought you deserved a little better fare than they might be offering at the mess hall or the officer's club," he said, already probing at the steak with his fork. "So I ordered up these two beauties."

We worked slowly and quietly through our lunch, the only conversation consisting of him asking how my steak was and me assuring him it was excellent.

Which it was. A rib eye, about an inch and a half thick, moist and pink in the center, seared buttery crisp on the fatty edges. With creamed spinach and a baked potato about the size of a softball slathered with butter, sour cream, and chives.

When the General finished, he sopped up the last of the steak's juices with what was left of a dinner roll, ate it, leaned back in his chair, removed the napkin and tossed it on the empty plate.

"Thing is," he said, pushing the plate a few inches toward the center of the table, "I was thinking on the way down here on the plane, we'd be doing this altogether differently a century ago."

He cocked his head back and scratched his leathery neck.

"Back then, Teddy Roosevelt would have had you to dinner in the White House, and given you a medal along with your beefsteak. And then he'd have said something about doing it on behalf of a grateful nation."

Then he was quiet for a long moment while he kept his squint-eyed attention focused on nothing in particular.

"I always liked that phrase. On behalf of a grateful nation. Of course, it doesn't mean diddly these days. And that's a shame. Nobody in the government is likely to thank people like you and me for a goddamned thing." He smiled. "At least not in public. Not on the record."

He looked back at me.

"But I want you to know this, son. On behalf of a very grateful nation, *I* appreciate what you did." Whereupon he tapped the medals on his chest with a stubby finger. Winked.

I nodded. Then so did he. And the awkward moment passed.

"So," he said, lifting himself up from the table, "no medal for you. To put with all those other medals you didn't get."

He stepped heavily over to his briefcase, lifted out a small package, and handed it to me.

I took a hardback book out of the paper bag. It was Graham Greene's *The Heart of the Matter.*"

"I remembered you wanting to meet him that time on Capri," the General said. "I asked the guy at a book shop in London if he had something by him that was a signed first edition." He pointed at the handsome volume that I was running my hand over. "He had that and something about glory and power or some bullshit."

He grinned.

"It won't come as any surprise to you that I haven't read either one, but I liked that title."

He reached back into the briefcase and brought out one of his cigars. Figuring, I suppose, to hell with the no smoking policy in the post headquarters. A steak as fine as the one he'd just consumed warranted a good smoke, he must have reasoned.

"That's what we do," he said as he fired up the big stogie, "people like us. We get directly to the fucking heart of the matter."

• • •

Later, when he'd called someone to drive me back to my jeep, he told me not to worry about Gomez or anything else. He told me my payment had already found its way into a secure bank account and he handed me a small sealed envelope that I knew contained the account number and access codes. He saw no need to remind me that the last few hours hadn't happened. Almost all of the meetings we'd ever been to together had fallen into that category.

"Go on home," he said. "Enjoy your retirement."

At the door, I turned and watched him go back over to the window and resume his inspection of the parade ground.

"That's it for me, sir," I said. "No more."

He didn't turn around. Didn't speak. Didn't nod. He was still standing at the window when I left.

• • •

I took the long way back. I left the top down and didn't hurry along the country roads, but let the fresh air whip along beside me and the rural landscape slide by.

But neither the weather nor the scenery could puncture what was so completely on my mind any more than a good steak or the handsome first edition still in its bag on the passenger's seat could. All I could see was the carefree kid I'd been paired with when we were teenagers and his gradual descent into confusion and guilt, finally stashed away in some secure place along with his secrets and his ghosts.

I'd foolishly convinced myself that my long-planned move to Galveston would erase that image, that a new life in a fine little house with windows open to the sea would be a strong enough bridge to deliver me from the dark side of the moon to a world that normal people live in. But two hours with the General confirmed what I should have already known, that such a bridge might not exist for people like Gomez. And me.

Ghosts can cross bridges too.

I hit Houston traffic about five, when one should definitely avoid hitting Houston traffic. Loop 610 barely crept along past the Astrodome. When I was a kid and came down with Donald, it seemed to take up the entire horizon; now it sat in the literal and figurative shadow of it immensely larger replacement.

Less than three miles and almost fifteen minutes later I made a quick decision to bypass the exit that would take me down I-45 to Galveston and stayed on the loop for another half hour before turning on I-10 toward Channelview.

It was dark by the time I pulled up at the bar. I knew that happy hour would be in full swing, so I wasn't surprised at the parking lot full of vehicles. Mostly pickups.

The twangy song that spilled out into the place from the jukebox might have been the same one that had been playing on my last visit. And the painted ladies at the bar might have been the same, along with the rednecks that leaned toward them. The cigarette smoke was thick, the talk was loud, the bar was cluttered with glasses and bottles and ashtrays. And Joyce wasn't behind it.

I had to wedge my way in between an old guy that had probably worked in one of the refineries for forty years and a younger one who would likely be there for forty more.

The bartender—a short, fat guy who happiness seemed to have bypassed for the present—finally came over and let a sour gaze suffice for asking me what I'd like to drink.

"Is Joyce working tonight?"

"Wahdayawant?"

"I want to know if Joyce is working tonight."

He sighed, pulled a towel off his shoulder and wiped up some spilled booze, and found his frown again.

"She ain't working tonight, or any other damned night. She ain't been in for four days and ain't even called. So if you see her, you can tell her to just stay wherever the hell she is."

"You know where she lives? Know her phone number?"

He ground out a short, raspy laugh.

"Look, you drinkin' or asking twenty questions? I got no time for this."

"Give me two packs of those Fritos and a Diet Coke to go." I laid down a twenty-dollar bill.

"And that phone number." I slid the twenty toward him.

"If you don't mind."

I tried the number on my cell phone in the jeep. No answer. No taped message.

So I headed out toward Galveston and had the stale Fritos and the lukewarm soda for supper.

Which was something of a comedown from lunch.

Thirty-Four

Jamaica Beach was pretty much shut down when I rolled through. The only activity seemed to be at the convenience store, where a couple of pickups sat at the gas pumps, each with small boats on trailers in tow. One guy from each truck was pumping and others were probably inside, stocking up on bags of chips and pretzels, beef sticks, and enough beer to see them through a night of fishing. In not too long they'd be heading down the Blue Water Highway for five or six miles to San Luis Pass, where maybe flounder would be running through the shallows under the big moon and a thousand stars.

The seafood place was closed. So was the Sand-n-Sea Liquor Hut. Ditto the washateria, the realty office, and the tube and surfboard rental place. They hadn't closed this early before, but the season was over. Summer renters and campers and day-trippers had migrated inland, leaving the tiny village and the beach to those of us who had settled at the edge of the sea, like driftwood washed up from the other direction. Soon, the scant few weeks of what passes for autumn on the gulf coast would commence, followed finally by the quiet, gray days of winter.

Gull Cottage was washed in pale silver moonlight. One lamp seemed to be all that was on in Tucker's place, where he was by now settled in his overstuffed armchair with his long legs stretched out on the big ottoman. He'd either be reading or watching television. Or he'd be napping, before waking up and moving into his bedroom.

Joyce's father's house was dark. I'd hoped to find her old car in its usual place, and Joyce inside the house, ready to talk. Ready to make a plan that would pull her back from whatever she had strayed into.

But she wasn't there.

Where she was was in my Adirondack chair on my front deck. And *what* she was was very, very high.

• • •

When the lights were all on and I'd gotten a couple of cups of strong coffee down her, Tucker was hovering over us at my table *tsk, tsk, tsk*ing.

I had called to ask if he'd seen or heard any vehicles at my house. Not much got by Tucker when it came to arrivals and departures. But he'd been out till well after dark, having had a craving for fried calamari and marinara sauce and the waitress who served them at a little place on the seawall. The waitress hadn't been there, but the calamari had, along with several bottles of cold beer.

Joyce leaned over the mug, her head tilting slowly one way and then the other. She hadn't said anything since I'd picked her up and carried her inside.

"I got back at . . . now, let me see, no later than nine, I guess," Tucker was saying. "You think she parked down the road and walked?"

Joyce watched him while he talked, her eyes fluttering, her bewilderment obvious. Wondering, probably, what he was saying. Wondering, probably, who the hell he was. She made an odd little noise and abandoned the effort. Her head plopped down on the tabletop, just missing the mug of coffee.

"She's running," Tucker said. "Maybe from the law. Maybe from those guys that showed up that time. She might have put the car somewhere else, and walked over here."

I shook my head.

"Somebody dumped her here. Hell, she *can't* walk. Somebody had to carry her up the steps and put her in that chair."

I rubbed the back of her neck softly.

"Do we need to take her to a hospital?"

Tucker thought a moment before answering.

"What we need to do is get her in bed. Let her sleep it off. Then she needs to go where they can get her peeled off of whatever the hell she's on. She needs a good, long stint in a damned good rehab facility, then maybe she can start putting the pieces back together."

So I carried her into the bathroom, washed her face and hands and arms, then put her into my bed and pulled the covers up to her chin.

She mumbled something entirely incoherent, thrashed around just a little, and held my hand hard when I offered it. I stayed with her until she dropped off to sleep. Which took all of about thirty seconds.

When I came out Tucker had found bottles of beer for each of us and his usual place on the couch. I dropped down into the recliner.

"Do you think Holly and that boy brought her here?"

It had already crossed my mind. But not for long. I shook my head and took a long pull on the cold beer.

"Holly has screwed up magnificently. I'll give you that. But she wouldn't do this. She wouldn't leave her on a doorstep, not in the shape she's in."

"Then who brought her?" he asked.

"I know who. So do you."

"But why?"

I polished off the rest of the beer and sat the bottle down on the side table. Then I leaned toward him.

"Only conjecture now, understand. But I'm betting Bonilla—that's Holly's father, from Dallas—somehow managed to lead Joyce down her old, bad road. And when she was screwed up good and proper, he put her where I would find her. Just to show me he still controls whatever he *wants* to control."

I leaned back, and ran the scenario out a little further.

"If I'd been here, he'd have just pushed her out in the driveway, or a little ways up the highway. But he got lucky. And got to leave her where I would be sure to get the message. Where I could see exactly what he'd done to her."

Tucker was listening carefully. Trying to make some sense of it.

"Could have happened," he said. "Or, like I said, she could have driven herself down here and parked the car under any number of empty beach houses."

I still didn't buy it.

"No way she drove anywhere. Not in that condition."

He got up to get us fresh beers.

"I was gone for the better part of three hours, Rafferty. She could have gotten plenty damned strung out sitting right out there on your porch in three hours."

I let it work its way around in my thinking a minute or two.

"I'm still betting on Bonilla. Creeps like that have some kind of radar when it comes to stepping back in at opportune moments."

He was back with the beers.

"Think about it," I said. "Holly was gone. I guess Joyce figured she was gone for good this time. And even if she showed back up, she realized that not even one of your magic phone calls would keep her in school now."

My guess was Joyce got around to the summing up that most people do, sooner or later. The checklist that puts it all in perspective about what their life really amounts to. And it must have been a pathetic bottom line for Joyce. Former user. And pusher. A screwup of a daughter who's hit the trail. A lousy job in a redneck honkytonk. Then Bonilla showed back up when she was flat on the floor and offered her something that would pick her back up.

We sat quietly for a few minutes.

"But, I'll tell you what," I said. "I'll drive around and see if there's anything to your theory about her parking the car somewhere else."

I stood up. Stretched.

"Can you keep an eye on her for a few minutes?"

● ● ●

I drove back toward town and looked beside and under fifteen or so houses, then turned around and headed toward San Luis Pass and the western tip of the island to inspect fifteen or so more.

Joyce's old car was nowhere to be seen.

But, parked way up between two big oleander bushes was the big Lincoln Town Car that I'd last seen in the alleyway behind a plumbing supply warehouse near the state fairgrounds in Dallas.

I rolled to a stop a couple of lots further on. My house was eight or nine houses further back. An easy stroll on a moonlit night.

So, he'd reconsidered just leaving her for me to see, or he'd intended all along to make an even stronger statement. He'd been watching from somewhere—from the dunes or the beach—hoping I'd come out or finally go to sleep, so he could make whatever move he had in mind.

I left the jeep where it was and ran through the shadows of the houses, stopping far enough away from his car to get a good look without being seen. I made my way in close enough to see that he wasn't in it.

As I had known he wouldn't be.

Because I had no doubt about where he was.

And I'd been stupid enough to let it happen.

Thirty-Five

I hoisted myself up along one of the corner stilts that the house sat on as quietly as I could. Gomez had always been better at stealthy approaches than I had. He was small and more limber. I, on the other hand, was six one, big framed, not one bit graceful, and tended to make more of an entrance than was healthy in certain situations.

Like this one.

When I was up to the window of my extra bedroom, I peeked in to see that the door to the hallway was closed. Which was good, in that it would hide my squeezing my way inside. And bad, in that I would have to navigate through the room in total darkness. But, unless I'd left something where it shouldn't be, which I didn't generally do, I knew where everything was. Luckily, I'd left the window unlocked and open a few inches at the bottom, to get some cross ventilation through the house the night before.

I nudged it up slowly, letting it do its squeaking in tiny increments. Then I pulled myself in as unobtrusively as I could manage and felt my way over to the door. Where I leaned in close and listened.

Not a creature was stirring.

Bonilla might be alone. Then again, he might have brought his goon duo with him. Probably not. The possibility of that many people being that quiet was improbable. Plus, this had the distinctive earmark of a personal vendetta.

Still, I couldn't go barging in like a bull. He'd turned the lights off and, assuming he was sedentary, he had the definite advantage in the event of a frontal assault. Especially if he had his gun. The one I'd borrowed once, to make the clever impression from the backseat of his car that landed us all in our current dilemma.

And he might just have the business end of that gun pressed against the head of one of the two people in there with him.

He was waiting for me. That, at least, I could bank on.

And, sooner or later, I'd have to oblige him.

I stood very quiet and very still for what seemed like one very long time. Then somebody—somebody heftier than Tucker—got up and took some cautious steps toward my bedroom.

I let him get to where he was going before I turned the door's knob gingerly and eased it back a few centimeters. Which gave me a clear view of Tucker, who lay in a heap on the floor.

Now was the time for calculation of the coldest sort. He was unconscious. Or he was dead. Either of which meant that I could take him out of the mix and focus entirely on Joyce.

I pulled the door open and moved quickly across the room, barely glancing at the glistening pool of blood by Tucker's head.

It was no time for caution now. Tucker had been dealt with, now it was probably Joyce's turn. If she hadn't been first. I threw the door open and saw that she was where I had left her: in my bed.

Then I didn't see anything else, compliments of the ringing blast at the base of my skull.

• • •

Bonilla came into focus slowly. Like the details of a tree tightening into sharper contrast as you walk towards it in a pea soup of a fog.

He was smiling. And he didn't look so much like Tony Soprano this time as like photos I'd seen of Al Capone. Probably because he was holding the big pistol, the one he had obviously employed to club me with. The fact that he had the gun most definitely caused me concern. The fact that he was smoking a cigar inside my house just plain pissed me off.

My hands were tied or taped to my ankles behind my back, leaving me on my side on the floor. The back of my head was spongy damp, and the inside felt like somebody had gone in and taken a jackhammer to the walls.

Bonilla leaned back comfortably in the chair by my bed and waved the gun in Joyce's direction.

"Your friend seems tired," he said. The thick accent—Brooklyn,

Hoboken, somewhere up there—reverberated in my ailing noggin. "She must of had a bad day."

My mouth was taped tightly shut. With my own duct tape, I suspected. I'd bought a big roll and lots of plastic sheeting a month or so before, in preparation for hurricane season. Extra wide, maximum strength, of course.

"I been thinkin' about the order of things on my checklist," he said, flicking some ashes from the cigar on my floor. "The old guy won't be a problem. He ain't goin' nowhere. Neither are you. Seein's how you're all tied up at the moment. "

He bellowed out a full-bodied, throaty guffaw that sent the ugly gold chain around his neck bouncing. The laughter bobbed along to its finish.

Then he was quiet as he looked over at the bed.

"And her," he finally said. He reached into the pocket of his bowling shirt and lifted out a plastic syringe.

"I filled her up with enough junk to make sure she won't wake up no more." He flipped the cover off the needle. "High octane. *Strong* shit."

He watched her for a long moment.

"You shoulda seen her when she was a kid. Holly's age. Now that was somethin'. That cute little ass movin' around in that warehouse. In my office. She was really . . ."

He took out a small vial. Apparently, the stroll down memory lane was concluded.

"As you can see," he rolled the vial around in his stubby fingers, "there's plenty left to go around. For you. Even for the old coon." He pointed behind him.

He carefully inserted the needle into the rubber stopper and filled it up.

He looked at his watch.

"Hate to run. Gotta' long drive, ya understand. And after . . . Well, you know. I have a little cleaning up to do. A little rearranging."

He smiled a particularly menacing smile.

"You'll be the lead story tomorrow, my friend. A double murder and a suicide. That's big stuff."

He got up and moved slowly toward me with the syringe.

"You'll go out with a real bang."

Not if I could keep from it, of course. That had been my rule even before I came in contact with the Rule. The distinct problem was that, this time, I didn't see *how* I could keep from it.

I could twist and turn. But the unavoidable fact was that I was bound up like a rodeo calf. And all Bonilla had to do was put one big foot on my side, jab the needle in my neck, and push its contents home.

Which is undoubtedly what he was about to do when the back of his head exploded.

Thirty-Six

Tucker was standing where Bonilla had been. Wobbly, with a dazed look on his face, but there nonetheless.

He let the fireplace poker slip from his hand to clatter on the wooden floor. Then he dropped more than leaned down to me and managed to pull the tape away from my mouth. Then from my hands. It was a monumental chore for him. He was breathing heavily, shaking, and the effort it had taken to save us had obviously drained every ounce of his energy.

I quickly unwrapped the tape from my ankles and went over to Bonilla. Just to make sure he was down for a while.

There were several things that needed doing immediately. So I went out and found the role of tape and returned the favor to Bonilla, to insure he didn't impede my progress.

I found my cell phone and called 911. I gave the girl at the other end of the line my address, told her there was an overdose and other injuries. Then I told her to send two—no, make that three—ambulances and the police.

I went to Joyce first. Her breathing was slow, way too damned slow. So was her pulse, when I finally located it.

Then Tucker. Who lay sprawled flat on his back.

When I leaned down close to tell him help was on the way, he dredged up just enough energy to whisper one word. One and a half times.

"Heart," he whispered. "Hear . . ."

• • •

The same doctor that had fixed me after my run in with Buster and Bubba fixed me again. In the same treatment room in the same hospital. He said I was lucky not to have a concussion but, considering the talk already spreading through the place, I was luckier to be alive. He cleaned the big gash at the back of my head, bandaged it up, and shot me full of a strong antibiotic. Which was preferable to what I had almost been shot full of a couple of hours before.

He said it would be a good idea for me to stay overnight at the hospital. But that it was my call.

Then I had a long sit-to with a detective lieutenant with the Galveston police department who had to hear the whole story all the way through twice before putting it all together. I even told him about the previous assault, and had to practically swear on a bible that I hadn't made the guys' names up.

Before we'd left the house, I'd told him he might want to be careful of the prints on the syringe and the vial that were on the floor beside Bonilla, who had started to come around. I'd watched the lieutenant scoop them into a plastic evidence bag.

When we were done—for that night, more questions and a formal deposition at the police station in the morning—I waited for the doctor to come into the waiting room with some news.

Later, we stood at the foot of Tucker's bed in the intensive care unit.

"We'll just have to wait now," the doctor said. "The head injury, and the drama of the evening, were enough to exasperate an already pretty bad heart condition. He had a double bypass a few years back."

He chuckled.

"If he'd heard that, he'd have said 'where'd you learn a big word like exasperate. You damn sure never paid enough attention in junior high school to learn a word like that'."

He closed the chart.

"I guess you knew he comes in here every Wednesday, like clockwork. Brings homemade cupcakes or cookies for the nurses, then does a couple of hours in the physical rehab center."

I watched Tucker sleep. I wished he'd wake up, look around, make his *tsk, tsk, tsk* sound, and say *What the hell is this all about?*

I wished for more late afternoons on my deck or his, while the sun dropped down over the salt grass. I wished for Tucker to lift his glass to the wide Gulf of Mexico and say "Here's to Her Majesty, looking particularly fine today, given her age."

I wished for it. But what I got, at the moment, was a sick old man in an oxygen mask. With a tangle of IV tubes hanging beside him like a honeysuckle vine gone berserk.

The doctor looked at the numbers and the jolting lines on the machines.

"He'll sleep all night," he said. "Which is what you ought to do, too."

I watched him a moment longer. Nodded.

"I think I'll see Joyce again," I said. "Then I'll go home."

• • •

Her eyes were closed. Her light brown hair was almost golden on her white pillow.

Her mouth looked unnatural without a cigarette. When I'd first met her, I'd wondered if her mouth could be manipulated into anything other than a frown. Then, as it found a few smiles, I'd come to the conclusion that it was as pretty a mouth as I had ever seen.

I watched her for a few minutes, then put just the tips of my thumb and index finger against her cheek and told her good night. To sleep well. To get a good rest. I might have told her out loud, and might not have. I was too tired to know.

Then I nodded to the man beside me, who zipped the plastic casing back up over her face and slid the shelf back into its refrigerated compartment, the locking mechanism echoing off the tile and stainless steel in the room.

It was almost four in the morning when I climbed into the jeep in the parking garage. The police would all be gone by now, and Gull Cottage would be dark and empty, waiting for my return. Waiting for the lord of the manor. The hunter, home from the hill; the sailor, home from the sea.

If I had a cat, it would be in the window, dozing, waking up occasionally to watch for me. Like Stormcloud used to do.

But I didn't have a cat, I remembered, with whatever coherent part of my brain was still functioning. And if I ever got one I wouldn't name it Stormcloud, I determined, as I rolled out of the parking garage into the dark, empty streets of Galveston.

That name had been retired.

Epilogue NOVEMBER, 2004

"We're wobbling," Tucker said, "don't you think?"

He held tight to the sides of the boat as I hauled down the jib, furled the sail into a bundle, and slipped the anchor over the side.

"There's a good deal of wobbling," he said again.

I told him it was just while we got squared away.

It was a glorious late afternoon, just before dusk. Galveston bay, stretching out all around us, was a tranquil mirror of a reddish golden sky that was slowly giving itself over to evening. The water's surface was almost motionless. As still, as the doomed captain of the doomed *Titanic* was supposed to have said of the North Atlantic just before all hell broke loose, as a millpond.

Tucker's feet were planted solidly and wide apart on the deck close to the ice chest we'd brought along in the *Joyce*—the name for the sailboat I had nurtured back to health had clinked naturally into place after so many weeks of none seeming good enough—and he leaned forward on his seat, facing me, ready to face any possibility in a boat that he considered too small in a body of water that he considered too large.

Once the anchor had dropped the several feet to the bottom and the craft had rocked herself to a calm mooring, he relaxed a little and watched me open the ice chest.

We should, of course, have brought a bottle of champagne, it being the traditional libation for celebration or remembrance.

But we'd reckoned we weren't all that traditional, old Tucker and myself. So I lifted out the silver shaker, the gin, and the vermouth. Tucker saw to the jar of olives, the toothpicks, and the pair of chilled martini glasses. I shoved the shaker half full of cracked ice, poured in the magical proportions, clamped down the silver top and stirred it energetically enough to cause the boat to rock and Tucker to grab the gunwales again.

In a moment, our drinks in hand, we watched the amber sun sink down on the horizon. I hoisted my glass.

"To absent friends," I said.

"Amen," Tucker said.

I knew full well that there are as few symbols in real life as there are were in modern fiction. Gone are the monstrous metaphors of Hawthorne and Melville, the beating and tolling reminders of mortality of Poe.

But, just then, in the little boat called *Joyce* in the wide, calm bay with the good man called Tucker, a sleek, shiny symbol sliding along beside us would have been welcomed.

Just one of my Uncle Donald's porpoises would have been nice.

The Sabine Series in Literature
SERIES EDITOR: J. BRUCE FULLER

The Sabine Series in Literature highlights work by authors born in or
working in Eastern Texas and/or Louisiana. There are no thematic
restrictions; Texas Review Press seeks the best writing possible by
authors from this unique region of the American South.

Books in this Series:

Cody Smith, *Gulf*
David Armand, *The Lord's Acre*